ISLAND OF RUIN

RUIN OR REDEMPTION TRILOGY BOOK 1

MARTI M. MCNAIR

REBSAM PUBLISHING

Copyright © 2023 by Marti M. McNair

All rights reserved.

No part of this book may be reproduced in any form or by any electronic or mechanical means, including information storage and retrieval systems, without written permission from the author, except for the use of brief quotations in a book review.

Island of Ruin is a work of fiction. Names, characters, places and incidents are a product of the author's imagination or are used fictitiously. Any resemblance to actual events, locales or persons, living or dead are purely coincidental.

No AI tools were used in the crafting of this book. The story was written completely from the author's imagination, from the planning stage to completion.

martimmcnair.com

Cover design by Jessica Bell of Jessica Bell Design

ISBN: 978-1-916721-02-9

To the memory of my beloved twin, Isabella Morrison Hannay King, affectionately known as Izzy to those who knew and loved her. I am grateful for the inspiration and encouragement she gave, guiding me throughout my writing journey with every single step.

CONTENTS

Chapter 1	1
Chapter 2	7
Chapter 3	21
Chapter 4	29
Chapter 5	37
Chapter 6	41
Chapter 7	51
Chapter 8	62
Chapter 9	71
Chapter 10	75
Chapter 11	80
Chapter 12	87
Chapter 13	100
Chapter 14	107
Chapter 15	114
Chapter 16	121
Chapter 17	131
Chapter 18	139
Chapter 19	150
Chapter 20	157
Chapter 21	170
Chapter 22	179
Chapter 23	187
Chapter 24	198
Chapter 25	215
Chapter 26	229
Chapter 27	240
Chapter 28	245
Acknowledgments	249
About the Author	251

1

It was the last thing we expected to find washed up on the shore.

Coral poked a bundle of rags with weathered driftwood, waving frantically with her free hand. 'Jasmine, over here,' she yelled, desperately trying to make herself heard over gusts of wind.

'Let me secure my nets first,' I called back, pegging them down with heavy stones from the rock pool before heading over. As I crunched over shingle and grit towards the vast shoreline, the relentless collision of waves against dark slate rock surrendered to a tranquil lapping of white surf meeting sand.

My brain stuttered at the sight, as if my eyes played tricks. 'I think she's dead,' Coral said, prodding the old woman again.

Sparse white hair sprouted in clusters from scabs on her scalp and her skin was wrinkled and worn. Soiled clothes clung to her and, tangled in seaweed, she conjured the image of a sea monster long lost to this world. I had never known a person to be so old.

'Where has she come from?' I asked, straining my eyes over the turbulent Pewter Sea. No watercraft was visible.

'How would I know? She must have fallen from her craft. She might be a poacher or a rebel.'

My gaze returned to the old woman. 'I don't see any weapons.'

Long bony fingers stretched out and brushed Coral's ankle. Shrieking, she jumped back, and reached for the spear strapped behind her back.

'It's okay,' I said, grabbing her arm. 'She's probably more scared of us than we are of her.'

I ditched my backpack and knelt down taking her fragile hand in mine. Her skin was paper thin, coated in sand and smelled of saline.

'You shouldn't touch her, she might be contaminated,' Coral warned.

'I've taken my anti-sickness tablets, and you should have too.'

'But who's to say they'll work? We could still be putting ourselves in unnecessary danger.'

I didn't care. Emotions we'd been taught to suppress stirred and stole my heart. Falling into them, I let them take over.

'Give me your water flask, Coral.'

'No way, Jasmine.'

'Don't argue with me. Give me your water flask, now.'

Coral usually obeyed without question, but today was different. Today, we'd found a person that didn't belong on Ruin, and every step I'd taken so far had broken our rules. Anger flashed from Coral's eyes. 'This is foolish. We'll get in trouble.'

'If you don't want to give me yours, pass mine from my backpack,' I said.

Coral sighed, rummaged through her bag and dumped her flask in my hand.

'We thought you were dead,' I said, to the old woman. She trembled as I helped her sit, so I let her lean on me while I placed the flask above her lips. She lapped droplets with a swollen tongue and thick saliva coating the corners of her mouth disappeared.

With a feeble shove, she pushed the flask away and tried to speak. Her voice was faint, murmuring in the old language. Coral's face muddied with tension as she inhaled a sharp breath. 'I'm sorry, we don't understand,' I said, eager to placate Coral's unease.

Nodding her head slowly, she tried again. 'Let me see your brand.'

Catching the sweater below the cuff of my furs and tugging them both back, I exposed the ink tattooed on my right wrist. It was a gift from our Government, given on the day we were born to help hide the scar from the microchip implant.

It was as though she had waited a long time for this moment, staring intensely at the purple and red contours. 'I've found you,' she said, her face paling. Even the blue tinge on her lips faded as her eyes rolled into white orbs. She flopped into my arms.

Coral edged further away. 'We should head back to Midpoint and report this. She could be contaminated.'

I asked myself why I didn't share Coral's fear. The old woman was confused, alone and looking for someone. Sharing Coral's concern was the proper course of action but doing the right thing didn't feel good.

'Did you hear what I said? We need to report this.'

Coral's unease was understandable, and I reasoned my lack of caution was a danger to us both. Living in a fragile world where sickness and death had been rife had constrained us. I pulled the small Geiger counter from my backpack and held it above her, breathing a huge sigh of relief. 'It's okay, she's not contaminated.'

Coral's expression remained taut and sullen. 'It doesn't change the fact, we have to tell.'

'No, we can't. They'll take her away and she'll be cleansed.'

'She has to be,' Coral argued. 'She's not from here. You know the rules.'

I knew them too well. Rules that tethered us to a belief system which I often questioned. Coral and I had been flogged for breaking one in the past, and although I was wary, my wayward spirit remained intact. 'Do you remember when we found the little red fox by the saplings?' I asked.

The words hung in the air like an accusation as her face contorted with pain.

'Do you think after what happened I could ever forget?'

'The wound on his leg was bad and he could barely walk. We checked him for radiation, and he wasn't contaminated. We did something special by helping him.'

There was a long pause before Coral's lips morphed into a sad smile. I hated the misery this memory brought. But, for some reason, I knew the old woman's presence was important and I needed Coral onside.

'Ash found the fox and reported him to Command,' I said.

Coral's gaze fell to the speckled pebbles at our feet. Clasping both her hands in mine, I spoke softly. 'They took him away. Sent him to be cleansed. Aconite had him burned.'

Her tears fell softly. She had blamed herself, believing had she not found him, his leg may have mended, and he'd have run off to wherever foxes lived on Ruin.

Our punishment still haunted my dreams. Strung like puppets, our wrists were chained high on a steel beam, our toes barely skimming the floor. Jeers from a bloodthirsty crowd had fuelled Aconite's wrath, each lash raining harder, the whip tearing flesh from our back.

'Do you want them to cleanse this old woman? Her only crime is, she doesn't belong here.'

A soft moan escaped her, and I could see the conflict play across her face. 'No,' she said, her tone resigned. 'I don't want her to be cleansed.'

'Then help me hide her. We can make a bed for her in the Black Cave. We'll take her deep into the cavern where nobody would ever think to look.'

The Black Cave was home to the Draconian, or so folklore had us believe. A hybrid breed turning from human to reptile feeding on anyone foolish enough to get too close. It was the safest place.

I gently hoisted the old woman from under her arms while Coral gingerly grabbed her legs, heading away from the shoreline and its salty spray.

The acrid smell of seaweed faded as we shuffled over an uneven path while the old woman's head lolled from side to side. A small wooden cross fell from her neckline mocking us from a thin string.

Coral stumbled, dropped her load and stared with wide eyes. 'This isn't good.' she said, gasping the words. 'Not good at all.'

Fear spurred my heart to a gallop, with goosebumps crowding my wrists to my elbows. I was unable to calm myself, never mind reassure Coral. Yet, I still clung to the old woman with all my might while we waited for retribution.

We waited . . . and waited, but nothing happened. I placed the old woman gently on the ground and wiped my brow. 'I think we're okay,' I said, in a shaky voice. 'Reprisal would have come by now.'

Breath caught in the back of Coral's throat causing her to splutter while her cheeks took on a purplish tinge.

I leaned towards her and clasped her forearm, speaking in a gentle but firm tone. 'Take a deep breath in through your nose, and out through your mouth. That's it,' I said, while she snorted in air. The strange colour on her cheeks faded to a ghostly white as I continued to assure her impending doom had passed.

My eyes drifted to the menacing cross resting on withered skin. Curiosity replaced fear and I placed the palm of my hand above it expecting to feel strange or disturbing sensations. There was nothing at all, only cold air.

Coral yelled loudly as I grabbed it between finger and thumb. The cross didn't sting, burn or blister, so I tugged it hard, freeing it from its cord and tossed it far towards the Pewter Sea.

2

The Black Cave was damp and dank, like a dark empty space waiting for something to be born. We settled the old woman on a makeshift bed of dry seaweed, leaving my furs behind as a blanket. Fungus spores disturbed by our clambering floated in the air. Their musty smell clung to us leaving a stale taste lingering in the back of my throat.

I couldn't stop thinking of the old woman as we traipsed back to Midpoint over a bleak and lifeless landscape. Every now and then a dead tree broke the skyline while black smoke rose from cracks in the hard packed clay.

Without furs, the bitter breeze bit into my bones having me crave for the warmth that Midpoint promised. It's granite walls beckoned from afar, casting a giant shadow creeping over barren and desolate land to meet us. The domed glass roof formed a giant bubble looking as if it reached the sky. It protected us from the many storms, sweltering heat and black rain that once fell toxic.

Midpoint was designed by experts prioritising health at the heart of their creation. Air was pumped in from the outside, analysed and purified through a ventilation system. It flowed freely from vents without worry of contamination, airborne viruses or anything that would bring harm.

Its structure was methodically divided into a maze of floors and tiers, each holding their own purpose. Those with high-ranking status slept and ate near the sky, while I slept and ate on tier three.

'Do you think she'll die?' Coral asked, as we arrived at the steel doors. 'She looks so old and frail.'

'I hope not. But she'll need plenty of rest and nourishment.'

Coral chewed her bottom lip. 'How will we manage this? It's not going to be easy.'

'Don't worry. I'll think of a plan, and we'll make it work,' I said, sounding more confident than I felt.

I placed my right wrist against the metal lock, feeling it tingle as the circuit board inside recognised my microchip and granted access. Midpoint was a bustling city, home to around fifty thousand individuals at the last count, all under the watchful guidance of Aconite.

He was the representative appointed by the Government on the mainland. It was he who selected the Elders to sit on the Council of Twelve, who helped oversee the law and management of the city. Some Elders became Section Commands, a slightly higher authority than the Elders who watched over us, with most carrying out menial tasks to ensure the working operations of the city. Collectively, they all maintained our compliance, keeping us in check.

Positions, regardless of gender, were bestowed upon those showing unwavering loyalty and devotion to the state. Our everyday existence was scrutinised for this purpose, as only the exceptional would be considered worthy of becoming future leaders. Most left the island when becoming of age, to take up assigned positions on the mainland or on other islands, only returning to Ruin if appointed to do so.

Citizens gathered by a table to our left, curious about artefacts brought back from an archaeological dig. An Elder stood guard, ready to answer questions on origin and history, before they were taken away.

A queue had formed by those wishing to hold gemstones, their hues captivating their audience. These were the best kind of finds sparking an air of excitement as beauty and colour were rare on our dull and lifeless world.

Pretty shells brought pleasure too, and I delved into my backpack to share one I'd found just before we'd stumbled upon the old woman. Its wide mouth and bulbous body looked as if it once homed something precious. I held it to my ear and heard the crashing waves of the Pewter Sea. Shivering with delight, I placed it on the table, happy for others to share my joy.

Animal bones brought much discussion, as it was unusual to find any living creature on Ruin. Only insects and spiders seemed to thrive, enjoying our brutal environment. Cows, sheep, pigs and hens were cloned before The End of Days and stabled underground. This part of Midpoint was off limits, so we never got to see them.

Another off-limits area was the Cellular Tissue Lab. Within its walls, scientist removed scrapings from the scant crops and fruit we managed to grow, manufacturing an array of vegetables. Their flavour never tasted as good as the real thing, but was a welcome compromise until the earth fully healed.

Copper and silver coins were piled on a table and went unnoticed. These were a common find, as well as broken pottery and glass bottles. Giant plasma screens lined the walls all through the city, beaming pictures of all relics, so everyone throughout Midpoint didn't miss out.

Coral and I entered the decontamination hall, a long glass corridor containing scanning pods. They reminded me of ominous sentinels guarding our city, their existence a reminder of the bleak threat of radiation. I stepped inside one of the sleek metallic frames placing my feet on the markers, and the palms of my hands on the back of my head. Dim flickering lights on a small panel emitted an eerie glow in the gloom. After a low hum, the pod fell into darkness, and a thin green light circled around me from head to toe. Once done, the familiar robotic voice confirmed I was free from contamination and allowed entry.

Stepping out on the other side I saw Coral leave her pod and run towards Willow, a girl from her year. A pang of uncertainty hit me as I watched her go. Would she tell Willow about the old woman? I shook off my doubt, having no option but to trust her. It would be tomorrow morning after prayers before I'd see her again.

Prayers were mandatory, with an Elder constantly present at Blessing Square to watch over us. We honoured our Goddess, Pax, twice a day. Most worshipped before or after breakfast and then again in the evening before bed. This helped prevent humanity fall back into wayward ways and having Pax curse the earth again.

She had been angry and brought The End of Days. First, she removed the ozone and the earth became sick. It was a gradual process with no place on the planet escaping her wrath, even plankton in the oceans perished. Rain eventually came, falling thick and black filled with acid from polluted clouds. Icecaps melted, plunging much of the earth's surface under murky water, so landmass changed. The earth was smaller, with people referring to Dominora, as the mainland, with several minor islands surrounding her shores. Pax took pity and offered mankind a second chance, reaching out to Government Officials whom she trusted to govern in her good grace.

* * *

The air always hung heavy in the dorm I slept in, even though it was brightly lit with long overhead lights. Every inch of space was perfectly filled and utilised. Metal bunkbeds jammed the walls on either side, allowing a narrow pathway down the centre.

Our dorm slept two hundred girls, each possessing a personal locker placed beside the bunks. These stored the meagre supply of clothes and shoes permitted, as well as our weapons and backpacks.

I headed for my bunk ignoring a girl sprawled on her bed. I hardly knew her. We were schooled in small clusters from an early age and tended to stick close to those in that group. Even so, we were instructed to be polite to those deserving of courtesy. I only knew Coral because I mentored her with tasks outside Midpoint's walls.

Working with Coral had inspired me, and the bond between us was strong. Perhaps the incident with the fox had sealed our friendship as others saw us as troublemakers. We were kind of stuck together now because of this.

I tossed my backpack and spear on my locker floor. After swapping boots for trainers, I grabbed clean underwear, joggers, and a hoodie before pulling my body warmer from its hanger. Its large pockets would help me stow away food. Hopefully the punishment for losing furs wouldn't be to forgo meals as access to the Be Thankful Hall was vital. It would be the only means to sneak food out for the old woman. First, I'd shower, then I'd eat and report my missing furs last.

* * *

My toes flinched from the chill on tiles as I stepped into the shower cubical. Hot steamy water tumbled, my muscles softening under its powerful spray as I lathered in plenty of soap.

The scars that crisscrossed my back beckoned like magnets,

my fingers stretching behind to trace their jagged welts. The touch of blemished skin emphasizing the new danger I brought to Coral.

Recalling the pain we had suffered, it surprised me how easy it had been to have her agree to help the old woman. But, of course, she had asked me to help her with the fox and now she returned the favour. It was that simple, and I was appalled at my selfishness.

Our rules had us shave our heads, keeping us free from lice infestation. As I massaged my bald skull I thought of the wispy silver strands that reached the old woman's shoulders.

The low beeping tone interrupted my thoughts, warning I had one-minute left before the water would cut out. Locking all thoughts from my mind, I tilted my face up and savoured the seconds I had left.

On leaving the shower, my gut twisted when I spotted two girls chatting by the doorway. Our past misdemeanour left Coral and I open game for pranks, some of them vicious. In our case, it was sanctioned, with hardly any Elders stepping in to stop it. Their aggression further marred the bleak existence we lived in.

I cast the girls a smile, hoping they didn't notice the anxiety that sat beneath it. If they had simply appeared to ogle my scarred back, I'd be happy.

The heat from their stares felt heavy while I dressed awkwardly, trying to hide visible skin with the towel at the same time. All the while I silently begged Pax to make them go away. Perhaps being bullied was part of her plan until her mercy would see it stop.

As I slipped my foot into one of my trainers, an unexpected sensation greeted me. It was the unmistakable feeling of stepping on to soggy toilet roll. Both girls sniggered while I chucked the sodden paper from both shoes in the waste bin and dried the insoles as best as I could.

I squelched towards the laundry chute to discard my dirty clothes and towel, making the moment last as long as possible. Anything to prolong the confrontation I felt the girls waited for.

The moment was charged with a mix of anger and fear and inhaling deeply, I strode towards them. They stood their ground confidently while I wore a false bravado, marching forward with clenched fists.

'Freak,' the larger of the two girls said.

Thankfully, they were both slightly younger than me and I was annoyed I had let their intimidation diminish my confidence. I barged past, slamming my shoulder hard into the gobby one hoping it would curb further harassment. It didn't work.

'You're nothing but an ugly freak,' she growled.

Leaning into her face, I pinned her with a feral stare and jabbed my finger into her shoulder. 'Mess with me again and it's the last thing you'll do. If you think I'm ugly, wait till you see the state of you by the time I'm finished if you give me any more of your crap.'

Deflated, her eyes fell to the floor, and side-stepping past, she darted towards her friend already backing away.

'My name is Jasmine, so don't ever call me a freak again,' I called after her.

Her courage magically re-appeared when out of reach. 'You better pray you leave Ruin soon, Jasmine, because the scars on your back will look pretty compared to what I'll do to you.'

At least she didn't refer to me as freak this time. I flipped her the finger without turning round to deliver my reply. 'Put toilet paper in my shoes again and I'll stuff them down your throat.'

Little did they realise I was desperate to leave Ruin too and put the past behind me. I was in my sixteenth year and a decision on my future would be made soon. Depending on progress, I'd become a breeder or worker for the state. Those who proved exceptional were handed prominent roles. Some were selected to become part of a holy order on the island of Mortem, but there's no way Pax would want me. I had tarnished any decent opportunity, and I think that's why helping the old woman had come so easily. I had nothing to lose.

* * *

Rowan caught my eye while I waited in line at the food court. She sat next to Lily waving enthusiastically through a mass of bodies. They were at the end of a table and if those beside them shuffled up, there'd be plenty room for me.

'Always be thankful,' the Elder said, handing me a tray, his tone aloof.

'May Pax receive my thanks,' I said, offering a smile which wasn't reciprocated.

Elders were everywhere, observing from the side-lines. The rigid white collars atop their black tunics looked uncomfortable, but the silver buttons down the front added a touch of brightness. Females sometimes wore black pleated skirts falling gracefully to their ankles, but more often, they opted for dark chinos matching the men's attire.

The Elders spanned a broad age spectrum too, with some as young as their early twenties, while others reached the age of fifty. This diversity served as a testament to the importance and longevity of the role they played on Ruin.

By the time I got to the end of the line, I had two hard boiled eggs, three slices of crusty bread, a chicken breast, a heap of greens, an apple, and a pitcher of water to wash it all down.

The Be Thankful Hall was one of my favourite places in Midpoint. It always buzzed with activity creating a vibrant and bustling atmosphere. Clattering cutlery, clinking glasses, bursts of laughter, scraping chairs, all lively and cheery sounds followed me as I weaved my way round busy tables.

'Are you cold?' Rowan asked, eyeing my padded body warmer. She missed nothing.

'I slipped on wet rocks and part of me landed in a black puddle. My furs got soaked, so I checked them over with my Geiger counter. The reading looked high, so I tossed them away. Obviously, it was a huge mistake, and I've been frozen all day.'

It was a poor lie but the first that entered my head, and I cursed silently for not being better prepared, especially with Rowan.

'That's not like you. You'll get punished,' she replied.

'I know. It all happened so fast, and I feel really bad by the way I handled the situation. Poor Coral was distraught.'

'You should have bagged them and brought them back to be cleansed. Not thinking is not an excuse. Not thinking is what will be your downfall. Not thinking will be...'

Lily interrupted Rowan's flow. 'Poor you, Jasmine, that's awful. No wonder you feel frozen, it was chilly this afternoon. Hopefully, you didn't hurt yourself and the rest of your day turned better.'

Lily's smile illuminated her kind blue eyes. From a distance, her face looked as smooth as her bald head due to sparse blond eyelashes and eyebrows. Even her short stumpy nose and thin lips seemed out of place on her long pale face.

In contrast, Rowan possessed a vibrant complexion. Her green eyes were framed with thick amber lashes and complemented by a dense set of eyebrows. A dark mole resided slightly above her plump ruby lips, enhancing her perfect pearly teeth.

'I saw your chart. You were down by Section Twenty on the beach. Did anything interesting wash up?' Rowan asked.

If only she knew, and I could imagine her face exploding had I told her.

'Nope, nothing at all,' I said.

Rowan's voice took on a dreamy tone. 'Don't you just love working on the beach, especially after a storm when the Pewter Sea spits out all the old stuff. It's one of my favourite places to be tasked. Not that I miss the menial jobs command hands out. There're much more important issues for skilled citizens of my calibre, than to be busy with mundane jobs between schooling.'

Our tasks and much of our daily routines came from the Central Office, which was run by Commanders and supervised by Section Commanders, answering directly to the Council of Twelve.

While Rowan continued to boast, Lily caught my gaze and rolled her eyes. To be honest, I was more than happy to let Rowan prattle on as it saved me from answering awkward questions and having to lie.

'Well, Jasmine, did you find anything?' Rowan asked.

'I found a nice shell that sounds like the sea. It's on the table if you'd like to see it. Wouldn't it be awesome if we found life in the rock pools? The waters tested are clear of radiation but are still dark. Imagine being the first to discover the rebirth of sea urchins or starfish.'

'I loved that class lesson,' Lily said, her eyes glazing tenderly. 'My favourite was the seahorse. They looked so majestic and beautiful gliding in a turquoise sea.'

'Guess black waters are not to their liking,' Rowan quipped. 'So, if your Geiger counter showed clear readings in the rock pools, how come you managed to misread it when you fell and threw away your furs?'

I was speechless at my folly, but Lily swooped in to save me again. 'The saplings in the east have taken root. It's way too early to tell if they'll mature, but they're looking good now.

Perhaps Aconite may allow a small festival if we have some success? It would be lovely to have something to celebrate.'

'Are you hungry? You seem to have an awful lot to eat.' Rowan asked.

'I'm starving,' I replied. 'Must be the salt air.'

Our early years in the nursery introduced us to many principles before integrating fully into Midpoint. Pax despised gluttony, and we were taught to respect a minimal diet. Having food piled on my plate would cause suspicion, and the last thing I needed was to be accused of gluttony.

'What about you, Rowan? Any sign of outsiders finding their way to our island?' I asked, trying to distract her from my stacked tray. Giving her something to brag about would do the job.

'None since the last one. Perhaps the rebels have heard of me and are too scared to venture to Ruin. Don't worry, I'll keep you all safe.'

Rowan had wounded a stranger and brought him back to Midpoint. After a long and painful interrogation, he confessed to being part of the rebellion on the mainland. His capture was an outstanding achievement, promising Rowan a bright future. The cleansing process was horrific and transmitted on every screen in Midpoint. I'll never forget the roaring inferno, with flames leaping and cracking towards him. Thick plumes of smoke billowed, suffocating the sound of his high-pitched screams. The foul odour of burning and singed flesh will stay with me forever too.

'Am I boring you? You look a million miles away.'

'No, not at all. I was just wondering . . . do you think all those who come uninvited to our island mean us harm? How can we be sure that they're all bad?'

Rowan tilted her head back and chuckled. 'Don't be so naïve. The rebels are sub-human, they stand against every one of our teachings. Of course, they mean us harm.'

'But can we be sure? Have we ever stopped to ask why they come in the first place? There could be other reasons than just to cause trouble.'

'They must mean us harm, or they'd apply for visitation rights and wouldn't go behind our Government's back,' Lily added.

It was difficult trying to keep errant thoughts to myself, that if we tried to understand our differences, we may learn to live beside them in peace.

'Why cleanse them? Surely, we could find a better punishment that would help serve the state.'

Rowan nodded methodically. 'Good point, but cleansing is a deterrent, and shows those who take a stand against us, our Government means business.' She looked around, leaned in, and lowered her voice. 'I've heard that the womenfolk caught are sometimes used as breeders. Only if they're healthy.'

Rowan sat back, forking beef into her mouth. She began to splutter. Lily jumped to her feet and loyally patted her back while Rowan grappled in her pocket pulling out a tissue. A small white plastic card came with it, falling to the floor. Lilly plucked it up quickly. 'This looks official,' she said, holding it out for me to see while Rowan composed herself. 'It has Aconite's stamp on it.'

Rowan lunged, grabbed it from Lily's grasp and packed it back in her pocket.

'What is it?' Lily asked.

'Nothing that concerns you,' she said, her face livid.

Lily shuffled awkwardly, uncomfortable with Rowan's reaction. 'I was only asking,' she said.

Rowan's voice took on a milder tone. 'It's no big deal, and I'm sorry if you felt I was rather harsh. I was asked to take part in a special project by the Council of Twelve, and the card is my membership. The reason I didn't want you or Jasmine to know was because I didn't want you both being more jealous of my achievements than you already are.'

I was about to quiz Rowan further when Salix appeared, dumping his tray on the table. Water splashed from his mug, and he cursed under his breath.

'I'll be right back,' he said, marching off to a nearby dispenser pulling a handful of napkins. We watched amused as he mopped up the mess.

'Can I join you?' he asked, sitting beside me before we had the chance to reply. I adored Salix. He was the only person in my year who'd offered any sympathy after the incident with the fox. With Salix's help, I restored friendships with my small group and life became bearable again. Coral didn't have it as easy. Her only support was Willow, and was still shunned by most in her year.

'You look happy, Salix,' Rowan said. She always appeared less hostile when boys were around.

'I was training with Ash and Spindle in the Hall of Exercise. Look at the success board next time you're in. You'll see I'm still leading the fitness charts, and I've managed to knock two minutes off my stamina records.'

'That'll please Ash,' Rowan chuckled.

Salix grinned. 'He wasn't happy at all.'

Exercise was encouraged, believing it sharpened the mind as well as keeping us fit. I took part grudgingly, often joking I'd rather attend the Medic to have toenails pulled. My envy of Rowan was evident, as she held the highest scores in our year for girls, never failing to remind us all.

Rowan's hand snaked out from under the table, her palm resting on the top of Salix's hand. I stared in disbelief, and Salix noticed. His handsome faced turned crimson as he pulled himself free. If an Elder noticed, they'd both have gotten into serious trouble.

I chewed slowly on a piece of chicken listening to my

friend's gossip, only too glad when they said their goodbyes and left. Looking round to make sure no one was watching, I wrapped the uneaten bread, apples and boiled eggs in napkins and packed them in my pockets.

Heading to the dorm to stowaway stolen food, I ran the words through my head that I'd use for my confession of lost furs, hoping the punishment wouldn't be too harsh.

3

Furs were manufactured on a different island. Made from fibres collected from polymers, they were blended with chemicals to make them warm and robust against our haphazard weather. Traders brought them to us, along with uniforms, shoes and toiletries. In return, we passed some crops we managed to grow.

Traders had mastered the art of sailing the adverse conditions of the Pewter Sea, tirelessly travelling from the mainland, Dominora, to surrounding islands ensuring the flow of provisions. Sadly, we rarely interacted with them as their dealings were reserved to the Elders, or the Council of Twelve. It would have been wonderful to hear of captivating adventures outside of Ruin.

Having to admit I'd lost my furs had me in turmoil and my confidence waned. I felt sickly, like I had a gaping hole in my gut that couldn't be plugged.

On the way to the Giver of Goods, I passed the nursery unit where we lived until year five. Section Commanders had taken care of us, teaching us how to work as one for the good of Pax. I don't know why, but other than learning much of our doctrines, I don't remember much of the time spent there.

One recollection was Naming Day, a special occasion where numbers were shed, and names were given of something beautiful from the old world. I was handed a picture of a magnificent flower with long white petals, and took its name, Jasmine. With our new identities, we integrated into Midpoint's society vowing to practice virtues worthy of Pax. To this day, the picture was still my prized possession and hung on the wall by my bunk.

My pulse quickened when I spotted Rowan chatting with Ash and Spindle outside the Hall of Knowledge. Hoping to scurry past, I put my head down and stepped up a gear as the last thing I needed was further scrutiny from Rowan. My luck was awful.

'Jasmine, over here,' she called signalling for me to join them.

Hoping my smile appeared genuine, I waved my hand and wandered over. 'Hey, I didn't see you there.'

'How strange. I was just telling Ash and Spindle about your missing furs when *poof*, you appear like magic,' she said.

I folded my arms across my chest and snapped back. 'It's no big deal. The only person making something of it is you. It was an accident and accidents happen. I'm on the way right now to collect new furs, so unless there's another possible route I don't know of, I was bound to pass this way.'

I couldn't help but feel she had set the whole scene up bringing Ash and Spindle to help gloat at my misfortune.

'I hope you're as brave when you confront the Giver of Goods,' Ash said, throwing a sympathetic look.

Spindle smirked which wasn't a surprise. I knew he disliked me well before the incident with the fox, but I could never fathom why.

'It'll be fine. It's not like I ever lost furs before.'

'It's not like you to lose anything. You're usually so careful. What came over you?' Rowan asked.

Her fault-finding was tedious, covering the same ground we had at dinner for her new audience. It didn't help, I was wary of Ash, carrying scars on my back for his betrayal.

'I panicked, that's all. I'll deal with the consequences and be more careful in future. It must be wonderful being perfect, so don't let my stupidity worry you.' I stole a glance at Ash. 'I'll always be fine, no matter how many times someone has a go at me or cracks a whip.' Blood rushed to my face, and I bit on my lip to stop further words coming that I'd regret.

'I'll come with you,' Ash said. 'It's been a while since we've chatted, and I think you could use some support.'

Rowan's mouth formed an o shape and I swear she'd have stabbed me in the stomach if she had something sharp in her hand.

'Honestly, I don't need a babysitter. I'm more than capable of going on my own.'

'I'd like to tag along.' Ash said. 'I want to see if you'll handle the Giver of Goods the same way you just did us. I swear your tongue is getting sharper than Salix's spear.'

Rowan flexed her fingers, and if flames had burst from her nose, I wouldn't have been surprised.

'Evening prayers are soon, and you don't want to be last in at Blessing Square, Ash. Jasmine deserves whatever punishment is served, but you would be wise to avoid becoming entangled in her web of foolishness,' Rowan whined.

His eyes were soft as he looked at Rowan, placing a hand over his heart. 'You go on and I'll meet you and Spindle there later. I promise not to be too late. And don't forget, you said you'd help Lily with her navigation skills. She's probably looking for you right now.'

Spindle fixed me with a disdainful gaze, his icy blue eyes piercing through me, while his face brimmed with contempt.

He tugged on Rowan's elbow. 'Come on,' he said. 'I'll walk with you to find Lily. She really does need help.'

Rowan shot a deadly look in my direction before stomping off with Spindle. Ash and I walked in the opposite direction. My brain felt like mush as I grappled for something logical to say. As much as I was horrified at Ash's offer, I also felt an inner glow I couldn't explain.

'What was all that about?' I asked. 'Rowan acting all territorial and then charging off.'

Ash chuckled. 'It's her hormones kicking into overdrive.'

'What's hormones?'

'We're born with them, and they help how we develop physically. Some kick in later causing our bodies to change. That's why Salix, Spindle and I have to shave our faces as well as our heads,' he said, rubbing his chin. 'They can cause fluctuations in your mood too and make you act strange. That's what's probably up with Rowan.'

'Like what's happening now,' I said. 'Because you offering to come to the Giver of Goods and wanting to help is certainly strange.'

He gave a lop-sided grin that made my stomach flip. 'Hormones make you feel and do some very odd things apparently, and the last thing our Government needs is for people to be acting foolishly. Don't worry about them though, as scientists have engineered a pill to suppress them. We'll be given them soon and the whole hormone problem will go away.' he said, in a matter-of-fact manner.

'How do you know about all this stuff?'

'I hear things,' he said. 'And remember them for future use.'

'That could get you into trouble.'

He sucked in his cheeks and screwed up his face. 'Says the girl who misplaced her furs.'

His attempt at humour made me smile and I felt myself warming to his charm. It didn't last long.

'How's Coral doing? She seems to be coping better now.'

'Is that another thing you hear?' I asked. Him saying her name snapped me back to reality. It was his fault she was left with only Willow as a friend. Being with him and enjoying his company was a betrayal to her. Coral hated Ash. I did too.

An awkward silence hung between us until Ash broke it. 'It had to be done. I'm not proud of it, but I'm not ashamed either.'

'What are you talking about now?'

'Reporting you and Coral to the Council. I had no choice in the matter.'

I didn't know what to say, other than point out I would never have told on him. I was wondering how to phrase it when he took me by surprise.

'I never got to say how sorry I was, and I never thought for one minute you'd be flogged. It was a cruel punishment and no person should be treated that way.'

My eyes met his and I could see the sorrow in them. It had never occurred to me he felt regret.

'Knowing how much Coral and I suffered, would you report us again?' I asked.

He looked appalled. 'Surely you wouldn't be so stupid though. Did you not learn anything from the last time?'

'If I helped a poor wounded creature again and you found out, would you report me knowing how much pain the punishment would bring? It's a simple question.'

Watching him ponder the question methodically made my blood boil. I was about to tell him to forget it when he answered, his face sombre and his tone subdued.

'It's for the good of us all. If we don't obey the rules, then we're no better than the rebels from the caves. Yes, I'd report you again.'

I opened my mouth to argue, but he placed his hands over his ears and shook his head, making a joke of the matter. The fact he could equate the pain we suffered as being good for us all made my heart heavy and an uncontrollable urge to punch him in the face surged. If we hadn't arrived at the Giver of Goods, I don't know what damage I could have done.

An Elder by the name of Birch watched with beady eyes as we crossed the room to the counter where he stood. He cleared his throat with a husky cough. 'How can I help you?'

My hands were clammy, and I fought to control the quiver in my voice. I took a deep breath, was about to say the words, but didn't get the chance.

'While out on patrol today, I slipped and fell,' Ash said. 'My furs got muddy and wet, so I took them off and placed them on a rock to dry. It was a busy day, and I was all over the place. Anyway, when I returned to retrieve them, I couldn't remember where I'd left them. I searched for hours but eventually had to return to Midpoint without them. I'm so sorry and really embarrassed by the whole saga.'

While the lies slipped easily from his mouth, my breath came in short spurts. My mind raced frantically wondering how to rectify the situation without landing us both in trouble. 'Ash, you don't...'

He flapped his hand, swatting my feeble attempt away. 'I'm grateful for your support in coming with me. But its fine, and I must deal with this in my own way.'

Half of me wanted to do somersaults while the other half raged at his stupidity. There was nothing I could do. Birch had his tape measure out measuring Ash's length and girth. 'You do realise this must be reported to the Council,' he muttered, tapping sizes into the keypad of his computer.

'Yes, absolutely, and I'll take any punishment assigned without complaint. It's the least I can do for my foolishness.'

Birch drummed his long skeletal fingers on the counter. 'Let your Section Command know of the area you were tasking and to keep an eye out for them. If they're found, they'll need to be brought back and cleansed. Goodness knows what vermin might sabotage them, given the chance.'

Ash nodded gratefully. 'I'll let him know at once.'

'Now place your brand here,' Birch said, pointing to the bar chip on his monitor. Ash placed his right wrist against the screen and we heard a low hum, as it registered the procurement, documenting Ash's brand against new furs. Birch disappeared through a door that led to the warehouse, leaving me to gawp at Ash.

'Why did you do that?' I asked.

He didn't get a chance to reply as Birch returned with a sealed cloth bag. 'Take this and be more careful in future. You'll be notified of your punishment shortly.'

Ash thanked Birch, apologizing again as we left the store.

'Why did you do that?' I asked again, as we headed towards Blessing Square.

His voice cracked when he spoke. 'I don't know, it just happened. I guess it was something I felt I needed to do.' He handed me the furs. 'Take this and don't lose it, okay.'

My hands shook as I accepted them. Ash beamed, and my heart flipped over.

'They won't punish me the way they will you. I'm one of their bright hopefuls, remember?'

Had he claimed to be a bright hopeful at any other time, I'd have thought him smug, but saying it now was the perfect way to make me feel better. We wandered on, my mind toiling over his act of kindness which left little room for the light conversation he made.

Prayers had already begun with a huge crowd gathered at Blessing Square. Aconite spoke from a marble pulpit, his solemn face etched with resilience and his words carrying an undeniable power, demanding our attention.

He dressed for the part too, hooded and draped in opulent teal robes. Their richness magnified by a striking emblem of

Pax's all-seeing eye brilliantly stitched across his chest in vivid yellow.

The same emblem loomed in the air above, projected in colossal form, a reminder nothing went unnoticed. I wondered what Pax would make of Ash confessing to my wrongdoing, and if she'd seek reprisal.

With hands by my side, I bowed my head and whispered the prayer taught to us before words even formed. The whispers inside my head differed, as I begged Pax to be lenient and show mercy to Ash. At that exact moment, Ash's fingers stretched over and brushed against mine. A strange and wonderful tingle ran up my spine.

4

My sleep was restless. I was back in the cave with the old woman trying to prise her free from iron shackles that chained her to the cavern wall.

'Can you hear them?' she asked.

'Hear who?'

'The Draconian. They'll eat my flesh and suck my bones.'

I stopped pulling at her constraints and strained my ears. 'It's nothing. There's no one there,' I said, after a few seconds.

'Listen,' she urged.

My heartbeat quickened as a figure lurched from the gloom. It was Ash, but he looked different, warped, covered in green scales; he sniffed the air with a flat nose. 'I smell your fear.' He stared eagerly from cold, calculating amber slits while his forked tongue probed the air.

I turned frantically to the old woman, but she was gone. Coral hung in her place, her head sagged awkwardly to the side while Aconite thrashed his whip on her back.

'Old wounds,' Coral mumbled, over and over.

Blood seeped through the cloth on Coral's back firing

Draconian Ash's hunger. 'You broke the rules again. Coral must be punished.'

'Please no, not Coral, not this time,' I begged. 'Punish me. It was my idea.'

A taloned claw seized my elbow, the sharp pain throwing me from sleep. I sat bolt upright, soaked in sweat and stared into Lily's face. It was her fingers that tethered my arm and had shaken me from my nightmare.

'Are you okay? You were calling out for Coral.'

I pulled my arm free from her grasp and wiped my forehead with a shaky hand.

I looked around the dimness of the dorm, the rhythmic breaths and gentle snores confirming it was only Lily I'd woken. 'I'm fine, it was just a bad dream.'

'You were tossing and turning so bad the whole bunk shook. It woke me up. Do you want to talk about it?'

I shook my head. 'No, I'm fine, honestly.' The clock on the far side wall welcomed the new morning but it was still early. 'We should try and go back to sleep for a little while. I feel bad I disturbed you.'

Lily tilted her head and gave a little smile. 'I'm worried about you. You don't seem to be yourself at the minute. You know I'm here for you if you need to talk.'

'I'm tired. That's all. Please don't worry.'

Her lips tightened. 'Okay, I'll try not to, but no more nightmares.'

She climbed the ladder back to her bunk, leaving me alone with my thoughts. I was too scared to close my eyes in fear of falling into another nightmare, so I stared blankly at the space between mine and Lily's bed.

The sound of peaceful sleep charmed the air, soft murmuring breaths, occasional sighs, and the creaking of Lily's mattress as she settled. I was envious of such contentment.

The events since finding the old woman played over in my

mind. Coral helping me carry her to the cave. Rowan being critical of me in the Be Thankful Hall. Ash claiming my punishment. Guilt crept in too, as I hadn't asked Lily about her problems. Ash had intimated to Rowan she was struggling and needed help. Lily had been kind, had offered to be there for me and I hadn't returned the sentiment. I took a mental note to rectify this as soon as possible.

* * *

Ash wasn't at morning prayers, or not that I could see. I scanned the room for him more than I'd care to admit. Rowan stood with Salix and Spindle, scowling in my direction, apparently harbouring annoyance from the night before. There was no sign of Lily either, so I prayed alone before heading for breakfast.

* * *

Every morning, prior to heading out on assigned tasks, we took anti-sickness tablets. Despite the gradual decrease in radiation levels over generations, the Government remained cautious, not allowing us to take any chances.

We collected our tablets via a medical vending chute located near the steel doors. You simply placed your brand against the bar code scanner, and it dispensed your daily dose. This was where Coral and I usually met before heading out of Midpoint.

She was always pleased to see me, and we enjoyed our time spent together. She commended my mentoring skills, comparing them to horrible stories heard from Willow. Claims of bullying, and the mentor skiving off, leaving the novice to complete tasks on their own was common. I would never dream of asking Coral to do something I wasn't prepared to do myself, no matter how much I hated the chore.

Coral also heard rumours of younger children going missing. They simply vanished with no questions asked, with the mentor unperturbed when assigned a new junior. It took some convincing for Coral to believe this was gossip designed to frighten juniors into behaving.

We trudged our usual path of rugged terrain, each step taking us closer to the Black Cave, and for me a sense of adventure to find out about the old woman. The air was fresh with a scent of salt as we neared the beach.

Coral walked quietly, carrying a bleakness that robbed our usual morning conversation. Dark shadows lay beneath her eyes, so I guessed she hadn't slept much either. Letting her have her silence, I waited a while before I spoke. 'Thanks, Coral.'

'What for?'

'For not saying anything about the old woman.'

'How do you know I haven't?'

'Because Aconite's guards would've come for me by now.'

'You kept my secret. It's only fair I keep yours.'

Gloomy clouds loomed above casting a dullness over land that seemed to match Coral's mood.

'Do you think she'll still be alive?' Coral asked.

'I don't know. It was cold last night, and she didn't look good when we left her.'

'I've been thinking, what if she does have the sickness. Will we catch it and die too?'

I shook my head fiercely. 'She didn't show any sign of contamination. In all my years, I've never heard of sickness being reported, so I think it's something of the past. Radiation levels are reducing, so even if she has something wrong with her, I don't think it will be infectious. Anyway, the tablets we take should keep us immune.'

It didn't matter how many times I tried to rationalise it, our belief system kept us in continual fear, reminding us of suffering from the past. Excruciating pain and racking nausea. Internal bleeding and bodies plagued with leaking boils, the pus so pungent you could smell the sick for miles.

'What are we going to do with her? Next week our rota changes and we won't be down by the beach.'

This problem had occurred to me, but I'd been too scared to plan too far ahead. She was barely alive when we left her. 'Let's just take it a day at a time,' I said.

Breaking free from the confines of her bleak mood our conversation began to flow. 'How did it go with the Giver of Goods? Your new furs look a bit big,' she said chirpily, eyeing me up and down.

Although I welcomed the change of subject, my worry now turned to Ash. There was no way I could tell Coral he'd come to my rescue. Not only that, it was unfair of me to ask her to keep another secret.

We laughed at my made-up account of Birch incorrectly measuring my size, and how ridiculous I looked. It wasn't long till we heard the distant roar of waves crashing against the black slate rocks, and stood peering into the jaws of the Black Cave.

Coral followed my footfall, my fingers tracing the curve of damp rock while my eyes adjusted to the gloom. We moved as fast as the darkness would allow through the narrow passage, the stalactites hanging like daggers, guarding the cavern where the old woman slept.

As we cautiously approached the ledge, the sound of her rasping breath grew louder. She clutched the furs I had left with her, seeking warmth in their embrace. Kneeling down on the floor, I tenderly stroked her cheek, exploring the intricate lines that mapped her face.

'Hello, it's me,' I said. 'We've come to see how you are.'

A small groan escaped her lips as her eyes flickered open.

Her gaze darted nervously back and forth between Coral and me, and then to space of her surroundings.

'It's okay, please don't be frightened. We found you washed up on the shore and when you passed out, we brought you here. This is a safe place where nobody will find you.'

She offered a slight smile which made her look familiar, but I couldn't think why.

'Are you hungry?' I asked.

'Thirsty,' she croaked.

She took my arm, and I helped her sit. Coral passed the water flask from my backpack without having to be asked and I handed it to her. Putting it to her mouth she gulped back its contents. Within seconds she retched, heaving water up as quick as it had gone down, splattering on the cave floor.

'It's the sickness. She has the sickness,' Coral shrieked stepping back.

I prised the flask from the old woman's grasp and trying not to gag, wiped the sour mess with dried seaweed from the makeshift bed. 'Don't panic, it's not the sickness. It's because she drank too quickly.'

Coral looked ready to bolt at any minute.

'I'm sorry child,' the old woman said, wiping her mouth with the thin skin of her hand.

'Sip slowly, only a little drop at a time,' I said, handing her back the flask with the little water it had left.

Coral bit her bottom lip, watching warily and I was at a loss on how to calm her fear. Rummaging through my backpack, I pulled out some bread and hard-boiled eggs. 'You should try and eat,' I said, peeling one of the shells.

The old woman screwed her face. 'I'm not hungry.'

'I'll leave it here.' I placed the food on a rock beside her, hoping the sight of it would encourage her appetite.

'What's your name?' Coral asked.

'Mary.'

Coral's brow knitted as she stepped towards me, leaning close and keeping her voice low. 'What kind of name is Mary?'

With no plausible answer, I shrugged my shoulders. Naming Day brought great excitement at Midpoint, as every now and then an unusual one would emerge. We'd all gather round to see the picture and admire what it looked like. I had never heard or saw the name Mary.

The old woman's eyes drooped. 'I'm so tired,' she said, sliding back down on the ledge and pulling my furs tight.

Her brow was clammy to touch, and her breath came in short distinct pants.

'What do you think is wrong with her?' Coral asked.

'She needs to rest for her body to heal.'

'Let's go and tend to our tasks. We'll come back in a little while to check on how she's doing.'

I worried about leaving food on the rock, afraid it would attract ants or other creepy bugs. Yet, to have her wake and be hungry was the option I favoured less.

* * *

It was blustery along the shoreline. Gusts of wind whipped up sand, making our tasks more challenging. As we tried to cast our nets into the shallows, the wind blew them in the opposite direction. With each attempt, they twisted and tangled, regardless of our efforts to rectify their movements. Frustrated, I left Coral to fix them while I headed to check the rockpools.

Our aim was to hopefully find living creatures to cultivate the oceans once more, as sea life was the only food we'd been unable to replicate. Kneeling on cold damp slate, I lifted my net and checked the black water for movement or ripples. I delicately probed the nooks between stones with finger tools, tapping gently. If life was present, I didn't want to scare it to death.

All the while, I did my best to keep the old woman from mind. It was useless, as thoughts of her wormed their way in along with so many questions. Having a name made her presence more real, even if it was one that didn't have a visual concept.

It was nearly time to head back to Midpoint, so we stopped our tasks and trekked back to the Black Cave for a final check on Mary. Her sleep was sound with light snores breaking the silence of her tomb.

'Look.' Coral said, pointing to the rock.

The food was gone and in its place were symbols Mary must have scratched with flint.

> Thank You.

We had no clue of their meaning but stood side by side admiring the curves and shapes.

We left the remainder of food on top of the symbols along with my flask. As much as it grieved me, we headed back to Midpoint leaving Mary alone for a second night.

5

Ash sat alone on a bench outside the Be Thankful Hall. He looked deep in thought, and I wondered why he wasn't inside eating with Salix and Spindle. His face was well chiselled, with dark brown eyes like saucers draped with thick black lashes. It was difficult not to admire his good looks.

I was tempted to go over and speak with him rather than head to the dorm to hide pilfered food. My face flushed when he caught me looking and flashed one of his brilliant smiles.

'Jasmine, how's things?' he said, his voice light and friendly.

A whirlwind of emotion took hold and I strode over, unable to hide my concern and leaving myself emotionally exposed. 'Thank goodness I've found you. I've been worried all day. Why were you not at prayers or breakfast, and why are you sitting here all on your own?'

His grin broadened. 'You shouldn't have worried. I told you I'd be fine.'

The fact he could be so calm while being at odds with the Elders was beyond me.

'What's going on?' I asked.

He patted the bench beside him, and I eased myself down.

'Well, what happened?'

'Nothing much.'

I clenched my jaw, annoyed I was having to prise information from him. 'What do you mean by nothing much? You've been missing all day.'

He gave my shoulder a playful shove. 'So, not only were you worried, but you were looking for me too. Should I feel honoured?'

'Stop messing around and tell me what happened.'

His skewed smile and raised eyebrow wreaked havoc with my gut. The sensation was strange, making it difficult to think straight. I was about to badger him further when he eased my worry.

'Everything's fine. I was called before the Elders, and they looked at my faultless records as well as all my good endeavours. They told me they were disappointed I lost *my* furs but decided not to be too harsh because I've never been in trouble before. My Section Command also put in a good word.'

'So, you didn't get punished at all?' I asked, fumbling over this revelation.

'No, I didn't say that. I said the punishment wasn't really that bad. I had to stay up all night and do a stocktake of furs.'

Frowning, I rubbed my chin. 'So why did you miss breakfast this morning and why are you not in there eating now?' I said, pointing to the Be Thankful Hall.

'I've been ordered to fast until I hear otherwise, so you won't find me in the Be Thankful Hall until the Elders let me back in. But . . . you could look me out at Blessing Square. Only if you want to.'

Blood rushed to my face as our eyes locked. Not only was Ash delighted at my concern, but he was asking me to seek him out. I fretted over his punishment, feeling guilty he'd been up all night and hadn't eaten.

'I have some food,' I blurted. 'I want you to have it.'

'Why would you have food, you've just eaten?'

His tone was hesitant, and I wondered what had possessed me to be so open with him.

'Jasmine?'

Thinking of a feasible reason was paramount and my brain churned for an answer. I didn't realise how stupid it was till I said it out loud. 'I keep some spare for emergencies.'

He looked confused. 'What emergencies do you need to keep food for?'

I tried a different tactic. 'You need to eat. It's not good to go without food.

'Jeez, who keeps spare food? Are you guilty of gluttony?' His jaw flexed, and a disdainful gaze emanated from his eyes.

The voice in my head screamed for me to play to his ego, to make it all about him, tell him what I thought he'd want to hear. 'I didn't eat last night, or this morning, because I was so worried about *you*. When I didn't see you around in the Be Thankful Hall, I thought I'd help out. I took the food for *you*, so you wouldn't go hungry. It was the least I could do, after you took my punishment. I didn't want to say all that at first, because I didn't want you to feel guilty about me breaking more rules. So there you have it, the truth.'

His face softened. 'You have to be careful. You can't keep doing stuff like this. I took your punishment to make up for what you suffered last time. I didn't take it so you could break more rules.'

'I'm sorry. I won't do it again. Do you want the food or not?'

He shook his head. 'No, return it to the Be Thankful Hall and no more foolishness. I'll eat when the Elders tell me I can.'

His arrogance was tedious. Not only that, but the punishment he received was nothing in comparison to what Coral and I suffered. Counting furs was no big deal compared to having a skinless back. I truly hated him.

He stretched out his arm, pointing the way to Blessing

Square. 'Do you want to walk with me?' he asked, catching me off guard. His gaze held mine and I felt as if I were falling into his eyes. I rose from the bench and inched closer to him with a burning desire to run the tips of my fingers over his flawless face. Spindle appeared from nowhere and swivelled between us barging me to the side. His presence felt intrusive and the magical moment was gone.

'Where have you been?' he asked, without glancing in my direction. 'Come on, you can tell me on the way to Blessing Square.'

My heart sunk as they strode off, and I had a feeling I'd been cheated out of something special.

6

Coral's complexion was pale and her eyes weary. Doubled over, she clutched her sides spraying puke all over her shoes. Mary was gone, except for a chilling pile of bones, a stark reminder she was actually here. I laid a hand on Coral's back feeling the unsettling sensation of damp fabric as blood seeped through her shirt.

Ash stood closely behind me, his flickering forked tongue darting in and out of his mouth, striking my neck. I spun to face him. 'What have you done with Mary?'

His sharp taloned claw circled his stomach. 'She was extremely tasty. That's what happens when you leave a helpless old woman in a cave with Draconian,' he said, his tongue slithering over his lips. 'You can't blame me. Taking your punishment left me without food. What was I supposed to do, steal some from the Be Thankful Hall?'

My hands cradled my ears, fingers pressing tightly against the side of my head to block out his taunts. 'This isn't happening. It's not real.'

Ash's cackle bounced round the cavern. 'You caused all this, Jasmine.'

'We should've had her cleansed,' Coral said. 'I'd rather she burned alive than have Ash eat her.'

'Mary,' I screamed, leaping from the nightmare. Constricted lungs had me gasp for breath and my heart bounced against my ribs. The whole of my body trembled and it took a few minutes for it to stop. Thankfully, not a single soul stirred, all in the dorm oblivious to my night terror. Faint snores mingled with the gentle hum of the air purifying system creating a harmonious backdrop that all was well.

* * *

The Be Thankful Hall seemed quieter than its usual bustling atmosphere as I made my way to the table where Rowan and Lily sat chatting. 'Can I join you?' I asked.

Rowan's frosty face eyed my tray suspiciously. 'The table's all yours,' she said, picking up her tray and turning to Lily. 'Come on, we're finished now. Time to go.'

Lily had just spooned a mouthful of porridge from a half-eaten plate. She swallowed quickly, her gaze flitting between me and Rowan.

'What's wrong?' I asked. 'Are you still upset because Ash came with me to get furs?'

'Why would you think that, as I don't really care? It's just a shame he's not around to see you filling your tray as if you're feeding an army.'

Rowan gathered her belongings and marched off without another word. Lily tidied leftover food onto her tray. 'Sorry about that. I'll go and check she's okay. You know what she can be like,' she said, tottering off after Rowan.

Feeling alienated, I ate alone wondering how long Rowan would hold on to our silly quarrel. Salix waved from across the hall, which helped brighten a miserable morning.

* * *

Coral waited by the steel doors, eager and ready to go. As we headed out, I spotted Ash and Rowan hunched together by the scanning pods. Her hand clutched his elbow possessively while she whispered in his ear. The commotion and bustle of the morning crowd vanished as my attention became solely fixed on them.

Over the span of space, Ash's cold and serious eyes met mine. They bore into me with a chilling gaze triggering a churning deep in my belly. I couldn't help but wonder what Rowan had said.

* * *

Coral chatted endlessly about the mystery surrounding Mary, but I scarcely paid attention. It was only the sight of Mary propped on her ledge with a haunted stillness that jolted me back to problems that actually mattered. She had eaten the food we'd left and drunk all the water.

'How are you feeling?' I asked.

'I'm much better and extremely grateful to you both,' she said, her voice still strained. There was an awkward moment where none of us knew what to do or say, but Mary put that right. Prising herself from the ledge, she closed the distance between us and drew me into her embrace, her moist lips touching my cheek.

A sense of unease settled and my arms hung like lumps of lead, as I was unsure what to do or how to respond to such actions.

Mary performed the same ritual on Coral and to my surprise, she only flinched a little.

'Come and join me,' Mary said, leading the way to her

ledge. I sat cross-legged on the cold floor while Coral unpacked Mary's food.

'What does a Mary look like?' she asked.

'It's just a name, child, it doesn't look like anything.'

'It must look like something.' Coral said. 'All our names look like something,'

Mary pulled my furs over her legs running her fingers through the texture as she spoke. 'My name was one given from the old language. Before The End of Days, names didn't have to look like nature, they were simply names, although some had meaning behind them.'

Coral and I exchanged glances.

'Does your name have meaning?' Coral asked.

Mary nodded. 'Yes, it means Sea of Bitterness.'

Coral looked as though she'd swallowed acid.

'Just like the Pewter Sea.' I remarked, before Coral responded with something awkward. I also wanted to give her a picture, even if it wasn't the prettiest of images.

Coral shrugged and moved on. 'Where are you from?'

'I live on the mainland in a place called Safe Haven.'

'How did you get here?' I asked. 'We couldn't find your watercraft.'

We looked while working along the shoreline earlier but assumed it must have drifted off or crashed on rocks at Hazzard Bay. No sightings of wreckage had been reported, which was good for Mary, as nobody would be looking for an outsider.

'I hitched a ride from a friend and not wanting to get him in trouble, he dropped me off as near to the shore as possible.'

'You nearly drowned,' Coral scolded.

Hearing Mary's story of how she smuggled herself onto our island only confirmed the danger we had placed ourselves in by hiding her.

'Why are you here, Mary?' My voice trembled as I asked.

Her revelation when we found her had held me captive. She thought she knew me, had come looking for me.

'I came to find you, child,' she said, gazing at me with tears clouding her eyes.

'But, why?'

Mary sighed. 'Let me start at the beginning.'

Coral was curious too and sunk down on the cave floor beside me.

'I had a daughter, her name was Laura.'

'What's a daughter?' I asked.

Mary furrowed her brow slightly and her gaze drifted inward as if she were gathering thoughts. It wasn't going to be easy for us if she kept using words from the old language, and she must have realised this.

Mary clasped her hands and leaned forward. 'Before breeders became the new normal, people lived in what was known as a family unit. Some were married or lived with the partner of their choice. I gave birth to a beautiful baby girl, and we called her Laura. I was her mother, my husband was her father, and Laura was my daughter. If I had given birth to a boy, he would have been my son. A son and a daughter are a brother and sister to each other. That best describes the basis of a family unit. Do you understand?'

It was difficult to grasp but I nodded, hoping clarity would come as the story unfolded. Coral wasn't so easily appeased.

'But that was the way they lived before The End of Days,' she said. 'The family unit you talk of has not existed in your lifetime. So, why would you have a daughter?'

'What happened to Laura?' I interrupted, liking the way the strange name rolled off my tongue. I also hoped Coral wouldn't need a meaning for the name and would let Mary get on with telling her story.

'Laura was taken from me many years ago by the Government Guard who raided our caves.'

In a split second, Coral sprung up, her hand instinctively reached for the spear fastened to her back. 'You lied. You told us you were from a place called Safe Haven. You didn't mention caves,' Coral uttered, her muscles taut and her posture adjusting to confront her perceived danger. 'Its only rebels who live in the caves.'

Mary's hands trembled as she extended her palms in our direction. 'It's okay, child. Those who came before me named them this because that's what they were, a safe place, free from tyranny. We live there with our families, trying to create a similar life before The End of Days'.

Coral's reaction was normal, as time and time again we heard tales of those who defied our way of life and had fled to the caves creating an improper existence. Their barbarism and opposing ideals with a desire to undermine and overpower, was a constant threat and challenge to our Government.

Yet, talking with Mary, I could never imagine her as a violent person. She wasn't a savage, and I was certain she didn't mean us any harm. 'Put your spear away and sit down. At least let Mary finish her story.'

Coral stood firm, her wild eyes fixed on Mary. 'No way. She has to be taken to Midpoint right now.' Her voice was sharp as she spat the words. 'She's dangerous.'

We knew little of anything from the mainland, other than what the Elders told us. This was a chance to find answers, and if nothing else, put an end to the doubts I had about our teachings. I was also desperate to know why Mary had come looking for me. Resting my hand on Coral's shoulder, I looked deep into her eyes. 'Coral, please. I'm begging you to give Mary a chance. If you're still not happy after you hear what she has to say, I promise to hand her over to the Elders myself.'

Coral sighed and sunk back to the floor, her face sombre and her hand still grasping her spear. 'Just so we're clear. I'm putting my trust in you, not this monster from the caves.'

Mary sagged against the cold wall of the cavern and took a deep, shallow breath. 'We had just celebrated Laura's eighteenth birthday when the guards took her.'

Coral shot Mary a blank look. 'What's a birthday?'

'A birthday is a celebration of the day a child is born. Look, I know this is difficult for you to understand because life here is so different from the life we live in the caves. We don't part with our offspring. We keep them in our family unit where they are loved and cherished. They grow with free will, whereas you don't. You're taken from the breeder, raised without love in an environment that makes you sleepwalkers, obeying those who govern without question. It's wrong on so many levels.' She paused, rubbed her chin and shook off the anger that simmered on her face. Composing herself, her voice took on a calmer tone. 'The Government Guards took Laura to a breeding camp. They shaved her beautiful ebony curls. Began stripping her life away to transform her into what they wanted her to become. Laura was lucky because she fell in love with one of the Medics in the camp and he loved her right back.'

A dull ache pulsed in my forehead and I tried to massage it away. 'What's this love you speak of that makes a person lucky?' I asked.

Mary gave a sad smile. 'It's one of the most powerful emotions that's been stolen from you. It comes in all different forms. The love of a parent to a child. The love of a man and a woman. The love between friends. Even the love between same sex couples. Your conditioning by the state has created breeders who are coupled without emotion to produce a slave for the state. With love, no mother would freely give up her child.'

It was all too much, too many new words describing scenarios we couldn't begin to imagine. Those who coupled together being allowed to live with each other as a family unit. It was unheard of.

'The Medic's name was Larch and he promised Laura he'd

find a way to free her and return her to the caves. Larch's father was a powerful man holding high rank inside the Government. Learning his son had fallen for a prisoner brought much embarrassment and anger. He forbade Larch to have any further contact with Laura. However, they had already coupled, and Laura was with child.'

Mary wiped away tears and I could tell her heart hurt badly. She clearly missed her daughter. The sad wistfulness of her tone was hypnotic as we hung on every tragic word. 'Laura told Larch how to find us and he made contact. After building up trust, we began to plan her rescue with him. However, it didn't go as planned as Laura's child came early. We had little time to improvise, so, I shaved my head, put on a birthing uniform Larch had given me and with his help, sneaked into the birthing chamber passing as one of the midwifes. We hoped I could smuggle the child away and Laura and Larch would follow later.'

Coral's spear now lay at her feet, her face slack, all hostility gone. 'How did Larch know who his father was and how come he had a father and not a breeder?' It was a good question, and being so absorbed in Mary's tale, one I hadn't thought of.

Mary tutted. 'Your entire existence is built upon falsehoods. The ruling elite who enforce the law reside in ancestral homes that have sheltered their family units for generations. They are branded with distinct symbols, selecting partners to live with exclusively from their inner circle, to keep their bloodlines pure. So, you can imagine Larch's father's rage, knowing his son had given seed to a slave,' Mary said, her voice rising with each syllable. She sucked in air and lowered her voice. 'My people have embarked on a relentless quest to find their hidden homes and expose their hypocrisy once and for all. Why do you think they fear us so much and try to crush our rebellion?'

Mary coughed dryly, and Coral pulled the flask from my

backpack and handed it to her. She smiled gratefully, took a few sips and cleared her hoarseness away. 'It was a difficult birth, and Laura was bleeding heavily.' Mary leaned forward and took my hands. 'When you came into the world it was the happiest moment of her life.'

An unexpected shiver exploded at the bottom of my spine and ran all the way up. Coral gasped, her stare darting from Mary to me.

'You were no sooner snuggled in your mother's arms when Larch's father burst into the room and tore you from her. I was given strict instructions to carry you, under armed guard, to the branding room. A small incision was made on your wrist, allowing the insertion of their implant, followed by the branding of the tattoo on your skin. I felt powerless. Hearing you scream and not being able to save you was one of the worst moments of my life. The colours,' she halted, her voice faltering as she tenderly brushed her thumb over the mark on my skin. 'And this shape have been seared into my memory ever since.'

A wave of tremors coursed through my entire being as my mind processed this revelation. I was Laura's child. I had a family and Mary had come to claim me.

'What happened next?' I asked.

'The Guards took you from me, boarded you on a watercraft bound for Ruin with all the other new-borns of that day. It broke my heart to let you go, but I had no choice. I returned to the birthing room to find out Larch's father wouldn't allow Laura a blood transfusion that would save her life. As she lay dying in my arms, your mother made me promise to find you and bring you home.'

Her hands fell from mine and clasping her head in them she sobbed uncontrollably. Coral and I were at a loss for how to console her, so we remained seated in silence, gazing intently until her tears gradually subsided.

'One of the guards overheard our conversation and I was arrested immediately. It took a long time before my people found and helped me escape.' Mary leaned forward again, her fingers cupping my face, her misty eyes staring intently. 'I'm sorry it took me so long, but I'm here now, *my beautiful darling boy.*'

7

In a single moment, the future I yearend for was whipped away. There was no explanation for the great loss I felt or the profound affect Mary's mistake had made on me.

'Boy,' I gasped, staggering back from her touch.

'Yes, my beautiful grandson,' she said, her brow knitting.

'Oh, Mary,' I said, 'You've got it wrong.'

Thinking logically, it was an easy mistake to make. We were dressed in thick bulky furs, had bald heads, and could easily be mistaken for the opposite sex. Mary had been desperate to unite with her grandson and saw what she wanted to see.

'Jasmine is a girl's name. I'm a girl.'

Mary's face crumpled as my words settled. Her eyes widened, searching for understanding, not believing the harsh reality. The thought of losing her grandson all over again was too much.

'It can't be,' she croaked. 'You have Laura's eyes and I recognise that mark on your wrist.'

I was devastated too, the wonderful sense of belonging shattered by mistaken identity. I'd have done anything to be that child.

'It's your eyes, and you look the right age. Your brand is the same too,' she muttered over and over.

Falling into my arms, I held her close whispering softly in her ear. 'I'm so sorry. The boy you're looking for must share my eye colour and have a similar brand. There are many of us at Midpoint.'

I'm not sure how long it took before Mary's tears ceased and her body turned limp. Eventually, she rose from my hold, picked up my furs and draped them over her shoulders. 'I'll go now,' she said, shuffling towards the tunnel that would lead her from the cave.

'And where exactly are you going to go?' I asked.

She stopped, half turned, and spoke in a defeated tone. 'To find my grandson. Where else would I go?'

Snatching Coral's spear from the floor, it was me who now posed a defensive stance. 'If you take one more step, you're as good as dead.' I said, my arm held high and taking aim.

* * *

Convincing Mary to stay in the cave hadn't been easy. She was stubborn, but quickly realised our fear was not only for her, but for Coral and me too.

Coral didn't say much as we hurried with tasks. We never had much to report anyway, so for once I was grateful for our mundane existence.

'Who do you think Mary's grandson is?' Coral asked.

'I've not got a clue. It could be anyone.'

'If you were to take a guess, who would you pick?'

'We don't even know half the boys in Midpoint so it's a stupid question to ask.'

Coral stirred black water in a rock pool with her spear and watched it ripple. 'What if there's a way to find him? Then we wouldn't need to guess.'

'You're just being silly now,' I said, fed up of such nonsense. 'Keep quiet and get on with your tasks.'

Coral let out a long whistle. 'Stop being so snappy, and have some faith. It should be me mentoring you, for your lack of imagination. You were keen when you thought the stolen baby was you, and now you just want to rid the matter from mind. I never had you pegged as selfish.'

Coral was right, I felt a mix of sadness as well as frustration that I wasn't the stolen baby. Her straight talking penetrated my bleak mood and I threw my disappointment to the side. Coral never failed to amaze me, being vibrant and enthusiastic, and her willingness to take unimaginable risks. Thinking of Mary's story, I realised Coral was the closest person I could call family.

'Go on then,' I said, in a happier tone. 'How would you go about finding him?'

Her face glowed with anticipation. 'We know he has your eye colour and a similar brand. We study all the boys who are in or near your year, have a look at their brand and compare it to yours.'

If only it were that simple. Most citizens wore long sleeves, and it would be difficult to catch a glimpse, let alone study and compare. It would also be rude to ask as most saw their brand as a personal gift from the Government. Not only did it hide the tiny scar from the microchip, but it recorded bloodlines for whatever reason.

'You have to remember, Coral, this happened a long time ago. Mary only thinks he looks like me because that's what she wants to believe. She was dehydrated and confused when we found her and has a connection with me because I helped her. If you ask me, her mind is playing tricks.'

Coral kicked some seaweed to the side and began scraping a hole in the pebbled sand with her heel. 'I can't believe you threatened to use my spear on her.'

'It was the first thing that came into my head to make her stay. You know I'd never have hurt her.'

Coral nodded. 'So, what happens next. She's getting better and can't stay in the Black Cave forever. Each new day she'll be tempted to head out and find him.'

That was true, and Mary was not our prisoner. Our rota would be changing soon and we'd no longer be on the beach. Whatever happened, a resolution would need to be found soon.

'When we visit her tomorrow, I'll see if she can give us the name of the trader who brought her here. Perhaps we can find a way to make contact and ask him to give her safe passage back to the mainland? I don't have a clue how we'll do that yet, but the longer she stays the more dangerous it will become for all of us.'

* * *

The thought of being snubbed by Rowan in the Be Thankful Hall made me nauseous, so I decided to visit the gym and eat later. My decision wasn't born from a desire to exercise, but from a need to find Salix as I wanted to ask him about Lily's problems in the hope I could help.

As I entered the gym, an automated voice welcomed me while I registered my presence on the monitor. It swiftly presented a condensed overview of my past endeavours, which didn't make pleasant reading. I quickly skimmed over it before examining the exercise routine the computer deemed suitable to assign me.

Air purifiers did little to mask the smell of stale sweat, while motivational slogans played on a loop from screens offering encouragement. *Today's pain is tomorrow's fitness* and *feel fit by looking fit.*

The gym resounded with beeping apparatuses, and a

collective chorus of grunts and groans as participants worked out. To me, it felt more like a den of torture than a gymnasium. Salix was nowhere to be seen.

I warmed up with a series of stretching exercises, gently rotating my shoulders and neck, reaching my arms skyward and extending my legs forward and backward.

The first machine on my workout was the exercise bike, and fortunately, the route was entirely flat, making it more manageable. Initially, my legs found a steady rhythm, but after a few minutes, each pedal rotation became increasingly challenging. If there had been any inclines, I'd have struggled more.

As I pedalled through the kilometres, I caught a glimpse of Salix and Spindle loosening up on the exercise mats. I kept my head down hoping they wouldn't glance over in my direction and witness my struggles. Spindle would be delighted, reporting back to Rowan as quick as he could about my lack of fitness.

Stealing a brief look at Salix, I couldn't help but admire him. His muscular arms moved in perfect harmony with his strong, well-defined legs, as he jogged on the spot.

Coral's words sprang to mind . . . the key to finding him was to simply look at their brand. If we were to search for Mary's grandson, this would be our starting point. It was a fleeting and somewhat foolish idea that caught me by surprise, so I promptly dismissed it, tucking it away to the back of my mind.

With each passing minute, I urged my feet to pedal faster, pushing myself to the limit as sweat poured from every pore. A sudden, sharp pain jabbed at my side, causing me to dismount the bike and catch my breath. Salix still worked on the mats, while Spindle moved to the opposite end of the hall, gathering dumbbells for his own exercise.

Draping a small towel around my neck, I ambled over. 'Hey, Salix, fancy seeing you here. I was just going to grab a drink from the cooler,' I said, trying to act casual. 'Can I fetch you one too?'

His smile truly dazzled, reaching his light brown eyes and lighting up his entire face. The shadow outline on his jaw warned the boy in him would soon be gone and that thought made me sad. We'd part ways and never see each other again.

He shook his head. 'No, I'm good just now, thanks. You're out your comfort zone. What brings you here?'

'How could I resist giving it a try after all your bragging. It's about time Rowan had some competition.'

'It's good to see you though, and I'm sure Rowan will appreciate you making an effort. She has it too easy,' he laughed.

The muscles beneath his t-shirt flexed as he stretched his left arm in an arc above his head. I followed it to the tip of his wrist and realised I'd get a good look at his brand when he swapped his stretch to the other side.

The unexpected desire for Salix to be Mary's grandson overwhelmed me and all thoughts of Lily's plight disappeared. Salix was kind, helpful and although we didn't have much in the way of nurture, he seemed to care about people.

Spindle forcefully barged in blocking my view of Salix arm. 'Rowan and Lily were looking for you. They said you didn't appear for dinner.'

'I wasn't hungry,' I replied with a shrug.

'I guess not,' he said. 'One of the perks of sneaking food out of the Be Thankful Hall. You better watch what you're doing or you'll be accused of gluttony.'

Speechless, I stumbled backward, filled with horror at the realisation Ash had gossiped to Spindle about me offering him food.

'You wouldn't do something like that, would you?' Salix asked, with a frown.

If Ash had told Spindle, he'd have told Rowan too. My heart quickened, and a fiery rage dimmed all sense of reason. I wanted to squeeze my hands around Spindle's neck and choke the life from him. Rushing past him, I sprinted from the gym afraid I'd do something terrible. Ash had now found himself back at the top of my hate list.

* * *

Unable to face Rowan's nagging, I headed for the dorm and lounged on my bunk. If only it were possible to sneak out to the Black Cave. Mary would have greeted me, held me close and told me everything would be alright.

Her custom to embrace was wonderful and made me feel safe, showing a hint of the love she told us of. She wasn't like our Elders, who never interacted with us unless to solve a dispute. It niggled that there was more to Mary's people than our leaders allowed us to know.

Girls I barely knew trickled in and began getting ready for sleep. Why was getting acquainted with them such a bad thing? Why was the prospect of friendships forming and falling in love so terrifying for those who governed us?

Mary had gone to great lengths to find someone she loved, had almost sacrificed her life doing so. Yet, here on Ruin, we were draped in heavy furs, sent out to complete a variety of tasks without concern for our welfare or a plea for us to return safely or soon. A heavy weariness settled upon me, and as I closed my eyes, I drifted off to sleep.

The watercraft glided through a calm Pewter Sea, sailing towards the mainland. Thousands of tiny stars dotted the dark expanse of the night sky while the shimmering moonlight lit our way. We were going home.

Having had a deep and peaceful sleep, I woke with a light heart - until I caught sight of Rowan's grim pout directed towards me. Hoping to ease the tension, I smiled over, only to have her ignore my efforts.

'Time to get ready, Lily,' she called.

Lily descended the bunk ladder glancing at me quickly as she passed by. Her eyes were red and marked with worry, her shoulders slumped as if weighed down by a hefty burden.

'Is everything okay, Lily?' I asked.

Her eyes locked with mine as she reached inside her locker pulling out clean clothes for the day. 'Sure, everything's fine,' she said, though her words carried a hint of uncertainty.

'You don't look fine?'

She gave a casual shrug and looked away.

'Have I done something to upset you and Rowan? I feel things are strained between us.'

'Come on, Lily, time to go,' Rowan called impatiently.

'Sorry, we'll chat later,' she said, striding off with Rowan.

* * *

My appetite was low, but as I hadn't eaten from the night before, it made sense to try. I also needed to restock food for Mary. The Be Thankful Hall was mobbed and I scanned the room looking for a seat.

'Over here, Jasmine.' Salix called, waving his arm in the air. Ash and Spindle sat at the table with him, and my chest tightened at the thought of joining them. I navigated my way through the bustling tables perching myself beside Salix.

'Did you get your spear fixed?' Ash asked Salix.

'It's still with the Blacksmith. If they can't fix it, I'll get a new one. That's what happens when you hit your target too hard,' Salix said, his tone lighthearted.

Ash turned his attention to me. 'Have you been abducted by a body snatcher?' he asked. 'Salix was telling me you were at the gym.'

I felt my cheeks redden as I shrunk from his gaze. My stomach did that unusual fluttering, but I did my best to keep my voice casual. 'Salix was telling me how well he was doing, holding all the best records. So, I thought I'd pop along and catch him in action. I must admit, I was very impressed.'

Salix beamed brightly at my comment. Ash on the other hand looked as if he'd been smacked on the face by a brick. This secretly pleased me for reasons I couldn't comprehend.

'Perhaps Salix should be your private coach,' Spindle scoffed. 'I checked your report after you left and was embarrassed for you. You were appalling. You only attempted one machine and I doubt if you even broke sweat. Was it too difficult?'

It would have been kinder if the walls of Midpoint crashed down on top of me rather than suffer Spindle's humiliation.

Ash's leg flew out in a swift calculating kick which he thought was hidden from prying eyes.

'What was that for?' Spindle yelped, rubbing his shin vigorously.

'My foot slipped,' Ash mocked.

'Lucky for me, you kick like a girl,' Spindle replied staring hard at Ash.

'If you mean kick like Rowan, I'll take that as a compliment. She'd have booted you into next year,' Ash said. His eyes held a gentle warmth as they met mine. 'Ignore him. He's just teasing. The more you exercise, the easier you'll find it. Now you've started you have to keep going.'

Ash had me baffled, fluctuating between nice and supportive one minute to solemn and stern the next.

'Did I hear someone mention my name?' Rowan said, throwing a tight smile in my direction. She dumped her tray on the table and squeezed herself in beside Ash. She was another strange character blowing nice to nasty all the time. Poor Lily hovered awkwardly shuffling from foot to foot searching for a place to sit.

'Here, have this seat.' I said, gathering my belongings. 'I'm finished anyway.'

'But you've hardly eaten anything,' Rowan said, firing a smug look at Ash.

Not giving her the satisfaction of an argument, I marched off with determination, the weight of their lingering stares following me.

Luck was on my side as the Elder at the waste disposal unit was stacking trays further down the hall. Standing behind a pillar, I began to pack the uneaten food into napkins and then into my pockets.

'Jasmine,' Ash said, lightly tapping my shoulder.

Startled, I almost hit the ceiling, and was also horrified I'd been caught. My stomach tightened at the intensity of his gaze, undermining my resolve.

'What's going on with you?' he asked.

'Leave me alone,' I said, stepping round him, realising he hadn't saw me steal food.

His steps matched mine to the walk lanes outside. Grabbing my arm, he spun me round.

'Let me go,' I said, straining against his grip.

'Not till you tell me what's going on with you?'

He rubbed a hand over his taut face. 'Speak to me. If you don't tell me what's wrong, I won't be able to help.'

Hot tears burned my eyes and I looked away, not wanting him to see me cry. Inhaling deeply, I pulled myself together. 'I don't know what's wrong. I feel strange, that's all.'

His stance relaxed and he softened the hold on my arm, leading me away from the lively flow of citizens, their hurried footsteps and endless chatter. We sat on a bench, just off the main walkway.

'Do you think you should see a Medic?' he asked, his voice laced with concern. 'They might be able to give you something.'

'I'm not sick. I've just got a lot on my mind just now. Don't ask me to explain because I can't.'

'You don't need to explain anything. We can all see you're not yourself. Rowan is really worried about you. She spoke to me the other morning.'

I faced him square on. 'Really, Rowan is worried?' It was the last thing I expected to hear.

'Yes, we're all worried. Lily say's you've not been sleeping, and Rowan's noticed you're filling your tray full of food but not eating. That's why I was confused when you offered me some. I asked Spindle if he thought this was strange, but he said I was overthinking, and to let you be.'

I couldn't hide the ecstatic grin that gripped my cheeks. My friends weren't plotting against me, they were simply concerned. Since Mary's arrival I'd become paranoid and perhaps a little irrational. 'Don't worry. I'll be fine,' I said, feeling an overwhelming sense of relief wash over me. 'I need to go and find Coral.'

'If you need to talk to someone, you know I'm a good listener,' Ash said. 'I'll always be here for you.'

'Thanks. If I ever do, I'll come find you.' I leapt up leaving with newfound confidence.

As I sped off to meet Coral, my heart soared by the simple offer Ash had made, to be there for me.

8

Fog rolled in from the Pewter Sea, drifting inland as a ghostly mantle and cloaking the slate grey rocks in a misty veil. Down by the water's edge movement was barely visible, but there was no denying someone was there. I grabbed Coral's arm pulling her to a stop as we squinted for a better view. It was Mary and breathing a sigh of relief we strode swiftly towards her.

She was on all fours, picking up stones frantically, turning them over and chucking them to the side. Her eyes darted from place to place as her search grew more erratic.

'What are you doing?' I said, dumping my spear and backpack and dropping down beside her. 'You shouldn't be outside? Do you realise what would happen if someone saw you?'

Her mind was far from us as she dug her fingers below shingle and sand muttering urgently in the old language.

Coral reached out and shook Mary's shoulder tenderly, only to have Mary brush her hand aside.

'Mary,' I said, my tone taking a stern turn. 'What's going on?'

Island of Ruin 63

'I can't find it,' she moaned.

'Find what?' I asked.

'My cross, it's gone. It must have fallen off when I landed here. I really need to find it.' Her eyes welled with raw tears as she wilted into my arms. 'It was attached to this,' she said, pulling the grey string that circled her neck. 'It's a small wooden cross and I wore it all the time. I remember clasping it while praying . . . when I thought I was going to die. It was just before you found me.'

Guilt bore down on me, as it was me who'd thrown it away. I couldn't tell her, not when she was in such an erratic state.

Coral scattered pebbles with her spear, her glum face searching strewn stones. 'It could be anywhere.'

Her frankness had Mary weep again and I knew we had to move her before she became hysterical. 'We need to go back to the cave,' I said, my voice carrying a sense of urgency. 'It's too dangerous for you to be out here and if someone saw, we'd all be in trouble. Coral and I will come down and have a look later.'

Mary shook her head. 'You don't understand. It's all I have left of Laura. When she and Larch made their plans to escape, she gave him the cross to bring to me. It was a sign from her that we could trust him.'

'We need to move her now. The fog is lifting,' Coral said, her eyes sweeping across the shoreline.

With a firm grip, I pulled Mary to her feet. Cupping her face in both hands, I met her sorrowful eyes. 'Come back to the cave. I promise Coral and I will find your cross, and I've been thinking about your grandson. With Coral's help, we'll find him too and do whatever it takes to bring him to you.'

Mary folded against me, and I felt the wet sensation of her tears on my face. 'Thank you,' she whispered through sobs.

We trudged back to the cave in unison, Mary in the middle

and our arms entwined with one another. Our hearts now bound by a promise to find her grandson.

Coral came to an abrupt halt at the mouth of the cave, her gaze fixed on the ground. 'What's this?' she asked, bending down to pick something up. 'Have a look,' she said, handing it to me.

It was a small plastic card with Aconite's stamp on it, similar to the one Rowan dropped in the Be Thankful Hall. It had been Lily who'd retrieved it, so I didn't manage a proper look. Had Rowan been here and found our secret?

Still hindered by foggy patches, I skimmed the long length of the beach.

'Is everything okay?' Coral asked.

'It's fine. Let's get Mary inside,' I said, sliding the card into my pocket.

The air was musty in the cave and the hint of moisture brought a dampness you could almost taste. Mary continued to fiddle with the empty string around her neck as we settled her on her ledge.

Coral fixed a solemn gaze upon Mary. 'You do realise having a cross is blasphemous. It's a symbol from the old God, and a lost world. We're taught in lessons such things anger Pax.'

Mary scoffed disdainfully. 'If Pax were real, or as powerful as you claim, why hasn't she ended the rebellion?'

Coral matched Mary's unwavering determination, refusing to back down. 'That's a bold statement. How can a Goddess that's not real bring about The End of Days? It didn't happen by itself.'

Mary tutted. 'It was man himself who brought about The End of Days. Honestly, they've done a fantastic job filling your heads with nonsense.'

'That kind of talk could get you cleansed,' I said.

Mary grumbled under her breath. Rather than fuel a quarrel, I changed the subject. 'You left us a message, what was its meaning?' I asked, pointing to the etchings on the rock beside her.

'It says thank you. I scratched them there to let you know how grateful I was for the food you left,' she said, tracing her finger over the lines. 'In my community, we learn to write letters and numbers at an early age. It's a skill passed down from those who first fled to the caves. They made an oath to never forget what life was like before the new world order took over, and passed their stories down through many generations with carvings on the rock face.'

The craft of writing had been lost to us as symbols came from tablets and computers. Until now, I'd never really thought of life prior to The End of Days.

'What stories do the carvings tell?' I asked, as Coral and I settled ourselves cosily at Mary's feet.

'They tell of history, so those who come after will always know the truth.'

'And what truth would that be?' Coral asked.

Perhaps it was our sudden interest in Mary's definition of life that perked her mood as she flitted to the role of teacher. 'Before the world died, there were many mainlands called countries. They spoke their own language, had their own Gods, and believe it or not, some had no God at all. Some became superpowers with technology beyond our greatest imagination, which was probably the beginning of when it started to go wrong. Scientists found a way to manipulate weather and a race to weaponise the elements began between superpowers.'

It sounded too bizarre and swapping glances with Coral, I could tell she shared my sense of disbelief.

'Peace was fragile and war inevitable. One country would bring mass flooding to their neighbour and in return the neighbour would trigger forest fires. Battles were brutal - hurricane winds, battering hail or blistering heat. Toxic chemicals leaked into the atmosphere and poisoned the ozone, leaving the earth with no protection from the sun. The world began to wilt.'

Coral expressed her doubt with a furrowed brow, her scepticism evident in her voice. 'It was Pax who brought The End of Days, not countries or their leaders. Pax saved us, appointing trustworthy Elders to form a Government and make sure we didn't stray from her path ever again.'

'Pax isn't real, at least not in the way you perceive it,' Mary retorted, defiantly raising her chin.

'What do you mean by that?' Coral asked, her mouth slightly ajar.

'In ancient times, there was a mighty empire known as Rome, who worshiped numerous deities. Among them was Pax, the revered Goddess of peace. However, this empire fell, and all their mythical Gods with them. Following The End of Days, the new world order resurrected Pax as a tool of manipulation, falsely attributing Earth's miseries to her influence.' Mary chuckled. 'And look how successful they were because you're both shaking in your shoes. Terrified she'll hear us blaspheme and throw a bolt of lightning to strike you down.'

Coral shook her head frantically, the tension slightly rising in her voice. 'But if it wasn't planned by Pax, how did civilisation manage to rise again? Only a Goddess would have the power to breathe life into the world after annihilation.'

Mary waved her hand dismissively. 'Weather manipulation was taking its toll, with the superpowers now believing there would be only one outcome. To have the world governed under the control of a one world order. The superpower countries set their sight on the most powerful energy source known, as whoever controlled the sun would control the planet. Scientists named the project SIAJ. I don't know what it stood for, but the common man called it Star in a Jar.'

Coral's brow creased. 'How on earth could man possibly do that?

Mary's gaze was unwavering. 'Chemicals were mixed together and fired into space causing a nuclear fusion which should have enabled the sun to be harnessed. Rather than go as planned, it caused a nuclear explosion which tipped the world on its axis making the landmass and weather pattern as it is today.' Mary paused briefly, allowing the weight of her words to settle. 'Before this happened, you couldn't look directly at the sun. Now, you can stare at it for hours without having to cover your eyes. Those at the forefront took over, taking charge of rebuilding the world using the survivors as slaves. Perhaps if we can reverse what they did, the world would heal.'

I shuddered at their duplicity. 'Why did powerful countries want war? Why couldn't they live in peace,' I asked.

Mary raised an eyebrow. 'They wanted to own the world and everything in it. Some countries had landmass and resources others were jealous of. Precious metals and oil, or black gold as it was known. The leaders back then were every bit the psychopaths we have now. It's just you've been conditioned not to see it.'

'So, if your God's real, why didn't he step in and do something?' I asked, not wanting to offend another deity. 'Surely, he must have been aware of their intentions.'

Mary's shoulders rose gently. 'We have many different faiths in the caves, as well as some who don't believe at all. Religion isn't forced, but we all work together regardless for the good of us all. We don't wait for Gods to intervene. Instead, we live life as best as we can. Unless you break away from your brainwashing, you'll continue to believe the lies you are told and will never be free.'

Coral caught me off guard with her unexpected curiosity, having opposed Mary most of the way through her discussion. 'What happened to the people after the nuclear explosion?' she asked, with a hint of compassion.

Mary slumped back against the damp rock, her eyes

misting over as she recalled the horrors passed down to her. 'The first few days were the worst. Survivors gathered in small herds scavenging among the dead. Rain fell thick and black on the third day. Those who could looked skywards with open mouths to quench their thirst. Little did they know they filled themselves with poison. Many lost their lives to the sickness radiation brought. The new world leaders eventually emerged from underground bunkers to enforce a new way of life. It didn't take many generations for them to eradicate the memory of normality. However, some realised humanity was being manipulated and took to the caves. In doing so, the rebellion was born.'

'Is that why you pray with your cross?' Coral asked. 'So your God will give strength to the rebellion to overthrow our Government?'

I felt myself grow anxious at the mention of Mary's cross, worried she'd begin to fret again. Coral shouldn't have mentioned it. However, Mary simply shook her head and smiled. 'I don't need my cross to pray. I just like to have it with me as it brings me comfort.'

'If this is all true, I think it's terrible world leaders hid in bunkers while people suffered,' I said.

Coral nodded her agreement. 'Not only that, but those who suffered badly were made to build a world which enslaved them. I guess they must have been desperate to belong to any kind of creation than belong to nothing at all.'

Mary pointed her thin finger at my head emphasizing the gravity of our situation. 'You do realise you've surrendered your identity. You'll never be the person you should've been. One language is spoken and all must worship Pax. You obey every command without question.'

Coral exhaled loudly. 'If it's that bad, why didn't everyone revolt?'

A heavy sigh escaped Mary. 'It took a while before people

woke up to what was happening. The breeding programme brought the first murmurs of discontent. Technology allowed screening for birth defects, so those showing healthy genes were forced to couple and produce children that would belong to the state.'

'But how did the Government keep people onside without everyone defecting to the caves?' Coral asked.

Mary leaned closer towards Coral, gently placing her hand on her shoulder. 'Scientists created a pill which suppressed emotions allowing total control of the mind. It was tested over several generations till perfected. They prescribe them at the coming of age as it prevents reproduction if given too early, and has terrible side effects. Have you ever wondered why you and your friends smile, laugh, cry ... yet, Elders in charge always wear the same po-faced look? It's because they're medicated, which makes them easier to control.'

Ash had touched on this briefly but it sounded more sinister coming from Mary. Her hand fell away from Coral. 'They'll give them to you soon, Jasmine, and you'll become a shadow of yourself,' she said, with a look of concern. 'Had Larch been taking them, he'd never have fallen in love with Laura. Those high within the Government and their families don't medicate. They live normal lives, while others pay the price for their twisted principles. I was born in the caves and thank God every day for my freedom.'

The dark gloom of the cavern mirrored the misery we felt, it was a tragic tale of lost humanity.

Coral cocked her head slightly to the side. 'Why do your people come to hunt and steal from us? I know you said we're children of the state, Mary, but that's what we are ... children. Why not keep your fight to those on the mainland and with those who you claim are the oppressor?'

Mary's jaw clenched. 'We don't come to hunt or steal from

you. We come to find our stolen offspring and take them home. I'm not the only person that's ventured to Ruin to find my kin.'

Coral jolted swiftly to her feet. 'Hello, is someone there?' she called, her eyes wide and fixed on the dark passage that led to the mouth of the cave. Her face held a sharp look of alertness.

Coral pivoted to face me, her face stamped with worry. 'Jasmine, I'm sure I heard someone.

9

We left the cave without seeing any sign of life on the shoreline, or evidence we were being followed on our hike back to Midpoint. I couldn't shake the thought someone was watching, and the mere thought made my skin crawl. Coral began to relax, her logic that if we were truly in danger, we would have been apprehended by now.

While I was apprehensive, Coral was filled with excitement as we planned how to find Mary's grandson. She memorised every line, shape and colour of the brand on my wrist, and we'd head to the gym and compare with boys around my age and eye colour and look for matching tattoos.

Spindle's account of my last visit had been accurate, and I cringed involuntarily reading the report. However, my newfound enthusiasm was endless, as I'd gladly do a hundred workouts if it led me to Mary's grandson.

Salix and Spindle worked inside the illusion dome, a captivating construction made of sturdy glass panels. They wore thick goggle masks which projected them to strange and dangerous worlds only they could see, while a computerised process rated their survival efforts. Only top students were allowed inside, but it was fun to watch their antics as they waded through chilling adventures only they were privy to.

Many times, Salix captivated us with stories of the virtual landscapes they found themselves in, from snow-capped mountains, scorching deserts and lush green forests. They would hear the rustling of leaves, knowing formidable creatures were lurking in shadows, stalking them. Armed with virtual weapons, they'd defeat the monsters, or be thrown from the illusion.

Steadying myself against the wall, I pulled on my ankle to stretch my thigh. As always, Elders watched our progress from the shadows, their faces masked with the same indifference. The thought of losing my mind and having my emotions manipulated was terrifying.

Three boys in my year began their warmup beside me and my attention fell to their brand. It took a good five minutes to catch a proper look with none of them replicating mine. That was the moment I realised the huge undertaking of my promise and hoped Coral was having better luck.

I followed my assigned route to the weight bench adding the lightest of barbells, straining as I pushed them up above my head. As the boy next to me was much younger, there was no point checking. Concentrating on my movements, I controlled my breath and let my mind wander.

I hardly recognised myself in my mind's eye. Dark coiled locks tumbled down my back, and as I moved, vibrant coloured fabrics flowed around me. People gathered round a crackling open fire and beckoned for me to join them.

We laughed and gossiped until my gaze was drawn to a boy idling across from me, his presence flickering through the flames. It took a few seconds for me to recognise him, and when I did, my heart sunk. It was Ash, and I cursed him for gate-crashing my daydream, snapping me back to our mundane reality.

A waft of cool air beckoned from the archery room as I headed towards the craft rower. I stopped to savour the breeze stealing a look inside. Ash stood with Rowan, her fingers soaring the length of his arm in deliberate confident strokes as she corrected his aim. It wasn't unusual, as she had tutored him many times. Yet, watching them now brought an awful sinking sensation in my stomach. The enormity hit me. I didn't hate Ash. I was in love with him.

No matter how much I threw myself into each apparatus while scrutinising boys' brands along the way, I couldn't rid myself of the searing gut wrench that took root. It festered all the way through the session and by the time it ended, I was emotionally and physically drained.

The only good that had come from it was, my performance had improved, and a glowing report greeted my efforts.

'Any luck?' Coral asked, sidling up behind me wiping her brow with a towel.

'Nope,' I said shaking my head.

There was no need to ask how Coral had got on as the disappointment on her face told it all.

* * *

After our shower, Coral and I ate together devising a rota to take turns in sneaking food out for Mary. That way, my friends would be less suspicious. When we finished, Coral excused herself as she wanted to meet with Willow before prayers. My muscles ached and I was glad to see her go, eager for an early bed.

Blessing Square wasn't busy when I arrived and I loitered as far from the pulpit as I could, mumbling the usual words. Now, I knew in my heart, Pax was a false Goddess, a figment, part of the elites' masterplan to keep us in line. It took lots of willpower not to curse those who had us believe in her, and yell to all that Pax wasn't real.

* * *

Rowan and Lily were nowhere to be seen, so I flopped on my bunk happy to be alone. Morning couldn't come quick enough as I was desperate to head out and see Mary. The more I was with her, the more questions I had. My need to know about her and her people was like a hunger that couldn't be sated.

A picture of Rowan caressing Ash's arm flashed to mind, and I wondered if they were together. There was nothing I could do other than wish the ugly weight in my stomach away. Resigned to that fact, I stripped off my clothes and got ready for bed. I pulled back the sheet... and stopped dead.

Mary's little wooden cross lay on my crisp white sheet.

10

I scanned the dorm frantically, but nobody paid any attention or eyed me suspiciously. Creeping into bed, I hid under the covers and curled into a tight ball, feeling Mary's little cross dig into the palm of my hand.

Someone knew we were helping Mary. Cold sweat gathered at the back of my neck as my mind jostled for answers. After Ash had reported the incident with the fox, Coral and I had immediately been locked in cells awaiting punishment. Was this a test from the Elders to see what I'd do? Perhaps they were toying with me before coming for us.

Tears burned my eyes as I worried for Coral. Should I seek her out and warn her? I decided to stay put, realising looking for her would be a mistake. The cross had been placed in my bed, so Coral's involvement may not be known. I'd make the Elders believe I acted alone, and spare Coral the punishment that would inevitably follow.

Consumed with fear, I lay fretting for Mary too. She'd be beaten bloody, and the thought of her suffering was unbearable. She'd be cleansed, reduced to a pile of ashes, and would never meet her grandson or see her people again. I wept like a wretched coward unable to stop the trembling that commandeered my limbs. Sleep eventually came with a dream that took me to Blessing Square.

Aconite shoved me forcefully, propelling me into the midst of a clamouring crowd. He looked down at me from his long and unforgiving face. 'You will light the flames in the fire chamber. It will be your hand that cleanses Coral and the old woman. That will be your punishment,' he said, his mouth forming a sneer.

Ash stood by my side, his draconian form casting a shadow over me. His sharp claw gently caressed my cheek while his serpent tongue sensually brushed against my neck. Aconite, and others who gathered were oblivious to his presence. It was only me who saw him.

'You'll watch them burn and hear their screams,' Aconite roared over the racket from the angry masses.

Ash drew close, his face contorted into a sinister grin. 'Come with me. Take hold of my hand and let me take you away from this. Let me show you how the Draconian love. You wanted a family in the caves, so, come and be mine. We can suck on Coral and Mary's bones after the flames have eaten their flesh.'

The dream drifted, transporting me to the grim scorched confines of the Cleansing Chamber. I found myself staring into the terror filled eyes of Coral and Mary, tightly huddled together in a desolate corner on the cold concrete floor. Their torment made visible by the presence of deep purple bruises and tangible wounds.

'Save us, Jasmine,' Coral called desperately. 'Don't let Aconite do this.'

'Activate the switch,' Aconite bellowed with malicious delight. 'Ignite the cleansing fire.'

'Find my grandson,' Mary pleaded wretchedly, the burden

of not having found him imprinted on her face. 'Tell him how much I loved him and wanted to return him home.'

As voices surged from the crowed, Ash threw his head back and filled the air with hysterical laughter.

'Set the flames ablaze,' Aconite's voice rumbled once more.

Fire burst through the chamber like a blazing golden ball that blitzed Coral and Mary with it.

'Mary,' I cried out, jolting upright gasping for breath, escaping the clutches of the dream. Blinking rapidly, I struggled to regain my composure, startled by the sight of Rowan perched at the foot of my bunk.

'What's Mary?' she asked, her brow furrowed.

I didn't answer, only stared blankly while pulling myself together.

'You were talking in your sleep, and I thought you were going to fall flat on the floor with all your tossing and turning,' Rowan said.

'It was a night terror.'

'It sure was. Honestly, I've never heard someone fret or talk so much in their sleep.'

'What did I say?' I asked, twisting bed clothes through my fingers.

Rowan leaned forward *'I can't help you, Mary,'* she said, mimicking my voice.

Stalling, I rubbed sleep from my eyes while trying to figure out what to say that would satisfy her.

'You were so agitated. I'm surprised the whole of Midpoint didn't hear you. I came over to wake you as I was worried you'd hurt yourself. So, tell me, who or what is Mary?'

'I'm not exactly sure,' I mumbled with an empty mind. A sudden thought shined bright; I could use the experience from the past as a cover. 'Do you remember the fox Coral found? The one that got cleansed?'

Rowan stuck out her chin and nodded. 'Yes, how could we

forget? You and Coral doing what you did was the scandal of Midpoint. No wonder Aconite whipped you both.'

I felt myself stiffen and wondered why I tried to be nice to her at times. She had no concept of people's feelings as she continued to scold me sternly.

'Hopefully, Coral has learned her lesson and won't ever do anything so stupid again. I worry about you though. I think you look for reasons to break rules. Hopefully, Coral will be your conscience and keep you out of trouble.'

My insides felt as if they were spilling out. Was Rowan letting me know in her own twisted manner she knew about Mary, and it was she who placed the cross in my bed. Fear made me hasty. 'If you are going to report me, go ahead, but leave Coral out of it,' I snapped.

Rowan dithered, shrugged, and looked genuinely puzzled. 'What are you going on about? I'm only asking about your nightmare. Why would I report you for having a bad dream, or report Coral for that matter? Why are you always on the attack?'

Her sincerity seemed genuine, and I recognised I needed to get a grip on my emotions. 'Sorry, I'm still a little shaky,' I said. 'I was dreaming about the fox we'd found, and I gave it a silly name. I'm not even sure where I heard it, but I called it Mary of all things.'

I hoped I had convinced her. One thing for sure, Rowan hadn't placed the cross on my bed. She'd have mentioned it or would have taken it straight to the Elders.

'Why do you think you called it Mary? It's not a name we'd use.'

'I don't know. It must have been in my head for some reason. Who knows what the subconscious gives when you sleep?'

Rowan's eyes darted round the room. She leaned in close and whispered. 'Do you know who Mary is?'

'The fox from my dream,' I whispered back.

The corners of her mouth twitched up as she scanned the room again before pressing her lips against my ear. 'Mary is the mother of the old God.' She sat back and met my eyes.

'How do you know this?' I gasped.

Her tone was arrogant. 'Come on, you don't get to work in important places like I do and sit with your eyes and ears closed.'

Before I had the chance to ask further questions, Rowan pressed her mouth gently on mine. Her lips were soft and moist and when parted slightly, I tasted a hint of mint on her tongue.

She pulled back, looked deep in my eyes and tenderly caressed my cheek. 'Try to forget the fox. You're your own worst enemy at times. We'll be moving on soon and our lives here at Ruin will be nothing more than a distant memory. Don't let the past haunt you anymore. Now, try to get some sleep.'

Even after she hopped off my bunk, the lingering sensation of her lips and gentle caress of her hand on my face remained. I'm not sure if it was delightful or simply peculiar, but an uncanny sensation surged, sending shivering tingles across all my senses.

Confused and afraid, I reached under the pillow and found Mary's cross. Clasping it tight, I closed my eyes and prayed to any deity who would listen, that Mary would be safe, and Coral would never be punished again.

11

I woke with a stifling unease, but at least there were no guards hovering to drag me off for interrogation. Every muscle in my body ached and as much as the gym was the last place I wanted to be, I'd arranged to meet Coral there early. I hid Mary's cross at the bottom of my backpack and set off.

Rowan snored lightly as I passed her bunk. I pressed my fingers against my lips, remembering the intimate moment we had shared. A realisation struck me, perhaps the tension between us was my own doing. I decided to make more of an effort, and try to be a better friend.

Every step was gruelling as I lumbered towards the gym on stiff legs, struck with remorse at the danger I'd put Coral in. There was no option but to distance Coral from Mary as the risk was too great. I'd never forgive myself if anything happened to Coral and I was sure she'd see reason.

My session in the gym proved fruitless, as none of the boys exercising near me were possible candidates for Mary's grandson. I began to feel irritable at my lack of progress, and decided to abandon my efforts and head off to check our rota before setting out for the day. It would be good to know how much time we had left on the beach.

The Task Assignment Office was a large rectangle chamber, lined with plasma screens displaying schedules of individuals, specifying their locations, timings and class obligations. The only information absent was those on special projects entrusted by the Elders.

I scanned the display for Section Twenty discovering Coral and I had a duration of five days left before transferring to plant saplings in the east in a group task. This entailed trekking over a treacherous hour-long hike across rugged and hilly terrain, with numerous workstations along the way.

It wasn't as isolated as the beach and presented little opportunity for us to sneak off and supply Mary with food. Even a new hiding place nearby was out of the question. Mary would have to stay in the Black Cave until I could find a way to get her back to the mainland.

Salix stood in the doorway, and swivelled to let me pass 'What's with the long face?' he asked, smiling.

'I'm trying to reunite a mystery boy with his grandmother and transport them back to the mainland before anyone else finds out. I'd love that mystery boy to be you.'

That was what I wanted to say but opted for 'Just checking the rota for my next assignment.'

Salix fitted the profile, was the right age and had brown eyes. I couldn't explain the overwhelming desire for him to be the boy who I was looking for.

'I wish I was as organised as you,' he said. 'I'm here to upload my report from yesterday. I may be brilliant in the gym, but you're miles ahead with organisation skills.'

'Salix, can you show me your brand?' It was reckless, but the words escaped before I could contain them.

He looked puzzled. 'Why?'

I shut my mouth with a distinct snap, worried at what else

would come out, annoyed at orchestrating another awkward situation.

'You can't ask to see my brand and then stand in silence without explaining why?'

Taking a deep breath, I plunged right in, hoping if I played to his ego the way I'd done with Ash, the awkwardness would blow over. 'You're my closest friend on this island. You've always been there for me and never judged me for the incident with Coral and the fox. Life here would have been insufferable without you.'

He stared mutely, and as my anxiety surged to new heights, I gibbered on nervously. 'After everything we've been through, I don't have a clue what your brand looks like. Yes, this is personal to you, and to you alone. However, I feel our connection, and I think you do to. I just wanted to see it for myself before we move on from Ruin and to our new lives.'

The voice inside my head pleaded for silence and I listened, pressing my hand tightly over my mouth.

Salix crossed his arms over his chest. 'We're good friends, but I've never felt the need to see your brand. It's an odd request to ask of someone.'

I tried to shrug off the disappointment and looked away so he wouldn't see the mist gathering in my eyes. 'It doesn't matter. I didn't mean to offend you. I was just curious, that's all.'

Cursing my foolishness, I skulked off.

'Jasmine,' Salix called from behind. I turned to see him loosening his cuff, taking a step closer to me while extending his wrist toward my face. The scent of carbolic soap filling my senses.

I delicately traced the tattooed markings on his wrist, sensing a shiver run through him. The intricate design of emerald and blue contours formed a small crescent moon shape. It was beautiful, but proved Salix wasn't Mary's grandson.

'Salix,' Ash's voice was harsh.

Crimson faced, Salix hastily snatched his wrist back, his eyes darting nervously between me and Ash.

Ash appeared uneasy, and his tone lacked any warmth. 'Sorry to interrupt, but you've to report to the blacksmith as soon as you can. Your spear is fixed and he wants you to sign it out.'

Salix nodded. 'I'll go right now,' he said, marching off without glancing back.

It was an awkward moment and an uncomfortable silence fell between me and Ash. All I could do was smile sheepishly.

'You're lucky I'm not an Elder. You and Salix would be in serious trouble if you'd been caught,' Ash said eventually, stalking off before I could offer an explanation. It was futile to think any fabricated story could hide my wrongdoing as my wrongdoing was undeniable.

* * *

With an uncertain future looming over us, it was now Coral's turn to sneak food out, but I felt compelled to lend a hand as well. Everything was changing and I worried the little control we had left to help Mary was slipping away.

'What kept you?' Coral asked.

'Sorry. I got held up with Salix. He let me see his brand though,'

Her face brightened. 'Wow, fantastic... and?'

'It's not him.'

She took the news better than I had, as I'd envisioned him being Mary's grandson, even though it was a bit of a stretch.

'It would've been too easy if it were him,' she said.

'Coral, I've something important I need to tell you, but I don't want you to be scared.'

The muscles on her face tightened as she eyed me cagily. 'What's wrong?'

Coral listened intently as I told how someone had left Mary's cross on my bed, and we were most likely being watched.

'It doesn't make sense,' she said. 'If the Elders know, why haven't they come for us?'

This was a question I'd been asking myself. 'I don't know. Perhaps they're watching to see what we'll do now.'

'What do you mean?'

'We have to look at all possibilities. It might not be an Elder, and the person who knows might be waiting to see if we'll report Mary by ourselves.'

'So, what do we do?' she asked.

I knew Coral wouldn't like my idea, but I was prepared for her the objections that would follow. 'From now on you don't go near the cave. You go out and task on your own and I'll meet you before it's time to go back. You've never seen or heard of Mary and you've no idea what I'm doing. At worst, you'll get in trouble for not informing Command that I'm not mentoring the way I should.'

Coral stopped dead and grabbed my arm, yanking me round to face her. 'No way, Jasmine. I'm part of this whether you like it or not.'

'I can't have you harmed, Coral. I'd never be able to live with it. You're only in this because of me. You wanted to report Mary when we first found her, and you didn't because I asked you not to.'

Had I not sprinted ahead, Coral would have continued our argument. There was rarely a time when I felt uneasy around Coral, but her stubbornness annoyed me. Why couldn't she simply accept my wishes without protest. I sensed her jogging behind me, tapping my shoulder once she caught her breath.

'I think I might know who found Mary's cross,' she said.

I stared in disbelief. 'Who?'

'I was chatting to Poplar last night in the gym. It was kind of unusual as he rarely speaks to me, but he's friends with Willow, so we have her in common.'

'Go on,' I said.

'He was asking about our tasks and what it was like working on the beach. Anyway, Poplar's duties have been cancelled for a few days now and he's back in class. He said his mentor's been given a special project on the coastline. It was very official, as he was handed a special plastic card, just like the one we found by the cave.'

'Can you find out who his mentor is?' I asked.

Coral grinned. 'I don't need to. I already know who he is.'

'Who?'

'Ash.'

The colour drained from my face. 'You know the length of our shoreline, Coral. Ash could be working on a beach on the other side of the island. It doesn't mean the card we found was his.' I mulled it over, but it didn't make sense. 'It can't be him. How would Ash have gotten into my dorm to put Mary's cross in my bunk without being seen?'

'Perhaps he had help?' Coral said. 'There's only one way to find out for sure. You need to ask him.'

I thought of the conversation I had with Ash when he confessed he wouldn't hesitate to report any indiscretion to the Elders. 'But why hasn't he told? Why are we still walking free?'

'My guess, he's lost his special project card, which you still have, and he'll get in trouble for being careless. He'll be wanting it back before he does anything.'

Coral's theory was a possibility and made sense, especially since Ash had just received a punishment.

'What if I confront him and it's not him. What do we do then?'

Coral linked her arm through mine. 'Whatever happens, we'll deal with it together.'

No matter how hard I tried, I couldn't convince Coral to turn her back on Mary and stay away from the Black Cave. She was the bravest person I knew.

12

All my pent-up fear and doubt usually dispersed when Mary took me in her arms, but today her warm welcome did none of that. She rushed to meet us on hearing our footfall, her face filled with eagerness and hope.

'Have you found him yet?' she blurted. 'I know it's probably too early for good news as you've only begun to look, but please tell me of your progress.'

Coral was desperate to update Mary, carefully avoiding any hint the task was impossible. 'Not yet, but we're still looking. We've been able to rule out who it can't be, so we're narrowing it down. We'll keep trying,' she said, glancing at me sideways. 'A promise is a promise after all, isn't that right, Jasmine.'

'Come on, let's go inside and we'll talk more,' I said, pointing towards the cavern.

It was dreadful having to bring bad news and I waited until Mary settled comfortably on her ledge.

'We have a huge problem. We know someone apart from us knows you're here. It might be a boy called Ash, but we don't know for sure. As far as we know the Elders have not been alerted yet, but we must consider it's only a matter of time before they find you.'

Mary was quiet for a few moments and when she spoke, she was unable to hide the quiver in her voice. 'I've put you both in danger, and for that I'm terribly sorry. I can't be the means of you getting in trouble.'

'Can you give me the name of the trader who brought you, or anyone who comes to the Island that you know and trust? We can somehow try to arrange a crossing back to the mainland,' I asked. 'It's a long shot, but we have to try.'

Mary frowned, shook her head vigorously. 'Not without my grandson. I've come this far. I can't go back without him.'

'It's not *if* you'll be caught, it's *when*,' I moaned. 'The longer you stay here, the more we're all in danger. You don't have a choice.'

The cold rough floor of the cave scraped my knees as I knelt in front of her and took her hands in mine. 'We can keep looking for your grandson and when we find him, we'll tell him about you. If he's in my year, he'll leave Ruin soon anyway. The chances are he'll end up on the mainland and I'll tell him to come and find you in the caves.'

Her face contorted with a strangled look. 'By that time, you'll all be medicated and it will be too late. If I don't find him now, he'll be lost to me forever.'

It was the truth of it and one we couldn't deny. A fate befalling all of us unless we managed to escape to the caves.

'You've both done more than I could ever have asked,' Mary said. She reached out and stroked my cheek. 'Today, we'll say our goodbyes and I'll find a way to look for him on my own. You must forget that you found me and never come back near this cave.'

I pushed her hand from my face. 'You don't understand. You have no choice but to leave. Do you have any idea what they'll do to you if they find you?'

Mary shrugged. 'I don't care what they'll do. I'll take the chance knowing I did all in my power to find my kin.'

The implications of Mary being discovered filled me with sheer terror. She'd never be able to withstand the torture no matter how brave she thought she was. Eventually she'd confess we helped her.

I paced back and forth. 'They'll torture you. It will be painful and ugly and you'll die a horrible death. It's not like we can fight them with our spears and bows. They possess lasers capable of slicing through bone in an instant.'

Mary wrung her hands together, 'I don't want you to fight for me. I want you to leave and never come back.'

I was stunned, heartbroken Mary thought we'd willingly let her die.

Coral tried to soothe me. 'Don't be angry. Mary came here of her own accord and should be allowed to leave in the manner she wishes.' Stepping past me, she joined Mary on the ledge and fell into her arms. My heart ached at the bond they shared, knowing it was coming to a brutal end.

'One thing to think about, Mary,' Coral said. 'If you die, what good will you be to your grandson. He'd never know you and would never see the wonderful woman Jasmine and I have come to love. We need to think rationally as there must be something we can do?'

Coral's calm approach had me in awe, and once again I was impressed with the qualities she possessed.

'What if you speak to this boy. Do you think he'd help me? There must be a reason why he hasn't reported my existence to your leaders,' Mary said.

I could have given a thousand reasons why Ash would never help but I simply shook my head.

'Jasmine,' Coral said, still trying to find a way forward. 'I think you should talk to Ash, even to find out exactly what he does or doesn't know. He's different around you now. I've caught him looking at you in the Be Thankful Hall, and it's not in a mean way.'

Coral had been watching, and I wondered if she noticed the way I looked at him too. Blood rushed to my cheeks. 'I don't know. He was weird this morning,' I said, shuddering at the memory.

Mary cleared her throat noisily, 'You have to try.'

'Okay,' I sighed. 'I'll speak to him tonight. Remember though, we might be landing ourselves in more danger by doing so.'

There was no reason I could think of, as to why whoever knew about Mary had continued to keep our secret. Asking Ash was a long shot, but I'd do it to appease Coral and Mary.

'There are people on the mainland who secretly oppose the Government. Take the trader who brought me here as an example. He goes unnoticed, pretending to be emotionless, but he's not medicated. He manages to spy for us, and those who interact with him don't have a clue he's not on their side. Could there be Elders on Ruin who are against their leaders?' Mary asked.

I thought back to the day of our flogging when I was lying on the ground barely conscious. Through a haze of pain, I caught sight of Coral being dragged away by her ankles leaving a bloody trail. Our crime was helping a wounded animal. 'No, Mary. We're on our own. The Elders on Ruin are all as bad as Aconite.'

I dug deep into my backpack and pulled out Mary's cross. Her eyes lit up as I handed it to her.

'You found it,' she gasped, hugging me fiercely and planting tiny kisses on my cheek. 'You and Coral should come back with me to the caves and live with my people. When my grandson is found, we should look at a way to get us all home.'

I stared at her, stunned by such a wonderful proposal and one I had often daydreamed about. 'As much as I'd love to, I don't think it would ever be possible. It will be difficult enough trying to smuggle two people off of Ruin, never mind four.'

Coral's eyes begged from a face full of hope. Her existence on Ruin had been miserable, and the thought of being part of Mary's family must have appealed to her every bit as much as it did to me.

Mary motioned with a gentle wave of her hand, directing her attention towards me. 'You'd be able to live freely and be part of something much better than what you have now. The rebellion is growing, and those who manage to avoid medication or wean themselves from it find their way to us.'

I forced a smile on my lips. 'Let's concentrate on our current problems and then we can think about it.'

* * *

Darkness had fallen when we left the cave. Coral chatted excitedly about living with Mary's people and how wonderful it would be. I didn't want to dampen her mood and hated the disappointment I knew fate would bring.

To distract her I told of my encounter with Rowan. 'To be fair, I think she was trying to be friendly in some warped way. But I was shocked when she told me the old God had a mother. You'll never guess what her name was?'

'Go on, tell me.'

'Her name was Mary.'

'No way! I can't believe Rowan would know all this,' Coral gasped. 'Are you sure it's not her who knows our secret? Perhaps she's messing with us.'

'She's too ambitious not to tell. Believe me, she's climbing up the social ladder quicker than anyone at Midpoint.'

As Coral and I discussed the tender kiss Rowan had bestowed upon me, the whole incident seemed even more bizarre.

'It's certainly strange behaviour,' Coral agreed. 'But she must have learned all this from someone?'

'She works for Aconite on special projects, so who knows what information she's privy to in the vaults. Anyway, I'm going to make an effort to be nice to her.'

Coral nodded. 'Don't trust her too much though. There's something about her that freaks me out.'

Over the years I'd lost count of the number of times Rowan did something freaky. 'It's probably because she's perfect at everything she does, so when something comes along that's out of character, it's a hundred times odder.'

* * *

Time was now our enemy, so we decided to head straight for the gym. Ash wasn't there, so I left Coral to work out while I went to look for him. Salix was on the walkway outside the nursery unit examining his new spear with Spindle. He called me over.

'Hey, Jasmine, I'm looking for a target to try her out,' he said, rubbing the pointy tip with his finger. 'Fancy coming to the practice hall and running around for me,' he joked.

'Why do you call it her?' I asked, raising an eyebrow.

He laughed. 'Since there's nothing more vicious than Rowan with a spear, I thought I'd call it her. It would be too blatant and impolite to call it Rowan.'

I rolled my eyes, knowing Rowan would relish the attention. 'Have you any idea where Ash is?'

'He's with the Elders.' Spindle said.

'Why's he with the Elders?' I asked, hoping the tremor in my voice wasn't noticeable.

'He'd something to report on the project he's working on down on the beach and wanted to do it sooner than later,'

Spindle said. 'Because it was an official report, the Elders suggested he meet them at the Public Halls.'

'Did he say what it was about?' I asked.

With a dismissive shrug, Spindle's blue eyes narrowed, and his voice dripped with loathing. 'Why are you so nosey? What Ash does is his own business. You have an awful habit of interfering where you don't need to.'

I was wary of Spindle. Beneath his striking physique, a meanness lurked tainting his attractive face, making him difficult to like.

Salix tapped his spear on the floor. 'Don't be such a bore. Come with us to the practice hall.'

'If she doesn't want to come, don't force her,' Spindle said.

It wasn't as if Spindle was giving me an easy way out to be nice, he simply didn't like me and didn't want me around. I thought I'd make a conscious effort to tag along at some point just to spite him. 'I'll definitely pop by later, but tell Ash I'm looking for him if you see him before I do,' I said.

* * *

The Public Halls served as the appointed offices where grievances and reports found their voice. Though my visits were infrequent, their splendour left a lasting impression. As I advanced towards the halls, I caught sight of Ash walking along the walk lane coming towards me, his head down and shoulders hunched.

'Ash,' I called, closing the distance between us.

'What do you want?' he growled.

Now he'd asked the question, I wasn't sure how to answer and worried at how best to broach the subject of Mary.

'Well? I've not got all night.'

'I'd like to chat to you about something sensitive, if that's okay?'

'Are you sure it's not Salix you're looking for?' he said, and strode past.

'No, Ash, I need to speak with you. Can you slow down please?' I said, walking briskly to keep up.

He slackened the pace a little, but I was worried passers-by would see our disagreement and approach an Elder to intervene. 'Please, Ash, can we go somewhere quiet and sit down? I really need to speak with you. It's important.'

He came to an abrupt halt, and the tone of his voice made it clear his patience had drained. 'Just tell me what you have to say and then go and annoy someone else. I really don't think I should be around you right now.'

A wave of nausea churned my stomach and brought a bitter taste that lingered at the back of my throat. Was this his way of distancing himself before the guards swooped in and carted me off to the cells.

Words tripped from my tongue. 'You need to calm down. I can't say what needs to be said if you're going to be so angry.'

He took a left turn that would lead to the sport pitches. 'Come on, the basketball court should be quiet just now. There's plenty of benches there.'

Only two boys played, bouncing a ball back and forth. I hadn't thought till I saw them, but this was another place we could look for Mary's grandson.

Ash stared ahead, his body tense and stiff. 'What do you want?' he asked.

My mind was mush and I struggled to find the words to begin. He got up to leave; I grabbed his arm roughly and tugged him back down. 'I know you're angry at me,' I blurted out, hoping he'd deny it, and tell me everything was all right. This was more difficult than I imagined, and I cursed Coral and Mary for putting such a task on me.

'Anger is mild in comparison to how I feel right now. You can't seem to help yourself. You act without thinking and don't give a toss about how your actions affect others. Then you somehow manage to turn it all round to make out that it's never your fault.'

Hearing his accusations launched my anxiety to a whole new level. It had to be Ash who dropped the special project card by the cave. His anger, the tone of voice and the fury spread all over his face convinced me. 'Have you reported me? Is that why you were at the public halls? I know you found the cross and somehow put it in my bed and I know you've found the old woman we are hiding. But I need to know if you've told the Elders?'

To accuse him outright was a bold move but I needed to know in order to prepare for the aftermath.

Ash pivoted to face me; his eyes met mine in an intense gaze. The hesitation in his voice hinted at a struggle within him. 'Yes, I went to tell but for whatever reason, I couldn't do it. I reported that I lost my special project card instead. Don't ask me why I haven't told, because I keep asking myself the same thing.'

I wondered if he could hear the drumbeat from my heart as I pulled his card from my joggers' pocket. 'Tell them you found it in your locker, that you overlooked it while searching,' I said, handing it to him.

He glanced at the card before tucking it away. 'Putting the cross in your bed was supposed to scare you into going to the Elders on your own. I thought if you did that, they'd be lenient and wouldn't punish you severely. It was bad enough the last time, and I couldn't have that happen to you again.'

His hands rested on his knees and without thinking I reached out and placed one of mine on top of the nearest one to me. He didn't flinch, simply curled his palm around locking our fingers together. We gazed at bonded skin in silence, as if it were a work of art.

'Why didn't you speak to me about it?' I asked.

'I came to find you this morning,' he admitted. 'But you were with Salix. He's my best friend, and when I saw the way you touched him, I wanted to punch him. That was so wrong.'

I knew exactly how he felt. It was the same angst that seized me when I came across Rowan helping him with archery techniques. His revelation he felt the same way made my stomach flutter.

'I was only looking at his brand. There was nothing more to it.'

He squeezed my hand gently. 'It was the way you looked, the way you softly brushed his skin with your fingers. You know our brand is a personal gift. It's ours alone and only to be shared if you're coupled. Not only that, had an Elder saw you'd both have gotten into serious trouble.'

Ash was right, I had overstepped the mark. Our brands were part of the ritual between couples chosen for breeding and the offspring born would be given a blend of both the male and female's colours and shapes. I had trespassed on something that wasn't mine and I hadn't realised the enormity of my actions until now.

'How did you know which bunk was mine?' I asked. 'Can you imagine the uproar if you'd put the cross in the wrong one?'

His skewed grin had my heart hammering. 'I know lots of things about you,' he boasted. 'One of the special projects I worked on was to help tap into dream waves. Cameras were put into your dorm, so I know exactly where you sleep.'

His admission had my brain stuck on pause . . . we were being spied upon as we slept. I could only imagine the conversations Aconite was having over my recent nightmares. Ash must have felt me stiffen at his revelation.

'It's not perfected yet. However, Aconite's under a lot of pressure from the leaders on the mainland to get it done. Once dreams are decoded, they'll be able to go further, and track our every thought.'

'Why . . . why are they doing this?' I asked, shocked Ash didn't seem perturbed. Ignoring my question, he changed the subject.

'I think about you a lot. What you're doing, where you are, and mostly I worry about the trouble you attract. Perhaps that's why I couldn't help crossing over to section twenty when I was on the beach, as I knew you were tasking there.'

A flush of crimson spread across his face, as if he'd said too much. He returned quickly to the conversation of Aconite and our dreams. 'The technology used to tap into the brain is called neuro coding and it's done through microwavable energies. You must promise never to tell anyone,' he said, pressing his lips in a thin line. 'I'll get into so much trouble.'

'I promise. I'll never tell a living soul.'

We sat quietly as he contemplated my promise. I on the other hand, tried to comprehend a world where our leaders knew our every thought. It was further enslavement into a world of their making.

Ash chewed on his bottom lip. 'Please don't be scared when I tell you this, but for some reason Aconite has his eye on you. You were specifically chosen for the dream project and out of all the test subjects it's you he always asks about.'

I shivered from goosebumps prickling my arms. 'How does it work?'

'Someone from the special project unit watches, making sure tiny sensors above beds release the right setting of microwave energy to plug into the test subject's subconscious mind. The sensors are then sent to a deciphering lab on the mainland.'

He stroked my cheek cautiously with his free hand. 'Are you okay?' he asked. 'You've gone all pale.'

'I'll be fine,' I said, nodding slowly.

He tilted my face towards his and I closed my eyes, savouring the feel of his fingers on my face. My stomach dipped as I imagined his lips meeting mine, the same way Rowan's did, only more intense, lingering longer and harder.

'I've been taken off that task and someone else watches you now.'

The thought of someone spying, especially when you slept, was repulsive and I wanted to argue this point. However, the intimacy we shared overrode any logic or sensibility.

'You snore,' he said, bumping his shoulder gently against mine.

'No, I don't,' I said, bumping him back.

'It's just a little snore, but it's cute.'

This wonderful moment we shared scrambled my senses, reinforcing what our leaders stole from us. Holding hands was harmless, an innocent act between two people with feelings for each other. Yet, we'd be caned if caught. If we lived in the caves on the mainland nobody would look twice.

As if he read my mind, Ash asked about Mary. 'What are your plans for the woman in the Black Cave?'

'Can I tell you her story?'

He scrunched his face in a display of disbelief. 'No, I don't want to know, and I don't want involved. I only want to make sure you are bringing it all to an end.'

My voice trembled. 'Are you going to report me?'

'Don't be silly. As much as I know I should, I can't because of the way I feel about you. You'll be moving from the beach soon and whoever takes over from you will find her, or signs of her being there.'

I swallowed hard and coughed to clear the lump that gathered at the back of my throat.

'You could save yourself. Report her now and accuse her of lying if she points any blame at you. Or leave her be and hope someone like Rowan finishes her off before there's a chance of interrogation.'

I searched his face for any sign of reasoning. 'Do you have any idea of how I can get her off Ruin and back to the mainland?'

A hint of a smile formed. 'Seriously, do I look like the kind of person who'd know how to do that?'

We were so absorbed in each other we didn't notice Rowan and Spindle sneak up on us. Spindle didn't say anything, only scowled in my direction but Rowan was her usual sarcastic self. 'This looks cosy,' she said, her pout sullen as I pried my hand free from Ash's. 'We're off to the Be Thankful Hall. Are you two coming, or are you planning to stay here all night?'

Ash looked relaxed as he stood and offered me his hand. 'Shall we,' he said, flashing a stunning smile that sparkled all the way to his beautiful brown eyes.

Thrilled by his daring, I took it without hesitation. 'Why, thank you,' I said, smiling back. 'You're awfully kind.'

Holding my gaze, he carefully yanked me to my feet, his head tilting down closer to mine. A lump formed in the back of my throat while my mind froze. Time stood still as I struggled to process the intensity of my new found belief. The resemblance was uncanny, even when he frowned. I don't know why I hadn't noticed before now.

'What's up,' he asked. 'You look as if you've seen a ghost.'

'Something like that,' I said, unable to move. It was as if I was seeing him for the first time.

Rowan shuffled impatiently. 'Are you coming to the Be Thankful Hall, or not?'

'No ... no, you lot carry on,' I managed to say, pulling away and staggering back. 'I need to go and find Coral.'

Ash called after me as I ran but I didn't look back.

Ash was Mary's grandson.

13

Coral was on the treadmill, her face plastered with sweat. I waved frantically from the entrance and caught her eye. She mouthed the words five minutes left while holding five fingers in the air. It was the longest five minutes ever.

'Where's the fire,' she asked, gulping back water from her flask as I pulled her from the gym, ushering her to a quiet spot.

'You're not going to believe it?'

'What?'

'I've found him,' I blurted. 'I've found Mary's grandson.'

Coral's jaw dropped. 'You're kidding?'

I shook my head forcefully, placing my hands on her shoulders to stop myself dancing with excitement. 'It's Ash. He's Mary's grandson.'

Her face fell. 'Did you see his brand?'

'No, but I know it's him.'

Her disapproval bothered me as I thought she'd be happy. I knew she disliked Ash but she'd already admitted he'd changed.

Coral folded her arms across her chest. 'Just like you knew it was Salix,' she argued.

'I didn't know it was Salix, I only hoped it was him. I thought you'd be pleased. Let's set aside our frustrations and focus on creating a plan. We need to get organised because there's a lot we need to do.'

'Hang on a minute,' she said, cutting me off. 'You don't know for sure, and we won't until you see his brand. So don't be making any plans.'

Her unwillingness caught me off guard and I knew my anger would only add to her stubbornness. I took a deep breath. 'Let's both calm down as clashing will get us nowhere.'

Coral wrinkled her nose. 'Okay, what makes you so sure it's him?'

'He looks like her. From the moment we set eyes on Mary, she reminded me of someone. Picture the shape of her face and her features. I swear Coral, it must be him because Ash looks similar. Check him out, he's in the Be Thankful Hall with Rowan and Spindle. If you really look, you'll see it too.'

Coral chewed on her thumb nail for a few minutes. 'Would he show you his brand if you asked him?'

Ash had already made is feelings on branding clear, so I didn't have to think before answering. 'No, there's no way he'd let me see.'

Smacking my forehead with my hand, I eyed Coral eagerly. 'Why didn't I think of this before. We need to go to the 'Giver of Goods.'

'Why, What have you lost now?' Coral asked, her brow creasing.

Dragging her along, I began to tell her of Ash taking the blame for my missing furs. She must have thought me insane as the story came in incoherent bursts.

'We should pretend to need something, Coral. Let's go and ask for a fur pouch to put sapling seeds in. Birch will believe this because that's where we're headed next, after our stint on the beach.'

I tugged Coral along without considering her feelings until she swatted my hand away. 'I need a shower before I go anywhere,' she said, smelling her armpits. 'I stink.'

'Shower later. This is too important. We have a way to see Ash's brand without asking him. You'll have the proof you need, and then there's no doubt. We'll know for sure, and we'll be able to tell Mary we've found him.'

Raising her hands in submission, Coral nodded. 'Okay, I'll come with you now, but stop with pushing and pulling.'

I should have apologised but was too absorbed in my plight to prove myself right. 'When we go inside, try to distract Birch, so I can steal a look at his monitor.'

'Why, what's looking at a monitor going to prove?'

I chuckled happily, pleased we were eventually making progress. 'I'll pull up the stock take from the night Ash came with me, and see the brand the furs were assigned to.'

Coral gasped. 'Won't that take too long, and what if you get caught?'

'It's worth a shot if it proves Ash is who we are looking for. If I feel I'm in danger of getting caught, I promise to quit.'

It sounded easy until we were inside the store digging through a table piled high with hessian pouches.

Birch offered his assistance, a look of disdain clouding his face 'What do you need?' he asked.

'We're being sent to plant saplings for our next assignment, and Coral needs a pouch for seeds.'

'Put your arms out,' he ordered stooping down and measuring Coral's girth before seizing the perfect size which snuggled perfectly round her waste. I had hoped he'd disappear into the back store, the same way he had with Ash.

'Thank you,' Coral said, as he registered her brand on his screen. My heart was heavy as we skulked to the door.

'In the good name of, Pax,' Coral said, a little too boldly as we were about to step out. 'Would you believe it?' Shoving the pouch in my face, she continued to rant.

'It's no good. It has a hole in it. Look, right at the bottom,' she said, pushing her finger through the seam. 'I'm not having it, because it's me who'll get punished when all the seeds fall out.'

Birch stomped towards us, his eyes fixed on the pouch. 'Are you sure? It's a fresh batch and the seamstress is highly skilled.'

'Who does the quality control around here? It's shocking goods should reach us without being checked,' Coral said.

'Come back in, and let me see,' Birch said, grabbing the material, trying to pull it from Coral's grip. She held it tight and catching my eye, nodded towards Birch's desk.

'Let me show you,' she said, beginning a tug of war with the pouch, half in half out of the store.

'I'll see if I can find another from the table,' I said, striding back in and across the room.

'Look down at the bottom, in the left corner,' I heard her say, keeping hold of the pouch and making it difficult for Birch to check.

The monitor still showed the stock files, which would save me time. Glancing at the door, I checked Birch was still fixated on Coral before highlighting the date box and selecting the evening Ash and I paid our visit. There had only been a few transactions, so I didn't have loads to scroll through before the fur transaction blinked from the screen. The outline was slightly different, but there was no mistaking the interweaving purples and reds were similar. Ash had a tiny black star in the middle which mine lacked.

Switching the monitor off, I returned to rescue Birch from Coral. 'I couldn't see any others in your size Coral. Hand it over and I'll have a look.'

Turning the pouch inside out, I held it up to the light and poked my finger through the hole Coral had made. 'A needle and thread will fix this. I'm happy to do it and have it ready for our assignment.' I looked up at Birch. 'I'm truly sorry for all this, but I can understand Coral's concern, not wanting to get in trouble. We'll take this pouch and leave you in peace.'

Birch seemed more than happy to be rid of us and I hoped he was deaf to our laughter as we sprinted off as fast as our legs would take us.

'That was quick-thinking, Coral. I'm amazed at how well you played the part. I wish I could've captured the look on Birch's face. He didn't have a clue what to do with you.'

'Well, now that we've recovered from our hysterics. Is it him?' Coral asked.

'Our brands are similar, so much so I can understand why Mary thought they were the same. His is bolder in colours, but there's no doubt in my mind Ash is who we are looking for,' I beamed.

Coral bit her bottom lip. 'What do we do now?'

'I'll think of a way to get Ash to come to the cave so he can meet Mary. She'll win him over, the same way she did with us.'

* * *

Rowan lay sprawled on my bunk, and at first I thought she was chatting to Lily in the bed above. As I drew nearer I noticed her finger trace the outline of the jasmine picture stuck on the wall.

'The wanderer returns,' she said, through a tight smile.

'Sorry about earlier. I'd arranged to meet Coral.'

'Yes, you said. Ash didn't seem pleased you left. He sulked all through dinner.'

Heat spread through my chest, and I hoped Rowan didn't notice my secret delight.

'Where's Lily?' I asked, changing the subject.

Even though I wanted to make an effort with Rowan, I was

still wary of her and unsure of the way our friendship was evolving.

'She's with Spindle in the Hall of Knowledge. I hope he's more luck helping her than I had.' She sat up and patted the mattress. 'Come and sit, you look a bit defensive standing there.'

Feeling awkward, I stood my ground. 'What's Spindle helping her with?'

'She's not grasping Orienteering. Did you know she's on a last warning from the Elders? I think they'll take her mentoring position away from her if she gets lost again.'

'Lily got lost?'

'Yes, her and what's her name.'

'Willow. She mentors Coral's friend.'

Rowan nodded. 'Ah! Yes, that's her name. They ended up on a section of the beach, miles from where they should've been. How thick can she be if she can't use a compass.'

I swallowed hard, anxious another friend had been on the beach.

Rowan continued to berate Lily.

'Honestly, she's become such a pain with all her dithering recently. I'm distancing myself from her as I don't want the Elders to class me as an idiot too. My relationship with them is too precious to be damaged by Lily's friendship.'

'That's a bit harsh,' I said.

Rowan rubbed her chin. 'You may think its harsh but if you look at it with perspective, it's simply common sense.'

I turned away, rummaged in my locker for fresh sleepwear and felt her eyes roam the scars on my back as I undressed.

'So, what's the story with you and Ash?'

I felt blood rush to my cheeks as I turned to face her. 'There's no story. He's just a good friend.'

She dropped her voice a tone. 'Once you start taking the pills all these strange feelings will fade.'

'What are you talking about?' I asked, pretending not to have a clue about feelings.

Rowan slithered off my bed and my body stiffened as she moved in close, her breath tickling my ear. 'The pills are called Control, and I know you know about them, so don't play games. I see how you react when I'm with Ash and I know it guts you. When we start to take Control, none of us will care, and we'll probably forget each other as time moves on. For what it's worth, I'll miss you,' she said, kissing me on the cheek before slinking past.

I lay on my bed trying to fathom Rowan out. Lilly was her closest friend, yet she was cold towards her at a time when she needed her most. Poor Lily. I should've supported her better too, and only hoped she hadn't ventured near the Black Cave.

14

Rowan ate breakfast on her own and scanning the room, I couldn't see any sign of Lily. Her bed hadn't been slept in and I couldn't shift the unsettling flutter in my stomach.

I placed my tray on the table beside Rowan's. 'What's going on. Where's Lily?'

Rowan's eyes lit up, as if she was truly happy to see me. Leaning in, she kept her voice low. 'You know how I told you she was with Spindle last night?'

'Yes, studying in the Hall of Knowledge,' I said

'I met Spindle at Blessings Square this morning and he told me two members of the Council came for her, and she hasn't been seen since. Her bed's not been slept in either.'

'I noticed that too. I hope she's okay.'

Rowan cocked her head to the side. 'She's only got herself to blame.'

I screwed my face, annoyed she could be so heartless. Rowan dropped her spoon, sat back and folded her arms.

'Don't look at me like that. Perhaps if she stopped making up silly stories, as well as getting lost, she wouldn't be in trouble or having such a hard time,' Rowan said.

I stopped chewing on bread and met her gaze. 'What silly stories?'

Rowan's face glowed with delight. 'The other day when she got her and what's her name lost.'

'How many times do I have to tell you? Her name is Willow.'

'Whatever. Anyway, Lily claimed she found the body of a child.'

My jaw fell. Coral had mentioned rumours of missing children but I had dismissed it as fables to keep us in line. 'What did she do?' I asked.

'She came back and told the Elders a body was out there. Every child in the nursery unit could be accounted for, so no child from Ruin was missing.'

'What did Willow say about it?'

'She confirmed they got lost. Seemingly, Lily wandered around spaced out muttering to herself. She wouldn't accept Willow's help when she tried to put them back on the right track. I'm telling you; time to distance yourself.'

Being shunned was something I wouldn't wish for anyone, having first-hand experience of the impact it had. 'We're her friends, and we should stand by her. Especially if she's confused and needs help.'

'Then stand by her... at your own risk,' Rowan warned.

* * *

The sun shone in a bright blue sky, betrayed by the cold nip in the air. Coral was waiting patiently for me at our usual spot.

'Did you manage to speak with Ash this morning?' she asked.

'No, not yet. I'm still trying to figure out how to tell him who he actually is.'

'You need to tell him soon.'

'That's not our only problem.' I said, with a sigh. 'We need Mary to give us the name of someone she trusts who will take them back to the mainland. If we have the name of a trader, we can figure out how to make contact.'

My eyes were drawn to the zigzagging cracks scattered over hard packed clay as we walked. Our society was every bit as fractured as the damaged earth. Lily's current situation was a testament to that.

'How was Willow when you last spoke to her?' I asked.

'I guess you've heard things aren't good. Her tasks have been cancelled and she's back in class until they find another mentor.'

'Did you hear anything about them finding the body of a child?' I asked.

Coral's face flooded with concern. 'No, nothing like that. All Willow said was, they've wandered off route for a while now, but her memory of where to or what is sketchy. She gets a dull ache in her head anytime she tries to recall their movements. They were taken to a Medic for a check-up, but the Medic said they were both fine.'

'Did Willow ever say if she and Lily were involved in any specific tasks or special projects, working for Aconite personally?'

She took a few seconds to answer. 'No, and I'm sure she'd tell me if they were.'

We walked woefully the rest of the way.

* * *

It always took a few moments to adapt to the gloom of the cavern, but the more I visited Mary, the more the Black Cave felt like home.

'She's gone outside again,' Coral moaned.

I stooped beside Mary's makeshift bed gathering the blood-stained furs in my hands. Food and dried seaweed were strewn across the floor. A sickly feeling rose in my gut and leaping up, I spun to face Coral. 'We need to leave.'

'What about Mary?'

'There's nothing we can do for her, but we need to go right now before we're seen.'

Coral's eyes widened. 'They have her. Oh no! They have Mary.'

Clutching Coral's elbow in a vice-like grip, I pulled her through the twisting tunnel. My heart raced in my chest with every fibre of my being strained, as I propelled us both forward, driven by an overwhelming fear. Coral choked out a continuous garbled spiel of despair as we frantically rushed to the mouth of the cave.

As we emerged from the gloom, a figure stood silhouetted against the bright light, creating a formidable image. The details of his face hidden in shadows against the luminous backdrop, till our eyes adjusted to the brightness. Even before his features became visible, his wickedness and authority lingered in the air. It was Aconite.

Behind him stood a formation of guards, clad in black leather from head to toe. Their uniformity created an imposing image, while the dark visors on their helmets reflected our own fear back at us.

Aconite's long bony finger pointed in our direction, his voice was a low growl of command. 'Bring them.' The words cut through the air like a chilling wind.

The guards at either end of the formation broke rank and advanced towards Coral and me with determined strides. Instinct kicked in and kneeling down, I grasped a small stone in my hand, stepping towards the guard closest to me, hand raised and aiming for his neck. He cut me down with a swift blow to my middle while his comrade seized Coral, her eyes wide with horror.

'Let her go,' I hissed, bent over and catching the breath knocked from me.

Strong hands gripped my arm, aligning me with Coral as we began our gruelling trek back to Midpoint with Aconite taking the lead. His stately presence emphasized by the billowing of his majestic purple cape unfurling like a dark omen in the wind.

Relentless prods and shoves from the guards behind pushed me forward, my body stumbling under their forceful blows. With a sudden, brutal impact, a heavy thud struck my back, causing my knees to buckle beneath me. I crashed to the ground, the coarse grit biting into my flesh. Curled up in a protective ball, I shielded my head, unable to escape the sturdy boots that pummelled my defenceless body. Each strike brining a shooting pain that left me feeling utterly defeated.

'Get off her,' Coral yelled, her attempt to pull them off only bringing a barrage of blows on her.

'Enough,' Aconite roared. 'There will be time for payback later.'

The pain that exploded when yanked to my feet left me disoriented and dizzy. Hot tears streamed down my face as Coral fell into my side, holding me up like a ready-made crutch. As I gasped for air, each breath seared the back of my throat with an intense fiery pain.

'Jasmine,' she whispered. 'Are you okay?'

One of Coral's eyes were already blackening and I flinched at her swollen face.

'It's nothing,' she said, wiping blood from her nose. 'I got smacked while trying to pull them from you.'

It didn't matter how much my body ached, the pain was nothing in comparison to what I felt seeing her hurt.

No amount of physical pain could match the anguish I had witnessing Coral suffer.

'When we get back, I'll tell them you followed me to the

cave for the first time today,' I said, each word grating the back of my throat.

Coral shook her head frantically. 'No way. We're in this together.'

'Don't argue with me.'

'Mary might have already told them, so there's no point,' she said, her hold tightening around me.

Interrogations were brutal and Coral was right, the chances of Mary being able to stand against them were slim. Still, I had to hope. 'Try my way first. Promise me, Coral, you'll say you only came to the cave for the first time today.'

'Shut up,' the guard snarled from behind, his fist thumping the small of my back. Coral steadied me once again, and we limped the rest of the way in silence.

* * *

Midpoint appeared empty. Those on cleaning duty gawked curiously at our procession as we passed them by. Word of our treachery would soon spread and I wondered if Salix would stand by me this time?

We passed the warehouse where Birch stood at the doorway, his hand resting on Ash's shoulder. Ash was unable to hold my stare, guilt clearly pinned on his face. It was another agony harsher than what the guards had inflicted as my heart was cut in two.

We stopped outside the holding rooms where an elder waited at an open door. Aconite pointed at me. 'Put that one in here.' The elder bowed politely and took hold of my arm, pulling me from Coral.

'Don't you dare hurt her,' Coral yelled.

I reached for her with my free hand, fingers stretched long and wide. 'Promise me, Coral, you'll do this my way.'

She struck and kicked the guard who hauled her away,

screaming my name as loud as she could. Locked inside the cell, I slid down the cold wall mooring myself in a heap on the floor. The wail that escaped was savage bringing with it an explosion of new tears.

Ash had betrayed me again.

15

The cell was bleak, killing any trace of hope. It was a granite cube of concrete with a side room attached, home to a toilet, sink and shower. The dim lighting came from a single flickering strip which added to the oppressive atmosphere, its low hum exhausting my ears and without a window, the isolation was suffocating.

My efforts to clean my skinned knees drained me of energy so I crawled towards the rusted metal bedframe, the only piece of furniture in the cell. The mattress was hard and lumpy with the texture from the blankets like barbed wire against my skin. Even so, I pulled it up to my chin hoping to stop me tremble as shivering intensified the pain shooting through my body.

Coral haunted my thoughts and I stressed at her suffering. As much as it shamed me, I hoped Mary was already dead and she'd passed without confessing our part in hiding and supporting her. I cursed Ash for his deceit and then myself for trusting him. If only he knew the extent of his treachery, sending his grandmother to her death.

Food was passed through a rectangular slat at the bottom of

the cell door. Even though I wasn't hungry, my stomach managed to rumble. When had I last eaten and would meals be regular? With this in mind, I crept off the bed and towards the tray.

Chewing challenged my tender jaw. The fatty meat tasted like sweaty socks, or what I imagined sweaty socks to taste like. Blood oozed from it when prodded with a wooden fork and after two bites I washed it down with tepid milk.

The meat didn't want to stay down and dashing to the toilet I spewed the mouthfuls back up. Lapping cold water greedily from the sink tap flushed the sickly coat that clung to my tongue away. Feeling faint, I slouched on the floor with my head between my knees, worried at the sharp pain in my ribs which seemed to worsen with every breath.

The left side of my torso looked as if it had caved in. Dark purple bruising marked the trauma and I didn't need a Medic to tell me something was seriously wrong. Crawling back to bed, I lay still on my back, the disorientation and isolation transporting my mind to dark places.

Gripped with paranoia, I searched the room for hidden cameras, wondering if Aconite was watching. My stomach growled and I returned to the tray of food which now stank like sweaty socks too. Gagging, I returned to the bed.

One hard crack to the head would end my misery. I could do it, smash my skull against the sink in the bathroom and it would all be over. It was the thought of knowing I had to be there for Coral which kept me from such a dark escape.

I drifted in and out of sleep, waking confused and cold with bouts of shivering firing the pain. Trays of food came and went and although I tried to eat, it never stayed down long. Each day was the same, and I quickly lost track of time.

It wasn't just the cell that stunk. I did too. Unable to bear the sour odour any longer, I attempted to shower, balking as ice water plummeted over my head and down my body. My foot slipped as I leapt out of the shower crashing me to the floor and slamming my head against concrete.

My head spun as I surfaced, the dazzling strip light piercing my eyes as they flickered open. Vowing never to wash again, I cradled myself in a towel and scrambled back to bed, cursing fate for freeing me from oblivion.

Days rolled into one with little change to my tedious routine of roaming the cell like a forgotten ghost. Then the infestation came. I heard them before I saw them, their faint buzz growing louder to compete with the ceaseless sound from the strip lights. They crept from a tiny hole in the wall above my bed, forming a line that skulked down towards me. Some took flight, their tiny wings whirring an angry beat as they formed a massive swarm.

'Go away,' I yelled from under the blanket, pulling it tight to keep them out. It was no use, tiny feet found and stabbed bare skin like thousands of tiny pins. Pressing my eyes and lips tight, I clasped my hands over my ears dreading the moment they'd reach my nose. They began to clog my nostrils blocking the breath from the back of my throat. Tossing the cover, I flew off the bed with screams that drowned out their sound.

Doubled over and leaning against the wall, I scanned the empty, silent cell wondering where they went.

* * *

I rested in bed, rubbing skin raw from angry bites that didn't exist, when the cell door opened. Two high ranking Elders, who were part of the Council of Twelve, towered over me, making the room feel busy. The female looked familiar with an upturned nose giving her a snobbish look. She gaped blankly through green eyes. 'I'm Robinia,' she said, and half turned to the man beside her. 'And this is Quercus. We've been assigned guardianship in order to oversee your safety and wellbeing.'

Quercus clutched a parcel protectively to his chest, his dull eyes roaming the cell before settling on me. It was obvious he wasn't impressed.

'Place your brand here,' Robinia said, holding out her monitor.

As I offered my wrist, the cover slid off my body revealing my dirty crumpled clothes.

'This is more than you deserve,' Quercus said, dumping the parcel into my arms. 'Please be thankful.'

They left without saying goodbye, leaving me to gape at the brown cloth bundle tied with string. Tugging the knot free, I shook its contents on to the bed. Clean clothes, a block of soap, toothbrush, toothpaste and a small plastic tub with a symbol for painkillers. I popped it open to find two pills nestled inside. I stared wearily, wondering if they would have the desired effect, or if it was the drug Control offered in disguise. My pain was too intense for dithering so, I gulped the tablets back convincing myself I no longer cared. It didn't take long before the giddy numbness settled as the painkillers did their job. Today was the best of days.

Time dissolved in an endless expanse. Food was basic but I nibbled enough without retching and kept the hunger away. Clean clothes were delivered daily and the dirty ones taken. Showering didn't feel so bad, as I braced myself for the frozen torrent dipping in and out quickly. The bruising on my ribs had changed to a nasty yellow colour and the pain wasn't as bad.

I was obsessive, running my fingers over the crop of fuzz that covered my scalp, savouring its feel and wondering its colour. Mary had claimed our baldness prevented identities forming. Perhaps it was my imagination, but I felt more confident with every spurt of growth.

I don't recall when I started seeing them, but my friends became regular visitors to my cell. Their presence provided a glimmer of comfort in the bleakness of my surroundings. Lily would spend countless hours by my side, assuring me she had mastered the art of map reading and no longer found herself and Willow lost.

Salix in his reassuring manner, said he'd help rebuild my friendships. Even Spindle, known for his perpetual scowl made an unexpected appearance. As I scolded him off for his constant frown, something remarkable happened. A smile tugged at the corners of his lips transforming his face. The lines around his beautiful blue eyes crinkled and he bubbled with warmth and charm. Only Ash and Rowan failed to stop by.

The most cherished visits were the ones from Mary and Coral. They brought me so much joy. We'd talk continuously, sharing stories and memoires, Mary with her gentle voice recounting tales of her life in the caves. She filled our hearts with optimism, assuring our current suffering would end, and Coral and I would finally be free to find a way to her people on the mainland.

Robinia's sudden appearance startled me, interrupting my conversation with them. 'Who are you talking to?' she asked, her voice carrying a mix of curiosity and concern.

Mary and Coral vanished at the rude interruption and my contentment fled along with them. Uncrossing my legs, I got up from the floor and sat on the edge of the bed, clasping my hands on my lap.

'I have a nice surprise for you,' Robinia said, in a tone devoid of any enthusiasm. 'I think you should go and have a shower.'

'I've already washed today,' I said.

'Please do as I ask, and go and wash. We can never be too clean,' Robinia said.

***

I stepped into the shower with the usual rush of adrenalin, ready to leap out after seconds. Water tumbled from the showerhead, hot and steamy creating a gentle mist in the bathroom. I slid to the floor tilting my chin up to meet its wonderful spray.

I felt Robinia's presence through the damp curtain, as she watched from the open doorway while I relished its warmth, not hiding the grateful sobs that gushed from me. 'Thank you,' I said, over and over, until the faucet ran dry.

'Here, let me help you,' Robinia said, opening a large white fluffy towel which I stepped into, its wonderful softness hugging my wet skin. She led me to the sink, pointing at the tiny razor resting on its ceramic lip. 'You know what to do,' she said, looking at the growth on my head.

My hands clamped the little hair I had possessively. 'No, please. I don't want to. You can't make me do it.'

'You must. You have no choice,' she said, picking the razor up and handing it to me.

I searched for reason in her pitiless eyes, wondering at her cruelty, especially after having been so kind.

'Would you like to see how it looks,' she asked, taking me by surprise.

'Yes,' I said, rubbing my fingers over the stubble, treasuring its texture, astonished it had almost dried.

'What do you think you'll accomplish if you do?'

'I'll have glimpsed the person I would have been had we lived a different life,' I said, without hesitation.

Nothing on Robinia's face showed understanding. 'We don't encourage vanity, as it would only enrage Pax. Her wish is for every person to be the same.'

It took all my strength not to yell Pax wasn't real. Instead, I bit back the simmering anger, staring sullenly while she continued her lecture.

'There is no other way ... no alternative. This is the way we are governed, and it's how we must act and be.' Her eyes fell to the razor in my hand. 'You do it, or I'll order one of the guards to come and do it for you. Believe me, they'll not be gentle.'

* * *

Robinia sat on my bed gazing at her monitor when I returned. 'That's better,' she said, looking up and motioned for me to join her. My legs felt heavy and I was glad to take the weight off them. She handed me her monitor, now changed to a mirror setting.

'Have a look,' she said, encouragingly.

The gaunt ashen face staring back was unfamiliar. Its heavy fatigued eyes held a weight of weariness. Cracked lips, sat swollen and inflamed, while underneath, a delicate pink hairline scar traced the jawline.

'This is who we are, and what we are meant to look like. We are without vanity and ego. I will have a mirror placed above the sink so every time you look, you'll remember.' She pointed to my face in the monitor. 'Jasmine, you will always be this.'

16

Time began to move again. Quercus appeared after breakfast donned in the official black robes exclusively worn by members from the Council of Twelve. The large white, square collar and red sash draped across his chest offered a splash of colour. His arms were ladened with chains.

'Stand, please,' he said, grabbing my wrists and cuffing them the moment I was on my feet.

'Is this necessary?' I asked.

Bending down, he shackled my ankles, far too tight as the carbon steel pinched skin.

'What's all this for, Quercus. Where exactly do you think I'm going to run to?' I asked.

He pulled hard on the fetter that linked my arms and feet, and I yelped as the steel bands gripped my skin.

'Is everything all right?' Robinia asked, coming into the cell.

'There's plenty room for manoeuvre,' Quercus said, as Robinia side stepped past him. 'She shouldn't trip when walking.'

'Seriously, why the need for this?' I asked.

Robinia shrugged and flung a searching look. 'You tell me, it's you who's the criminal.'

'We're ready to go,' Quercus said, his voice flat.

'Go where?' I asked, trying to control the rush of panic. The thought of venturing out into open space was daunting. Quercus didn't mention our destination, he simply led the way while I shuffled beside Robinia on heavy legs. Four guards fell into line behind us on the walkway which I thought was ridiculous too. It became clear their presence was for my protection. Hateful jeers from a bloodthirsty mob could be heard as we neared Blessing Square. I couldn't block out the faces as we passed them by. One particular boy showed a state of heightened agitation, his nostrils flaring as he cursed my being. It was the intense hatred springing from narrowed dark eyes that revealed the depth of his loathing.

Most scowled, their mouths turned downwards and lips apart as they vented their anger, shaking their fists and pushing into the small safe space held by the guards. Spittle hit my face as we continued our jostle through the angry sea of people to the chants of '*Traitor.*'

Aconite waited at the pulpit, staring from cold and calculating grey eyes, his anger etched into every line of his long aging and angular face. His prominent brow creased and his square jawline taut. He appeared terrifying, even more so than the time before with the incident with the fox.

The chains that bound me restricted my ability to climb each stair to the stage. One of the guards stepped in and clumsily tugged me upward causing me to bump up each one. I gritted my teeth as pain tore through my restrained ankles and wrists.

Plasma screens burst to life projecting my wretched image all over Midpoint making me the focus of every person on the island. I sought and found the offending camera staring defiantly with hate-filled eyes. This time, I wouldn't let Aconite break my resolve, no matter how hard he tried. My fear turned to loathing, and I wanted to kill him.

Robinia laid her hand lightly on my shoulder. 'May Pax have mercy on you,' she muttered under her breath before striding off to sit at the side of the stage with Quercus and the other Council members.

Aconite strode across the stage, with powerful unhurried steps that placed him beside me. 'Welcome, citizens of Ruin.'

A clamorous noise erupted. As quickly as it came, a sudden hush fell over the gathering when Aconite tilted his face upwards mouthing words only Pax could hear. After several long minutes, he faced his devout followers with outstretched arms. 'We find ourselves seeking Mercy from the one true Goddess, Pax. Actions have consequences, and the insolence of those who refuse to obey our laws impact the many. Today we ask our gracious, Pax, to place her mercy on all of us.'

His hand landed heavy on my head, his fingers spreading over my skull reminding me of pictures we saw of starfish. I was glad his fingers didn't have suckers that would burrow deep inside in my head.

'We find ourselves faced with a child who has sinned in the past but has the audacity to sin again. She offers no respect for our values or community. Her transgression conveys the utmost severity, leaving no alternative but to notify our wonderful leaders on the mainland. A Government Official will travel to Ruin and personally pass judgement on this offender.'

Whispers from the crowd carried to the stage. I guess like me, they had never heard of anyone from the Government coming to Ruin. Aconite let his words hang for a few seconds before spewing more.

'It is their desire to know first-hand why we have raised an egotistical child who is cunning and manipulative, with the ability to encourage those in her charge to do the same.'

Pain clutched at my chest as the river of love I felt for Coral threatened to burst its banks. I shook my head free from Aconite's grip. 'Coral did nothing wrong. She shouldn't be punished,' I said, my fists clenched.

Aconite's foot shot out landing a hard blow to the back of my lower leg. With my hands chained, I couldn't break my fall and my face smacked hard on the wooden floor.

Blood ran from my nose, tracing a path down my chin. I managed to scramble upright on to my knees and with sheer willpower back to my feet. All the while, the voice inside my head shouted encouragement. *Don't show him any fear.*'

Aconite looked as if he was going to strike me again but continued with his spiel instead. 'Our Government leaders have instructed a new hall be erected where those who defy our Goddess will be publicly judged. The construction will be an honour to her, and will be known as The Justice of Pax. We shall investigate Jasmine's inner circle and analyse her duplicity. In doing this, we hope to deflect Pax's outrage at what has happened.' He stretched an open palm to his audience. 'You are the dutiful children of Ruin. We live free from Pax's wrath, but *only* if we *all* obey her will *collectively*. Those who stray from a righteous path brings Pax's wrath on all of us. May Pax have mercy on those that do nothing wrong, and only condemn the sinful.'

Aconite nodded to one of the guards who seized hold of me and led me from the stage. The initial ripple of applause soon swelled into a thunderous clap. I twisted my neck doing my best to keep Aconite in my line of sight, wanting him to look me in the eye and see my defiance.

* * *

The stillness of my cell was wonderful compared to the commotion at Blessing Square. Robinia had left a tub of ointment to help heal chafing and I rubbed generous dollops into my wrists and ankles. My face had ballooned to a grotesque shape and a dull ache throbbed at my temple.

Aconite's announcement of investigating my inner circle had taken me by surprise and there was no doubt my friends would turn against me. Thoughts of their rejection weighed heavy and perhaps that's why I found myself in a strange and vivid dream when drifting into a troubled sleep.

The six of us – Rowan, Lily, Ash, Spindle, Salix and myself, huddled together round a small table, seated on tiny plastic chairs. Scores of infants, in small groups sat too, all of us watching the Medics in pristine white coats. They wheeled trollies laden with vials of potions, wipes and needles. The room buzzed with apprehension. It was another Jab Day, a term coined by the Elders who watched over us.

'Let's all roll up our left sleeve so we're ready for the Medic to administer the medication, children. Remember, this is so we don't catch nasty bugs that will bring us harm,' the Section Command said.

I stubbornly rolled up my right sleeve instead. The section command swooped down swiftly and calmly righted my wrong. It was Robinia, and although much younger, I recognised her from her upturned nose.

'Surely you should know your left from your right by now,' she said, lightly tweaking my cheek.

Elders moved from table to table rubbing antiseptic wipes on the upper arms of children. In our group, Lily was the first to receive attention from the Medic. As the needle pierced her delicate skin, she burst into tears. The nursery soon filled with the sound of sobbing children. Salix fell from his chair, shaking violently while white froth bubbled over his lips and chin.

'We have a wriggler,' Robinia called, bending down and scooping him up. She passed him to a Medic who placed him on a trolly and carted him out. Salix wasn't the only one. Voices of Elders echoed from all corners of the large room, alerting the Medics of wrigglers.

It was my turn and I pushed the large hand of the Medic away. 'No,' I said, jumping to my feet with tiny fists balled at my sides.

Robinia pressed my squirming body against hers, holding me tightly in place. It took several attempts for the Medic to jab my arm successfully. As the potion entered my system, a shooting pain coursed through my body, with every nerve end burning.

'That wasn't so bad,' Robinia said, letting me go.

Refusing to cry, I looked round. A creepy hush fell over the room as little heads rested on desks as the children slept.

'You did this ... you hurt them. It's all your fault,' I yelled at Robinia.

She struck my face hard with the palm of her hand and that's when I jolted awake. I sat up slowly, rubbing the side of my face. The dream was intense, more like a memory secretly filed away. Checking my left arm, I looked for a puncture mark, or any sign that proved it real. There was nothing. Breathing deeply, I closed my eyes and tried to recall more. The only thing that came was a throbbing ache at the side of my head.

Caught in a vicious cycle, I began to fret over my friends again. Why had Ash betrayed me? Rowan would delight in my downfall and cast me aside the same as she had with Lily. Salix had forgiven me once, our rekindled friendships had brought life back to normal. Would he feel let down? I pushed my face into the pillow and allowed my cries to take over.

I'm not sure how long I lay there, but Robinia broke the monotony arriving with a tray of food, the aroma mouth-watering. Steam rose from the plate holding a variety of vegetables and chicken smothered in a mushroom sauce. My stomach groaned in anticipation.

'You must eat. The Elders have noticed how thin you've

become,' she said, passing a wooden knife and fork wrapped in a napkin. 'Aconite insists we must have you fit and healthy for the Official's arrival. We don't want anyone to think we neglect you here on Ruin.'

My appetite waned at the mention of Aconite's name. 'You can leave now. I'll be thankful and not waste any,' I said, shuffling food around the plate.

'I thought you might like some company,' Robinia said, her tone light and far too chatty for the mood I was in. 'Being locked on your own for a long time isn't good for you. It's time to talk to real people and not those conjured from imagination.'

I saw through the charade, showering me with hot water, good food, and company would make me appear extremely ungrateful in the eyes of the state.

Robinia pried the fork from my fingers, tilted it on its side and sliced through the meat. She held a piece at my mouth. 'Eat,' she ordered.

I chewed mechanically for a long time finding it difficult to swallow.

'You need to prepare yourself mentally for judgement day. The Government on the mainland have taken a great interest in your situation, and feel a need to understand how it could've happened,' she said, waving food at my face. 'It's unusual for any child to defy the state, never mind commit a second offence. You have no idea the outrage you and Coral have caused.'

As usual, the mention of Coral stabbed my heart. My lips trembled. 'Is she okay?' I asked.

Robinia nodded stiffly. 'She's as well as can be expected under such extreme circumstances. Coral was very protective of you and tried to convince the Elders you were following her instructions. We knew that was a lie.'

It took extreme willpower not to punch a hole in the wall at Coral's stupidity. However, I couldn't deny her bravery and loyalty. She would sacrifice herself for me, the same way I would for her. More than anything, I wanted to see and hold her close.

'Why haven't I been questioned?' I asked between bites. 'Why has Coral been able to give her version of events, but nobody has approached me to ask what really happened?'

Robinia stopped slicing meat and stared through narrowed eyes. 'You are unique. There has never been a citizen like you.' She reached out, and I flinched as her fingers gently brushed my face.

'It's okay, I'm not going to hurt you. There are technical problems today, so we aren't being watched as intensely. Is there anything you would like to ask and if it's in my remit, I'll answer? I might even put some questions your way too.'

I was trapped in a fog of confusion. Was this a game, a false sense of trust where I would spill the truth to Coral's detriment? The voice in my head told me to play along but be careful.

'What makes me unique?' I asked, figuring this was a good place to start. Mary had told us of many who defected, so breaking rules wasn't exclusive to me.

'The Elders study you. They have done for a while now.'

It wasn't riveting news as Ash had already confessed they watched me sleep. I thought of blurting that out and breaking my promise. As much as I hated Ash, unlike him, I stayed loyal. 'Are experiments carried out on Ruin? Do Medics go around sticking needles into the arms of vulnerable children? Do you physically hurt them when they refuse and what happens to those who experience side effects and fitting?'

Unperplexed, Robinia began spoon-feeding again. 'Time to eat some more,' she said.

'I'm only going to eat if you answer my questions?' I said, .

She sighed. 'You have a very colourful imagination. We monitor all infants and they are only medicated to prevent disease. We observe all on Ruin, from the day of arrival to the day you leave. We don't scrutinise every move, as if we did, we'd have known about the woman when you first found her. We learn a great deal from watching which helps to indicate what you'll become and how best you'll serve the Government. Now, eat.'

As I swallowed another bite, I returned to the compelling question. 'What sets me apart? Why does Aconite hold such a keen interest in me?'

Robinia's gaze never wavered from my face as she spoke, her eyes carefully assessing my reaction. 'During your early years in nursery, you displayed a talent for forging friendships in an unusual manner. While most children on Ruin settle for surface-level interactions, you possessed an ability to engage with others on a deeper level. This surpassed the boundaries of what you were taught.

'All this intrigue over an ability to form friendships. Is that why I'm unique? I thought it would be something far worse than that.'

Robinia didn't offer a reply or any explanation why friendships on Ruin posed such a threat. The plate was nearly empty and I still had so many questions. Robinia handed me a pitcher of water and I gulped some back. 'What have you done with Mary?' I asked, wiping my lips dry.

'I think that will be enough for today,' she said, returning the pitcher and plate to the tray.

'Please, I need to know. What's happened to her? If you tell me, I promise to do everything you ask from now on.'

She stopped by the door and half turned. 'Why make a promise we all know you won't keep? Anyway, I'm not permitted to discuss the woman with you. That's an out of bounds subject.'

'I thought you said we could speak freely,' I choked. 'Please, Robinia, I'm begging you. What happened to Mary?'

Robinia shook her head and tutted. 'This is what the Elders have noticed about you, and has played a huge part in your downfall. You don't accept orders, and this is not normal. I stated clearly that discussions pertaining to the woman are not allowed.' She looked down her nose. 'Instructions from Elders should be accepted without question, and that should be the end of it.'

Unable to stop myself, I leapt from the bed and strode towards her shaking my fist. 'Is Mary dead?' I roared, hoping Aconite would hear too. 'Has she been cleansed? Murderers, you're all murderers.'

Robinia simply slipped from the cell leaving me and my temper locked inside. I looked around for something hard to throw at the door, wanting to hear the smash, hoping she would too. There was nothing, only one pillow. I dove on to the bed and battered it with both fists, vowing over and over to avenge Mary's death.

17

Robinia visited most days and although I would never admit it, I began to enjoy her company. She never said much about Coral, no matter how much I begged, but some topics we did discuss; those such as technological and scientific advancements were interesting. I wasn't foolish enough to think of her as a friend, realising she merely did a job, reporting back to Aconite.

She brought gifts too, a lip balm for cracked lips and ointment for dry skin. Conditions had certainly improved since the early months of confinement as I now had three delicious meals a day and warm water to wash.

I slept soundly too, falling into dreamless sleeps, leading me to believe I had reconciled my actions, and made peace with my fate. Helping Mary had been the right thing to do, with the outcome for Coral being my only regret. I should have sent her off to task on her own and never involved her.

'How would you like to get out of here for a while?' Robinia asked, popping her head round the door.

I bit the ragged skin round my fingers, remembering the last trip she and Quercus took me on. 'I'd rather just stay here.

Chafed skin and a smacked head are not my idea of a good time.'

'It's okay, Quercus and his shackles are elsewhere today. Its only you and me,' she said, dismissing the trauma inflicted the last time.

The solitude and limited confinement of the cell had become a safe place, and I had no desire to leave. Robinia joined me sitting cross-legged on the floor. 'Most citizens are out on tasks or in lessons. There are a few Elders out and about, but they'll go about their business without bothering you.'

She nudged my arm gently, 'Come on, you're braver than this. Getting out will do you so much good.'

My palms felt sweaty as I followed Robinia to the cell door, but frozen with fear, I was unable to step outside. The thought of a ghastly mob hounding and ripping me apart was too much.

She laid a reassuring hand on my arm and coaxed me from the cell out into the walkway. It was the simple things that calmed me. The aroma of baking bread wafting from the kitchen and the sight of an epic blue sky through the glass dome. A tingle spread up my spine with a thought of the salt breeze brushing my face and the wind ruffling my furs.

For a short while, we walked in silence until my attention was drawn forward, and there it stood, glorious in its construction. The magnificence and sheer beauty of it captivated me completely. Without question, this was unmistakably the Judgement of Pax. Its presence left me breathless.

The immense ivory walls and curved layers depicted our entire history, from the catastrophic End of Days to the very heart of Pax's forgiveness, and her granting rebirth to our world. A set of twelve limestones steps ascended to a stone canopy supported by grand marble columns. The magnificent arched doorway beckoned an invitation.

'Shall we,' Robinia said, leading the way.

Each step forward would prepare me for the end that was coming, and my gut twisted at the concept. What if Pax were real, and my condemnation truly deserved? Why would our Government bother to erect such a magnificent construction if there were no truth behind her being?

Robinia saw me hesitate. 'Are you all right?' she asked.

I managed to give the merest of nods. Try as I might I couldn't swallow as my tongue felt as though it were glued to the roof of my mouth. 'Yes, I guess I'm just a little nervous.'

A majestic marble statue of Pax welcomed us at the door, her raised hand yielding her fiery rod, serving as a stern warning against any uprising. I held my breath in awe as I delicately traced the contours of her stone face. 'She truly is beautiful,' I said.

My passionate reaction should have delighted Robinia, or any person able to show emotions. However, Robinia simply led on without acknowledging my revelation.

Inside the hall, rows of sandstone benches stretched from one side to the other, interrupted solely by a central aisle leading towards a majestic stage. Cushions of emerald green and lilac scattered the sandstone, creating a complimentary softness.

Taking a seat at the end of a row, I extended my legs. 'Plenty of space here,' I said. 'At least the spectators will be comfortable.'

Sunk in the rear of each benches' backrest, was a small black monitor.

'What are those for?' I asked. 'They resemble mini plasma screens.'

Robinia shrugged. 'I'm not sure. Perhaps it's for those with difficulty seeing the stage from the back. There will be a reason though, as nothing is designed without purpose.'

We walked casually towards the large stage. Positioned within the platform, slightly to the left of centre was a meticulously sculpted wooden pulpit, partially surrounded by twelve grand, high-backed chairs made of granite.

Robinia followed my gaze. 'That's where the Council of Twelve will sit,' she said.

Swivelling, I gazed across the immense expanse of the hall as seen from the stage, awestruck at its impressive dimensions and sweeping curves. It truly was an architectural marvel. The chandelier lights suspended high in the ceiling cast a radiant illumination, bathing every nook in mesmerizing brilliance.

'Where did all this stone come from?' I asked.

'The stone was cut from the Dolomite hills on the mainland, shaped into blocks and shipped over to Ruin. Labourers of over five hundred men have come over from the mainland too, working night and day since your incarceration, delighted to be part of such an extraordinary build. It's not quite finished, but it will be soon.'

'Where will I sit?' I asked, looking round.

'Um, I not sure,' Robinia said, clearing her throat. 'That's one of the details that's still to be decided. Probably you and Coral...'

'Coral,' I said, stopping her flow. 'Will I be judged alongside her?'

Having kept us apart for so long, it hadn't occurred we'd attend the same trial. My heart sang at the thought of seeing her again, even under such horrible circumstances.

'Nothing has been fully decided but I imagine you'll be together. I'll let you know when the details are finalised.'

'When will that be?'

Ignoring my question, Robinia started to make her way towards the stage's far side, opposite from where we'd climbed. Along the way, we passed an offshoot exit leading to a backstage area. My attention was captured by a large object concealed beneath a dustsheet at the mouth of the corridor.

'What's hiding beneath that,' I said, pointing.

'Come and I'll show you,' Robinia said, walking over and yanking the cloth from its place.

'Wow,' I said, dazzled by yellow metal that shimmered with spectacular allure.

'It's a throne for the Government Official who'll come to oversee proceedings,' Robinia said, running her finger over the plush red velvet material adorning between metallic frames.

'What's it made from?' I asked, unable to tear my gaze away.

'It's a precious metal called gold,' she responded. 'What are your thoughts on it?'

Allowing my hand to fall on one of its armrests, I sighed. 'I've never seen anything like it before. It's stunning, but when you touch it, it feels cold.'

I tilted my head to the side and took all of the hall in once more. 'Every aspect of it is beautiful, from the sculpted pulpit to the intricately carved walls. The plush cushions and every colour and detail . . . its breath-taking. It's just a shame its being used to promote mine and Coral's trial. It could be used for something with a far greater purpose.'

Robinia took my elbow, guided me down the stairs and back along the aisle. 'There's no way of getting round that one. You and Coral are accused of a crime and must be judged. It's as simple as that. In this hall, more than any other in Midpoint, we will be near to Pax. By setting such a high example, she will atone for the wrong you have done, and your judgement in the hall will appease her without further need for wrath. Our obedience, and the efforts we take to show our loyalty will bring her happiness.'

Her words jolted me free from the trance I'd fallen into. 'How many people died digging for gold to make that throne? I demanded. 'Would Pax approve of their sacrifice made for the sake of providing others with precious metals. Isn't that why she destroyed the Earth in the first place? I take back every compliment I gave. There's nothing beautiful here, it's just an ugly sham. This so-called great hall is built on nothing but lies.'

Robinia seized my arm and flung me towards the wall. 'That's enough. Don't you dare anger Pax in the very building that's been constructed to bring justice upon you.'

Before I could protest, she clamped my mouth with her hand. 'I will not allow you to say another word against our Goddess or leaders. Is that clear?'

Confusion washed over me as I pondered the origins of her fury, as an Elder, and one on the drug Control, she shouldn't be capable of such blatant emotions. Perhaps those medicated were triggered when faced with a disregard for our teachings.

'Can you be respectful?' she asked.

I nodded and her hand fell from my face. We continued our descent of the stairs.

'Do you have any questions you want to ask about your trial?'

'No, not about the trial. I just can't get my head round the whole public display. If I'm to be honest, I feel it's one big spectacle, because I know I'll be found guilty anyway.'

Robinia sat on the bottom step and beckoned for me to do the same. Side by side, we looked out at Midpoint. Classes were beginning to empty, and to my relief those who passed by paid no attention.

'How do you feel knowing you'll be found guilty?' Robinia asked.

'I just want to get it all over with. My only regret is Coral,' I said, reaching out to touch Robinia's arm. My hand hovered and fell without contact. 'Would you do something really important for me?' I asked, in a shaky voice.

'Tell me what it is first before I make a decision. I hope you're not going to ask me to break the rules?' she said, raising an eyebrow.

I took a deep breath and let the words fall. 'When we first

found Mary on the beach, Coral wanted to come straight back to Midpoint and report it. I'll swear an oath right now to Pax if you need me to. Coral begged for me to tell.'

'Why didn't she tell?' Robinia asked, interrupting my intention.

I shrugged. 'I bullied her to the point where she was terrified. It's my fault she's in this terrible position and you've no idea the guilt I harbour. She was more afraid of what I'd do to her than she was of the Elders. Don't you see, it's all my fault.'

'I find that difficult to believe.'

Words came thick and fast, and I didn't care how bad they made me look as long as Coral was spared. 'You've been studying me since I've been locked up. You told me there's never been anyone like me before here on Ruin. If that's true, why is it so difficult to believe I was able to manipulate Coral?'

A furrow appeared on Robinia's brow. 'And why are you sharing this with me?' Her gaze pierced mine. 'What is it you expect me to do on her behalf?'

'Please convince Aconite and the Government Official Coral only did what she did because I forced her.' I asked, my voice cracking. 'I know you can't make her punishment disappear, but at least make it easier for her. She's been through enough.'

Robinia's gaze softened, or perhaps I only thought it did because I needed her sympathy. I looked away, not wanting her to see my tears.

Robinia squeezed my shoulder motioning for us to move. 'You ask for too much. Come on, it's time to head back,' she said, pulling me up from my seat.

'Why . . . why can't you do this for Coral? I don't care what happens to me, but Coral deserves another chance. She's just a child,' I begged, my words falling on deaf ears and failing to pierce her icy heart.

Gripped with frustration, I snatched her upper arm and

swung her round. 'Don't you dare let anything bad happen to Coral. I swear I'll...'

'You'll what,' Robinia said, swatting my hand away. 'You do realise you've just exposed your weakness. You care for others more than you care for yourself. Perhaps the best punishment would be for Coral to be cleansed while you carry on living a normal life. That would destroy you more than anything else the Government Official could think of. If you ever lay a hand on me again, I'll be sure to tell Aconite the best way he can break you.'

18

Robinia arrived the next day acting as if our spat hadn't happened. Since our conversation yesterday, my mind had gone into overdrive with a deep-rooted seed of fear planting itself inside my head, I'd made matters worse for Coral.

'Let's go,' Robinia said, holding the door. 'You have an appointment with a Medic today. He's come all the way from the mainland to see you, so be nice.'

As we ventured outside, my heart quickened as I caught a glimpse of someone lingering in the distance. It looked like Ash, but the space and fleeting nature of the sighting made it difficult to be certain.

The conversation on Robinia's side was blunt as we walked to the Medical Centre, and I began to think she was holding a grudge after all. She didn't answer any of my questions about Coral and was more mundane than usual.

We made our way towards the reception and Robinia gestured for me to place my wrist on top of the desk mounted compact monitor. A robotic voice acknowledged my appointment advising we should head to Medic Station Three.

We passed empty corridors until we found our destination which was dimly lit, with a lingering scent of antiseptic.

A cluster of mustard coloured chairs lined the small waiting area and I planted myself beside Robinia. 'Why do I need to see a Medic anyway?'

She didn't reply. Nothing in the room offered a sense of calm. Sickly sulphur walls invoked no sense of well-being, while a message droned in a loop from the plasma screen, emphasizing the significance of maintaining good health.

Leaning back on the chair, I tried once again to start a conversation. 'Is there really a need for me to be here? Why waste anyone's efforts to check my health when I'm going to be found guilty and probably cleansed? It doesn't make any sense.'

Robinia didn't entertain me, simply looked ahead clasping her hands on her knees. For a frightful moment I suspected she'd put her threat from yesterday into practice, and Aconite was making sure I was fit and well before having Coral cleansed. I dismissed that thought quickly, not wanting to dwell on it.

Tapping my foot rhythmically, my fingers drummed along the side of my chair.

'Quit fidgeting,' Robinia snapped.

I stopped for a good few minutes, but my foot soon found its tapping beat again.

Robinia's brow creased. 'What's up with you today?'

I sighed. 'I just don't see the need for this. It's a total waste of time.'

Her tome sour, Robinia said, 'Sit still and calm yourself. You'll be happy to know Coral was here too, and she's doing well.'

This news calmed me. 'Coral was here,' I said, leaning forward and looking round the room. 'So, you've not said anything to Aconite about having her killed to spite me.'

Robinia turned, looking me square on. 'No, I haven't said

anything to Aconite about our conversation regarding Coral. Her fate, as well as your own, is not for me to decide. My task is simply to observe and report back on issues worthy of Aconite's ear.'

There was no way to describe the relief I felt, yet, I still couldn't settle. The waiting room sent shivers down my spine. Unable to contain myself, I resorted to pacing the floor.

'I'm exhausted watching you. Sit down and stop being a nuisance.'

'I can't,' I said, continuing to pace. 'Something about this place doesn't feel right.'

Robinia's next words stung. 'Do you think I really want to be here too? There are other tasks I could be getting on with. If you don't settle down, I'll request Quercus take over. That way, I'll never have to see your sorry face or hear your grumbles again.'

Quercus was the last person I wanted to interact with. Grudgingly, I returned to my seat, closed my eyes and focused on summoning a sense of calm. I'm not sure if it was the abrupt hush or the deliberate inhales and exhales I mastered, but my mind unexpectedly summoned a vivid memory.

We were in the same waiting area, with the same familiar sickly sulphur walls and plastic chairs. I found myself sitting rigidly between Lily and Spindle. We were mere infants, our little legs swinging aimlessly as our feet couldn't reach the ground. The room seemed larger, perhaps because we were smaller. Lily began to sob and I impulsively grasped her hand in mine. Spindle noticed, and drawing near took my hand too. In that moment, I felt the three of us created an unbreakable bond.

'We'll all be brave together,' Spindle said, through a small hopeful smile.

The Section Command strode tenaciously towards us, cane looming high in the air. Towering above Spindle, she brought it crashing down on his head. He crumpled to the floor curling into a ball while she continued to strike him harder and harder. Crimson welts rose on his skinny arms as he struggled to block each blow. Her fury spent, she turned her attention to me, jabbing her cane painfully into my ribs. That's when I clearly saw and recognised her face. 'If I ever see you touch her again,' Robinia said, nodding towards Lily. 'I'll have the Medic chop off your hands.'

The recollection ended as quickly as it began, leaving me with a pounding pain at the side of my head. Was this the reason why Spindle acted coldly towards me? We had shared an act of kindness, with Robinia unleashing a vicious assault upon him, while my punishment was a jab in the ribs. His subconsciousness had likely buried the incident, leaving him wary in our interactions.

I nudged Robinia, unable to look at her cruel face. 'I really don't want to be here. Can you please take me back to my cell,' I asked, clutching my throat.

She rolled her eyes, and I could tell her patience was waning. 'Stop this ridiculous behaviour immediately. I'm not telling you again, now stay seated and get a grip. I don't think it will be much longer now.'

As if Robinia wished it, the door to the surgery swung ajar and the Medic stood reading notes from his tablet. His gaze eventually lifted to meet my own, and he broke the silence. 'Apologies for the delay, Jasmine, please do come in.'

I swallowed hard, trying to loosen the knot restricting my chest. It was as if all the air had been sucked out the room. As I staggered towards him, Robinia sat unmoving in her seat. 'Are you not coming with me?' I asked, hanging back, not just wanting her support but needing it too, even after remembering her cruel act.

'You're not a child anymore, and are more than capable of seeing the Medic on your own.'

Nervous tremors tingled at the bottom of my spine as I cautiously followed the Medic into the examination chamber. Air pumps sounded from a segment of the room partitioned off behind a blue curtain.

'What's behind there?' I asked, moving towards the noise. The Medic clutched my elbow and led me to the examination table at the other end of the room.

'Remove all your clothes and put that on,' he said, glancing at a medical robe hanging from a peg on the wall. 'Once you're done, pop on the table and let me know,' he said, pulling a screen round the table for privacy.

I stripped to my underwear, slipped on the robe and folded my clothes into a neat pile. Feeling vulnerable, I shuffled on top of the table and sat awkwardly. 'I'm ready,' I called.

I heard his footsteps, and he whisked away the screen. 'I'll just be one moment,' he said, returning to his desk, pulling small silver rimmed spectacles up on his nose, before looking at his tablet again.

Shifting my gaze, I checked out the room, taking in my surroundings. The walls were decorated with posters displaying health information. Looking at them helped keep my attention from wandering to the tiny silver instruments on the tray beside the table.

'Are you okay?' he asked.

'You tell me, you're the Medic.'

'I'm just pulling up your past medical assessments,' he said, studying the screen. 'This will let me compare your last check up to where we are now.'

'Bet it makes good reading.'

He looked up, peering through the thick glass of his spectacles. 'What do you mean by such a statement?'

'If those are my records, you'll see I had various lotions prescribed a few years back. Didn't help though. The scars on my back are still ugly whoppers. Do you want to see them?' I asked.

He shook his head. 'No, not unless the scar tissue is causing you pain.'

'The physical pain is long gone. They're simply a source of entertainment as many on Ruin like to ogle and laugh. Welcome to the Jasmine freak show. In fact, we're currently in the process of making a follow up, but I guess a fiery cleansing will do the job better than a good old whipping.'

He stretched his fingers into medical gloves. 'If you'd care to lie down, we can begin your examination.'

I swung my legs up and adjusted myself on the table, trying to still the tremors coursing through my body. He loomed over me, his face inches from mine while a penetrating beam of light pierced my eyes. He then caused a further jolt of pain when unexpectedly dropping a solution into them.

'I can't see,' I said, blinking as fast as I could in an attempt to find some vision.

'It's okay. It will only hurt for a few seconds. No need to worry,' the Medic said, as he jabbed a needle in my arm. 'It will all be over soon.'

My eyelids felt as if heavy weights were pulling them down and no matter how hard I fought to keep them open, it was impossible. The darkness crept in quickly and I was lost.

I woke gagging from the sharp ammonia placed under my nose on a cotton wool pad. The Medic had one hand placed firmly on my shoulder holding me still. 'Don't try to get up yet. Take a few minutes.'

Awareness began to return and my throat felt thick and dry.

'Easy now,' the Medic said, taking my arm and helping me sit. 'The dizziness will pass shortly,' he said, handing me a glass of water. 'Sip it slowly, or you'll make yourself sick.'

The Medic hurried back to his desk, his fingers tapping a staccato beat on the keyboard. 'There's no rush. Take your time getting dressed and when you're ready you may join your colleague in the waiting area.'

'Oh, she's not my colleague. She's my . . . guard, guardian, shrink or whatever. They probably want you to think she's my colleague. Come to think of it, they probably want you to think we're all one big happy community.'

His hand rubbed the grazed skin on his chin as he sat back and took me in. 'The rumours about you appear to be true,' he said. I almost thought I saw him smile.

'What rumours?'

'That you're insolent and don't heed what you're told by your Elders. It's not a common trait for a child of Ruin.'

'Did my examination show anything out of the ordinary?' I asked, changing the subject.

'You'll be happy to know all my findings registered wellbeing. You're a healthy specimen for a girl your age.'

'That's strange,' I said.

His face slackened with surprise, which was odd. I guessed the medication to suppress emotion worked on individuals differently depending on the roles they played. Robinia had already shown she was capable of anger.

'Do you want to have some kind of illness?' he asked, walking round and perching on his desk. He folded his arms and I got the feeling he was amused.

'The Elders say they've never had anyone on Ruin like me. According to Robinia, I'm unique. So, you must have found something?'

The smile he beamed nearly threw me from the table. It wasn't the lip twitch I imagined, but a huge gaping grin of pearly whites. 'You're definitely bold,' he said, with a chuckle. I was confused and my mind shot up a gear looking for answers. I thought of Larch. 'I guess you don't take the medication Control. Are you one of those Medics who have parents in high places and are allowed to live a normal life?'

The Medic crinkled his brow. 'Why don't you get dressed, and then you can tell me what you know about Control?'

I was treading dangerous ground, but had nothing to lose by speaking my mind. As I quickly threw clothes on, I could hear the methodical clicking of his keyboard and wondered what he'd report. More than anything, I knew I had to confront him.

'They suppress emotions,' I said, scraping a chair from the wall to join him at his desk. 'You just laughed out loud and if on them, you wouldn't feel the need to be happy. You're right about one thing, I'm certainly bold. But, then again, I'm far from stupid.'

His smile turned cruel. 'How would you feel if I prescribed Control for Coral. Snuff out her identity in seconds before she has a chance to truly know herself.'

My pulsed quickened. 'It's what you do best, and eventually happens to us all. Coral's still a child though, so you can't give it to her yet.'

I knew our session would end soon and I should make every minute with him count. 'Do you live with a family on the mainland while others scrape by on a sorrowful existence on our islands, living in Midpoints? I asked. 'You're pathetic. All of you. Traitors to humanity.'

'You don't get it,' he said, holding up his hands. 'The state can do whatever it likes. Yes, there are implications if Coral is medicated too early, but will anybody really care? Let's face it, she's spoiled goods simply by being associated with you, and the chances of her being put to death are extremely high,' he said, leaning back in his chair, his hands clasped on the desk.

'Why medicate? Why can't people live normal lives without supressing their true nature?'

He chuckled and the sound was alien coming from an Elder, never mind him being a Medic too. 'Isn't it obvious. Medication stops citizens like you.'

'Goodness, surely I'm not a threat.'

He rested his elbows on his desk and clasped his hands. 'You have a natural rebellious instinct, and that needs to be culled before you entice others to be the same. Medicating our population blocks such thoughts and allows us all to live in peace. It's the most effective way to keep people in their place, and most would say a solution which allows for the greater good.'

It was the Government who needed kept in line but I didn't tell him that. Instead, I tried to appeal to the healer in him. 'You're a Medic. You took an oath to save lives, yet dispense medication that could potentially cause harm. How does that allow for the greater good?'

'I don't do anything different from any other in my profession who took an oath to heal. What we practice has been done since the rebirth of humanity after The End of Days. The world is precarious enough without rebellion. Do you think there is a better way? If so, I'm willing to hear you out.'

I resisted the urge to discuss Mary's people and how they lived in fear of putting them in danger. 'You experiment on children,' I said changing the subject. 'And somehow make us forget.'

I caught him off guard, his gaze weighing heavily on mine with my accusation, his lips compressed in a taut line.

'What do you do with the children who go missing? Is there another island they're taken to? Who selects them and why?'

Clearing his throat, he coughed into his sleeve. 'There are matters you'll never be able to understand. Matters far beyond your capability.'

'I won't take your medication, and I'll tell everyone not to take it too,' I spat.

He clapped his hands loudly. 'Bravo, and what do you think that will accomplish? They'll slip it in the food or water supply.'

Without thinking, I propelled myself over the desk, an

untamed scream erupting from the back of my throat. My fingers gouged his face while my teeth found his ear, filling my mouth with a tang of thick metallic saltiness. I'd have bitten it right off had Robinia not crashed through the door and pulled me off.

'Stop this right now. What's gotten into you, Jasmine?' Robinia said, pulling me from him.

We fell to the floor with a thud. Twisting and turning, my limbs flailed as I tried to break free. Robinia tightened her grip.

'Help me, quick,' she gasped.

Cupping his bleeding ear with one hand and a syringe in the other, the Medic lunged quickly, thrusting the needle into my neck. A wooziness washed over me, its soothing giddiness speeding through my body on every cell.

Their voices became distant, yet seemed to linger close by me, and although I heard their words, they made little sense. I felt myself being lifted and carefully placed back on the examination table. Robinia gently wiped away saliva that dribbled down my chin. As much as I tried to speak, I couldn't seem to connect the words to my voice.

'What did you say to her?' Robinia asked.

'More than I probably should have, but before we proceed, we need certainty she fits our profile. Hot heads can be dangerous, so we'll need to find a way of ensuring outbursts are contained.'

'What provoked her attack?'

'It doesn't matter. I saw what I needed, Robinia, and you've done well. The others will be pleased.'

Through blurry eyes, I saw Robinia nod happily, she smiled, pointed to the side of the Medic's face.

'You better clean that mess before anyone asks awkward questions.'

'I'll clean and pack it now,' he said.

I watched him stroll toward the other end of the room, the

potent medication affecting my vision. It was like seeing his movements through a fragmented prism. Shapes and colours morphed and swirled while my head felt dizzy and light. I craned my head towards him, trying with all my might to focus, hearing the swish of the blue curtain being pulled back. My woozy eyes blinked rapidly.

Four tiny infants lay naked on beds, their skin glistening as if they'd been brushed in oil. Masks covered the full of their faces driving air into their lungs, their tiny chests rising and falling to the push of the pump.

'One thing's for sure,' the Medic said, rummaging through a drawer. 'Regardless if she fits our profile or not, she's perfect. I've never known a specimen like her, and yes, she's unique.'

19

I woke to unfamiliar surroundings with no memory of who I was. My stomach roiled with hunger but the thought of food made me gag.

'Where am I?' I asked, finding my throat dry and sore. Pressing the side of my neck, I found a tender lump. My muscles protested when I forced myself up and a throbbing ache pulsed through my head.

I looked round the concrete room, which only held the bed I woke from. There were two doors and I staggered towards the larger without a handle. My fingertips traced the edges trying to coax it open. 'Hello, is someone out there,' I called, knocking gently. 'Can you let me out?'

After a few minutes I opened the second door revealing a sparse washroom, with a toilet, sink and shower. The water from the tap was tepid, but at least it quenched my thirst. A plastic coated mirror hung above the sink. The reflection staring back didn't help jolt my memory. The reflection was a stranger in unkempt clothes with a slight crimson trail of blood on their neckline.

Returning to the bed, I patted the flat pillow and placed it beneath my head. I lay still, doing my best to fight off the panic of having a huge gaping hole for a mind. Tears eventually spilled, but I had no clue for whom or what.

A while later, a familiar voice spoke inside my head, but I couldn't place who it belonged to. *'You will always remember who you are.'* I thought of the stranger staring back from the mirror, and the voice came again. *'You are simply this.'*

The lost memories returned, a jumbled collection of remembrances cramming back inside my brain. Exhausted, I began to piece them together. The voice in my head belonged to Robinia and then, with new recognition, came a new swell of tears. I was Jasmine.

* * *

When I next awoke, a heavy chill had settled in the cell. I pulled the cover up to my chin and dug my hands deep in the pockets of my hoodie. At first, I thought it was frayed material that rested against my left hand, but it wasn't stitched to the cloth and flicked easily through my fingers.

I pulled it out, a small piece of paper that had been folded over and over and pressed into a tiny square.

Paper was a rare commodity, and the only piece I owned was my picture from Naming Day. More paranoid than ever, I scanned the ceiling for hidden cameras, afraid Aconite was watching. My heart hammered as I slipped under the covers to unfold my find.

It was a beautifully sketched picture of a Jasmine plant, much nicer than the image I already owned. Words from the old language were scribbled below, their bizarre loops and shapes alien but beautiful. I wished I understood their meaning.

'There is Hope'

I'm not sure how long I lay there but it must have been a while, tracing my finger over the line of every petal, leaf, and rune. It calmed me, and I knew deep in my soul this was a message from someone on my side. Although I had no idea what the words said, it gave me hope.

Mary had mentioned there were some from within opposing the world order, operating in secret to bring its downfall. Could there be such a person here to help?'

The door opened and I peeked from under the blanket to see Robinia striding towards me, a bundle of clean clothes neatly in her arms.

'What're you doing under there?' she asked.

'Hiding,' I replied.

Her brow knitted together. 'Don't be childish. That kind of behaviour is expected from those in the nursery unit, not someone nearly of age.'

I thought about sharing my note with her, but only for a second. It would have been an act of madness, and I'm glad the notion passed quickly.

'What was the name of the Medic who carried out my health check?' I asked, trying to keep my face impassive.

'Why?'

'He looked familiar, that's all,' I said, hoping she didn't notice the slight elation I was feeling. 'Has he worked here on Ruin before?'

'His name is Aspen, but you don't need to waste time worrying about such matters. Who he is, is of no relevance to you. His duty is simple, to make sure you remain fit for trial.' she said, placing the clothes on the bed. 'Now, time to wash and dress.'

Aspen was the sole person capable of slipping me the note. Although my memory had returned, the events of the examination remained frustratingly vague. I was probably given a shot to knock me out while he did what he had to do, but surely, I should be able to remember something. Even walking back to the cell, or my feelings afterwards. There was no recollection at all.

'Will I see the Medic again?' I asked, contemplating darting to the washroom and plunging fingers down my throat in an effort to make it happen.

Robinia ignored my question, offering other news that halted my desire to make myself puke. 'The Government Official has arrived from the mainland. You'll be presented to him tomorrow in the 'Justice of Pax' and all citizens who don't have priority tasks or lessons will attend. The Elders wanted me to advise you of this, so you'll be aware of large crowds attending. We can't have you freaking out.'

Their concern for my wellbeing was hysterical, in light of the fact they planned to burn me alive. 'That's very considerate of them. Can you thank them for me?' I said.

My attempt at sarcasm was lost on Robinia. Nodding her approval, she continued in her neutral tone. 'You've adopted a superb attitude, and I'm delighted to pass on your gratitude.'

I curbed the urge to scream, holding back a desire to knee her solidly in the gut. The violent thought stirred a memory I couldn't quite catch. It was on the cusp of my sub-conscious and felt important.

'Are you okay?' Robinia asked. 'You look as if you drifted off somewhere else.'

It would have been rude to tell her I saw myself slam her head against the cell wall. 'Yes, I'm fine. I guess I'm just tetchy with everything that's going on. You know, visiting the Medic yesterday and now the news the Official is here.'

Our gazes locked, and for several minutes, there was a silent exchange between us. Something in her expression led me to believe she genuinely cared. I guess it's what I wanted to believe, and saw it for that reason.

'It's understandable. There would be something wrong if all this hadn't affected you in some way.'

'Will Coral be there?'

'I'm not sure of all the details right now. Aconite is finalising them with the Government Official, but I'm sure you'll see her at some point tomorrow.'

I flung myself toward her, my trembling hands clenching one of hers in a desperate attempt to have her see it my way, have her understand. 'Do you remember I asked you to tell the Elders I bullied Coral, and she only helped Mary because she was terrified of me?'

'Let go of me,' she said, wrenching herself free and backing away.

Falling forward, I dropped to the floor and clasped my arms round her knees. 'Please don't let anything happen to Coral. Don't let them hurt her,' I begged over and over.

It was all a bit dramatic as I clung tightly to her, my face wet and sticky against her cotton trousers. Instead of kicking herself free, she dropped down beside me pulling me into her shoulder where I sobbed uncontrollably.

'Please tell them it was all my fault,' I said, between sniffles.

Robinia's heart drummed against my ear as she cradled me close, and I knew for sure I didn't imagine the sadness in her voice. 'I'm sorry, Jasmine, it's not possible. Coral has already spun a lie, saying she bribed you. Aconite knows you're both trying to deflect the blame from each other. There's nothing I can do.'

She gave a heavy sigh before releasing me from her arms and gathered herself together. 'Come on, enough of this. Get yourself washed and dressed.'

I took the clean clothes and skulked towards the toilet, flipping my head back to see her fix my bed. 'Will any of my friends be there tomorrow, to see me in the Justice of Pax?' I asked.

Whatever had softened her heart in those past few moments disappeared fast. 'Seriously. You think after what you've done ... you still have friends?'

'I guess not,' I said, feeling my mood sink further.

Robinia followed me through the open door. 'Perhaps I was a bit harsh. Is there anyone you'd particularly like to be present?'

Ash sprang to my mind which annoyed me, the fact he continually infiltrated my thoughts when I least expected. I shook my head vigorously. 'There's no one at all, like you said, I don't have friends anymore. It was silly of me to think otherwise.'

Perhaps Robinia was on a low dosage of Control as it seemed she was struggling with her emotions. Her voice softened. 'Do you need anything before I leave?' she asked. Her hand moved as if to caress my cheek, pulling back at the last minute. 'There's much to prepare before tomorrow, so I won't be able to return today.'

Perhaps the strange interaction between us was her way of saying goodbye, and even medicated, some kind of feelings could slip through. Her babysitting would soon be over, and she'd resume the role she played on the Council prior to my crime. I had stolen that from her, taking over her routine. I turned to face her. 'The only thing I will ever need is for Coral to be okay. But thanks. I want you to know I'm truly grateful to you.'

'What for?' she asked, with a faint look of surprise.

My smile was sincere. 'For all you've done for me, and for putting up with my moods. I know I've not been easy, but sometimes I enjoyed your company, and looked forward to your visits. If your job was to keep me sane, then you can let it go knowing you were amazing.'

She nodded towards the shower. 'Go get washed.'

Reflecting on that particular moment, I felt a strange peacefulness wash over me. As if knowing my end was near and there would be no more pain or worry. Amidst the cascading water of the shower, I thought I heard Robinia utter my name and wish me luck. I peeked through the damp fabric of the shower curtain, but she'd already gone.

* * *

Later as I lay contemplating my fate, a whirlwind of thoughts on Robinia flooded my mind. Her nature, both tender and ruthless left me unsettled. The vivid memory of her jabbing my ribs, and the awful beating she inflicted on Spindle haunted my thoughts.

If only I could reach out to Spindle, confront the past and set things right. Let him know his hate for me wasn't mine or his fault. He'd never understand or probably wouldn't want to, but it would be good to try.

20

It was Quercus who brought breakfast, causing a heightened bout of anxiety that I didn't expect. 'Where's Robinia,' I asked, unable to hide my worry. 'Why are you here and not her?'

He placed the tray of porridge and fruit on the floor. 'Eat this and then get ready. You'll be summoned soon.'

'Robinia usually brings me clean clothes, so I'm stuck until she appears. Where is she?' I asked again, through clenched teeth.

'I only have one pair of hands,' he said. 'I'll pass your uniform through the slat in the door shortly.'

'Robinia always managed,' I said. 'Look, can you please just tell me why Robinia's not here.'

It was clear Quercus was uncomfortable, trying to fathom a diplomatic reply to satisfy me without causing a scene. 'With all due respect, you are not the only responsibility Robinia has.'

Coral . . . Robinia had to be with her, which helped suppress my worry. I was about to ask him if this was the case but he scarpered out the door as fast as he'd come in.

My only consoling thought on Robinia's absence was she

was helping prepare Coral, and if true, I could accept not having her here with me now. I hated to admit it, but I had become attached to Robinia. I had a warped sense of neediness which had manifested over the time I spent with her, and I cursed myself for allowing it to affect me.

To pass time, I imagined what life would have brought if we hadn't found Mary, and how I would have gone on to serve the Government. Death itself didn't feel as fearsome now, because I knew living the way we did was not a life at all. The only future I'd have wanted was to be with Mary's people in the caves. Ash was her grandson, and he too could have been part of something wonderful, had he not betrayed me. My anger towards him seemed to have mellowed, leaving an overwhelming sadness in its place.

Bowing my head, I offered a prayer. It was a strange one, because I hadn't prayed for a long time and didn't use the usual words. It wasn't aimed at Pax, or any deity, or God, but I wanted to put it out there, into the universe. All I know is the words were sincere, coming from my heart.

I prayed for all of us, for our suffering to cease and for peace to be present in all lives. For an end to tyranny and for all people on Earth to have free will. My need for Coral to be safe was paramount, beseeching this above all other things. I would happily sacrifice my life to see her safe. I hoped Mary had not suffered much, that her God took her quickly and into his realm of rest. If she was looking down from her afterlife, I wanted her to know how much we had loved her in the short space of time we'd known her. It would have been wonderful to unite her with Ash, and have sent them home together, and I hoped she'd forgive our failings on this.

My prayer was still in flow when a cloth sack was pushed through the slat in the cell door. It was time to get dressed.

A nervous rash rose on my neck when Quercus appeared clad in robes crafted from a mix of silk and cotton, blending the colours of charcoal and pale grey. It was the official robes held for state occasions worn by the Council of Twelve.

Quercus muttered something incoherent, but I knew he meant it was time to go. I trailed behind him, leaving the cell into the empty walkway.

'No reception party to cheer me on,' I said, looking round. 'Where are the guards?'

'You don't need protection for now. Most people will be heading for the Justice of Pax, so you're perfectly safe.'

Quercus walked precisely two steps in front, his head snapping round every few minutes to make sure I was keeping up. I could only conclude he wanted to avoid answering awkward questions he knew I'd pose.

'Is Robinia with Coral?' I asked.

He answered after a few seconds. 'My orders are to deliver you promptly, not to engage in conversation,' he said, striding out and widening the space between us.

I stepped up a gear to keep pace, tugging on his arm and slowing him down. 'The Justice of Pax is that way,' I said, pointing back at the left turn we'd missed. 'Robinia took me when it was still being built, so I know the way.'

Quercus nodded thoughtfully. 'I have instructions to take you by a different route. Now, no more talking unless it's important, as I'll only ignore you.'

We departed from the main walkway into the depths of a lengthy corridor forbidden to most citizens. It gradually narrowed to a descent of spiral stone stairs. As we climbed down, the overhead lights cast a haunting glow, conjuring eerie shadows on the rugged brick walls. Delving deeper, a repugnant stench wafted upwards, forcing me to shield my mouth and nose. 'What's that smell?' I asked, as the putrid sourness attacked my eyes, causing them to water. It was so bad I almost gagged.

Quercus didn't reply. He seemed immune from the odour as

he strode through its unpleasantness. We reached the heart of a wide labyrinth, with the smell at its worst, and a strange deep lowing sound coming from one of the offshoots. If I had to put a name to it, I'd have called it the sound of despair.

'What's that noise?' I asked, feeling a cold shiver run through me.

Again, my question fell on deaf ears as we hurried through the gloomy tunnel with twist and turns and mud underfoot.

The voice in my head returned, joyfully claiming Quercus had left the note in my pocket and was prompting my escape. Why else would we travel such a strange route, and at such a fast pace?

Eventually the smell and depressing noise lessened and the path underfoot turned solid. We arrived at a door with symbols claiming it to be a holding pen. Quercus pushed it open, and we stepped into a dimly lit room.

Coral sat shackled to a bench inside a glass cage. Her face was pale and greasy under the poor light, and her gaunt eyes widened at my arrival.

She leapt to her feet, her face inches from the glass. 'Jasmine, it's really you,' she said, placing the palms against the toughened walls.

I pushed past Quercus, resting my hands on the glass to mirror hers. 'I've missed you so much, Coral, and thought of you every single day.'

'Me too,' she said, her eyes brimming with tears. 'It's so good to see you.'

I stared wordlessly taking her in. She looked smaller, thinner, and her blue eyes had lost their sparkle. Robinia waited beside a second cage, next to Coral's.

She watched our reunion with interest, and I thought I saw sadness flicker on her face. I turned to her.

'Thank you for looking after Coral,' I said, with a sincere smile. 'It means so much to me you were there for her.'

She shrugged off my gratefulness. 'Let me get you settled,' she said, ushering me into the cage.

'Not more shackles?' I said, screwing my face up at Quercus while Robinia cuffed me. 'It's not as if we can go anywhere locked in a cage.'

'Let's head over to the Justice of Pax now,' Robinia said, peering over her shoulder at Quercus. 'We should go and take our place with the other Council of Twelve.'

He nodded towards Coral and me. 'Don't you think we should wait till they depart. They shouldn't be left on their own.'

'It'll only be for a few moments. We should really go and take our place as we don't want to appear late. No harm can come of it, but if you are unsure I can have guards placed outside?'

'No, I'll accept your judgement. If you think it will be okay,' Quercus said, casting a final glance at Coral and me before stepping out into the passage. Robinia stopped at the door, turning to look at us one last time. The corners of her mouth were downturned, and a sad heaviness seemed to have taken over her usually emotionless face.

'What about us. How do we get to the Justice of Pax from here?' I asked.

'Don't worry, you'll be there sooner than you think,' she said, and mouthed the words '*Be strong,*' before finally leaving us on our own.

It was as if Coral and I had never been parted. Our conversation flowed as we did our best to catch up in the little time we had.

'Thank goodness they cut air holes in the cage, or we'd struggle to hear each other,' Coral said, peering up at the line of holes all the way round the top. 'Or suffocate before Aconite has time to kill us.'

Hearing her flippant remark about death brought back the guilt I hid. 'I'm so sorry you're in this situation because of me.'

Coral didn't give credence to my guilty conscience. 'Talk about breathing, what was that awful smell on the way here? It took ages for it to unclog from my nose. And that terrible noise. It sounded as if something was in pain.'

'Perhaps Robinia will tell us what it was if we ask her nicely,' I said.

We sat quietly for a moment, each of us lost in our own thoughts.

'What do you think they did to her?' Coral asked.

She hadn't said Mary's name, as if uttering it out loud would be too painful. I sighed, shook my head, and sagging down on the bench, curled my hands round my knees. 'I asked Robinia numerous times but she wouldn't tell me anything. She wouldn't even talk of you, no matter how much I pestered her.' My voice was low, sorrowful and trembled a little as I looked deep into her eyes. 'I'm so sorry, Coral, you have to believe me. I should never have gotten you into this and it was foolish of me to think we wouldn't be caught.' I said, brushing away a tear with a trembling hand. 'I hate what all this has done to you, and I'll never be able to forgive myself.'

Love radiated from Coral's face. 'I could've walked away at any time, but I chose to stay because of Mary. I wanted to help her just as much as you did. There's no fault from either of us as we did the right thing,' Coral said, offering a warm smile. 'Our rules are cruel and inhumane and I'd rather be sat here with you knowing I did some good, than have turned my back on Mary. You've nothing to feel guilty of, so stop with that right now.'

I bit my lip, wondering how I could force her to see things from my perspective. 'You can't tell them any of that, Coral. You must be submissive and play to the idea I bullied you. I know Aconite won't believe it, but others might. The Official from the mainland may take a totally different view, and I want that for you. I want you to live.'

'How many times do you have to hear it. We're in this together, no matter how it ends.'

I raised my voice. 'I'm trying to protect you.'

Coral rolled her eyes. 'I don't need protecting.'

Silence so thick it could smother you, fell. My heart broke that we bickered at a time when we should be drawing close.

'Did they hurt you?' I asked, steering away from the argument.

She shook her head. 'No, not at all. I was questioned by the Council, then locked up. Robinia visited most days and took me out once or twice. The isolation wasn't too bad either as other than you and Willow, I'm used to my own company.'

Hearing Coral's imprisonment hadn't been too bad didn't detract from how awful I felt, but it did make me feel a little better. 'Did you have a health check by a Medic called Aspen?' I asked.

'Funny you should ask because I did see one, but every time I try to recall it I get an awful pain here,' she said, rubbing her temple.'

Four loud metallic screeches pierced the air halting our conversation. The partitioned ceiling above each cage opened up with a swift thwack, exposing a long dark shaft.

'We're being lifted up to the hall, Coral,' I said, my voice a mix of surprise and fear. 'Whatever happens, know how much I love you.'

Our glass cages shuddered to life and we began to rise slowly towards inky blackness.

'I love you too,' Coral said, her eyes wide.

We held each other's gaze until Coral disappeared and I was alone in the blackness. As the cage ascended through the shaft, the chilled air was thick with a smell of oiled metal and aged dust. A rim of light peeked from above, bringing with it a cacophony of conversations blending together as one humming noise. My cage grounded to a halt on centre stage and my eyes fluttered rapidly adjusting to the shimmering brightness. The powerful bulbs not only blinded me but caught me under their intense heat.

* * *

There was an oppressive atmosphere that spurned all hope of justice. Since my last visit, the walls held surveillance cameras to record and witness our judgement.

Aconite stood at the pulpit looking every bit the cold figure of authority he portrayed himself to be. His body flitted from left to right, his arms stretched wide, his voice booming from the sound system as he welcomed everyone in. The Justice of Pax was packed, bodies crammed tightly together, with standing room only at the back. I stole a glance at Coral who crouched low on her bench with her head bowed.

'It's an honour to have our Government Official oversee this trial and I ask you all to show appreciation for his time,' Aconite said, his hand sweeping towards the gold throne placed near the arc of chairs where the Council of Twelve sat.

Thousands of hands struck together heartily making a thunderous noise that seemed to last forever. There was nothing unusual about the Official's rugged face, devoid of warmth or empathy. His neck was thick, his brow and chin square with a bulbous nose and thin lips. He wore purple robes similar in style to that of the Council of Twelve, with the Government crest stitched in red and yellow above his heart.

The strangest sight was the white peruke resting on top of his head, an elaborate wig of graceful grey curls, meticulously arranged. Perukes were only ever worn at extremely special events, and as these were such a rare occurrence, we hardly saw them. In my opinion, this only confirmed the twisted minds of our leaders. Why wear a head piece made of wool when real hair could be grown?

Aconite's voice resounded powerfully. 'The transgression of Jasmine and Coral is of the highest treason, and we gather in our new hall to honour Pax, to seek her mercy and guidance on such a terrible matter.'

My eyes swept across the rows of seats, to discover my friends settled together in the front row. Lily appeared as I imagined, her complexion pale and filled with sorrow. Rowan sat upright and resolute, fully engrossed in proceedings with a gleeful air. Salix wore a sombre expression, leaving me apprehensive about his thoughts on how he now felt about me. Slouched to the side, Spindle looked bored, probably desperate for my demise so he could rush off to the gym. Ash, my betrayer, remained composed. His gaze met mine directly.

Anger bubbled within me, the voice in my head wanting to scream *'Are you sorry now?'* His eyes broke away to focus on Aconite. Yet, I couldn't tear my gaze from him. It was as if a magnetic force drew me to him.

After his lengthy introduction, Aconite stretched his arm towards the Government Official. 'Please, dear Official, guide us through these troubling matters.'

The Official rose from his gold throne and strode across the stage picking up a microphone from its stand. His thin lips parted revealing a row of yellow teeth.

'Children of Ruin, thank you for honouring my presence with such a warm and hearty welcome. As much as I am the chief Official to our Government, I am happy for you to call me by my name, Malus. My devotion to our Government and our gracious Goddess, Pax, will hopefully be fruitful, and she will not punish all of us for the wrong of two tragic offenders.' He strode towards our enclosures. 'If we do nothing, and allow those who strive to violate our rules,' he paused, pointing a stubby finger at me. 'Pax will bring another End of Days. Children of Ruin, I ask you, do we do nothing?'

A hushed murmur rose from the benches, falling short of the heightened reaction Malus had hoped for. He posed the question again, this time his voice full of fervour. 'Do we do nothing?'

A smug smile played on his lips as cheers, whistles and bloodthirsty cries erupted from the ecstatic mob. If fury had the power to shatter glass, I'd have broken free from my restraints, and assaulted Malus with a vengeance. The seething rage engulfing me had become a familiar companion. I fixed my stare upon Malus, hoping he sensed the havoc I'd unleash if given the chance.

My heart galloped as I stole a quick glance at Ash, hoping he'd acknowledge my defiance too. I longed to scream at him, and make him know I wasn't a feeble coward like him. His head inclined towards Rowan as she whispered to him. I'd have given anything to know what she said. Lily wiped her eyes with the back of her hand, giving me hope her sadness was a sign I still had a friend. Salix would be there for her as he'd always been there for me.

Malus bellowed into the microphone demanding everyone's attention. 'Pax is merciful and therefore we must show mercy. The extent of Jasmine and Coral's treachery will be made known, and you, the children of Ruin, will judge their fate in the name of Pax. In doing so, her wrath will not fall upon us, as it is you who will see justice served.'

Malus had the crowd hooked. Thousands of hands pumped the air triumphantly, while a thunderous stomping of feet threatened to shake the foundations of Midpoint. The rumblings persisted till the colossal arch door swung open at the entrance.

Two guards trooped down the centre aisle dragging a ragged bundle between them.

'Oh, Pax, no. Please no.' I heard Coral say frantically. It was the first words she'd uttered since arriving in the Justice of Pax, and I leapt to my feet seeking the cause of her despair.

I never thought I would see Mary alive again, but here she was, being dragged down the passageway like a dirty sack. Skinny legs flailed as blood seeped from her battered body, smearing the polished floor. Her bloated blue face dangled at an unusual angle as the guards tugged her cruelly by her scrawny arms.

Tears stung my eyes as I banged hard on the glass yelling at Malus. 'I'll kill you. I'm going to kill all of you.'

Mary's body bumped up each step, every whack hammering a new blow. Hauled across the stage, they dumped her at Malus's feet. 'This is what they chose over you,' he said, firing his boot into Mary's side. She withered in agony.

'Enough!' I screamed, with an overwhelming urge to make it all stop.

Aconite watched with a twisted sense of satisfaction from the pulpit, a wicked grin pinned to his face, his hunger for cruelty sated from Mary's pain.

'Don't be fooled, good people,' Malus said, scowling down his nose at Mary. 'This is not human. It's an animal that lives in the caves on the mainland. Right now, our brave army of government guards are hunting them down, and before the end of this trial, they'll all be wiped out.'

What started as a faint hiss grew into a resounding hum, escalating until it reached fervent chants. *'Death to them all.'*

Malus bent down and curled a hand round Mary's hair tugging her swollen face from the ground, showing her off like a morbid trophy. 'This kind of animal would bring death to us all. But, we will obliterate her pack's existence before we let them destroy us.'

The crowd unleashed their fury, their disdainful jeers growing louder and louder, turning the air more toxic if that were possible. Mary turned her head towards our cages and spotted me through the bulging slit of one of her eyes. I pressed my hands on the glass. 'I'm so sorry, Mary.' I yelled over and over.

Coral screamed from her cage too, her voice thick with heavy sobs. Mary sucked in a huge breath, spread her arms from under her, edging her body slightly in our direction. Malus crashed his boot down hard on her back, and air escaped her in rasped gurgles. She lay deathly still. I threw myself against the glass, the chains on my hands gouging flesh painfully. I had to get out and help Mary.

Malus continued to preach, his message rumbling round the hall, revving up hysteria. I was oblivious to all he said. Coral was on her knees praying, and at first, I thought my eyes played tricks. Sure enough, when I glanced again, Coral clasped Mary's little wooden cross between shaky hands.

Mary still hadn't moved, and as much as it pained me, I hoped she was dead and her suffering over. Aconite rushed from the pulpit and beckoned Malus to join him with the Council of Twelve. As they huddled in conversation, Mary was hauled away from the Justice of Pax to the shouts and jeers of the crowd.

Tapping the glass of my cage, I caught Coral's attention and pointed at her hands. 'Where did you get that from?'

'I found it in my pocket after the examination by the Medic,' she said, between hiccups.

'Put it away now, before anyone sees,' I said, my eyes darting from Aconite to Malus.

'But, we have to pray for Mary,' Coral said, her voice full of grief.

'Put it away *now*,' I said.

As Coral slipped the cross back in her pocket, I searched for Robinia among the Council of Twelve but couldn't find her.

Could Robinia in some warped way be trying to help? And if so, could she help Mary if she was still alive?

Malus returned to the stage and took up the microphone once again. 'Having discussed the severity of matters with Aconite and your Council, and by the powers that be under the guidance of our gracious Goddess Pax,' he paused, his malicious gaze fixing intensely on me. 'I condemn the creature from the caves to be cleansed.'

It was as if his words were a long awaited announcement, as a flow of jubilation rippled through the Justice of Pax. We began our descent back to the holding pen, leaving the eruption of cheers from the crowd behind.

21

It was much cooler in the holding pen, probably because it didn't have massive stage lights blasting off heat. An invisible weight crushed on my chest and every breath felt constricted as I waited on Coral. I could hear engineers talk from above and inside her lift shaft. A runner had split causing her cage to stick. The ruckus from workers above gave hope she'd be with me soon.

I waited anxiously for Robinia to come too, desperately hoping she was the person who gave Mary's cross to Coral. If it wasn't her, I needed to find out who as soon as possible. The whole sad situation was a mess, and if Mary wasn't dead now, her life would soon end in the most horrific way. Discovering the note in my pocket, and Coral possessing Mary's cross, convinced me someone on Ruin was on our side.

'Are you okay, Coral?' I asked, as her cage emerged from the lift shaft. It was a stupid question as she clearly wasn't. Her swollen eyes were tinged red and tear lines streaked her face.

Her lips trembled as she spoke. 'I'm not sure how I feel anymore. I thought I could be strong, but seeing Mary...'

If only I could have held Coral in my arms and shared our

heartache. More than anything, I'd loved to have told her everything was going to be alright. 'Our leaders are evil. This trial is a sham and will be used throughout history to paint us as the wrongdoers, and how *they* saved everyone from another End of Days.'

Exhausted, I slouched on the bench with my elbows on my knees, resting my head in my hands. A dreadful realisation struck me, and I kept my voice low. 'We need to be careful of what we say as they could be listening in on us.'

'I wish they'd come and let us out,' Coral said, her voice shrill. 'My bladder's full and if they don't come soon, they'll have another mess to clean.'

We managed to laugh a little at her mockery. It lightened our mood and helped deflect from the horror we'd just been through.

Footsteps sounded from the corridor and my prayers were answered as Robinia entered the holding pen. She wasn't alone, Quercus lurked in her shadow, slithering through the door behind her. As soon as they entered, the room plunged into a veil of blackness. In the midst of the gloom, sparks erupted casting bright bursts of light like fleeting stars in a night sky.

'What's going on?' I asked, over the crackling pops and bangs, worried the room would catch fire.

'It's probably a power surge,' Robinia said, and turned to Quercus. 'Can you go and check to see if this is the only area affected?'

Through the flickering glow, I saw Quercus nod his head. 'I'll be right back as soon as I know what's going on.'

The room pulsated with each sparking flash as Quercus left, leaving Robinia alone to deal with us.

'We don't have much time,' Robinia said, removing a small compact gadget from her robe pocket. 'This is a frequency blocker. It won't cut the feed from the cameras, but it will block all sound. The technicians won't be able to find the fault for weeks as once I press in a code, the systems will be corrupted with a data-worm. At least in here, we now have a safe place to talk.'

My heart raced at such a speed I thought it was going to crash free from my ribs. Robinia was on our side. She would be our liberator. Coral was speechless, gaping wide eyed at her.

Concern radiated from Robinia's eyes as they clouded with worry. 'Are you okay?' she asked. 'It was pretty rough at times, but you both seemed to hold it together.'

Coral wasn't the only one who couldn't find her words. Although I nodded, inside my head, I struggled to fit the puzzling fragments together.

Robinia spoke, her voice urgent. 'There are some among us who are trying to bring about change, but it's a dangerous path and the less you know of it, the safer for everyone. We're doing our best to make matters easier for you. Do you understand what I'm saying?'

Coral had her doubts. 'After everything that's happened, how can you expect us to trust you?'

'Two things. The first being you don't have a choice. I am your only hope. The second . . . I put items in your pockets so when this day came, you would know I'm a friend.' Within three strides she was at Coral's cage. 'I gave you Mary's cross, and you must keep it hidden, always. Never be tempted to use it again, like you did today. That was extremely dangerous, and you're lucky it was only me who noticed. Right now, my people are trying to fudge recordings, so it won't show if played back.' She turned to me. 'I drew you a picture of a jasmine plant and wrote a message from the old language. It translates as there is hope. To write in the old language is a death sentence in itself, and my reason for doing so, was to build your trust.'

'Why only tell us now?' Coral argued. 'This would have been good to know earlier.'

Robinia inhaled deeply. 'We didn't know if saving you both

would jeopardise what we're accomplishing. Not only that, we had little time to plan. Matters are now escalating quicker than anticipated and we're running out of time.'

'So, you've only decided to help us recently? That's nice of you,' Coral grumbled.

My voice was firm. 'If you truly want to help us you need to stop Mary's cleansing. That should be your first priority.'

Robinia shook her head vehemently. 'Impossible. Nothing can be done for her. You must believe me when I say that.'

'Can you give this back to her?' Coral said, standing on her bench and passing the tiny cross through one of the air holes. 'It will help her through the nightmare that's to come. She lost it once before and fretted so much. I won't have her dying without it.'

'I'll do my best,' Robinia said, reaching up and taking it from her.

'Why didn't you tell me you were trying to help?' I asked. 'There were so many times I wondered, and was left confused.'

In a dazzling moment of brightness, light returned to the holding pen, dimming to its feeble glow. The electric sizzle ceased and the room became eerily quiet.

Robinia approached the door and cautiously peeked outside. 'We never know how much we are monitored when with you. I've had little opportunity and can't put our movement at risk. Aconite and appointed Elders don't watch or listen at all times, but because we don't know when, we simply can't take chances. I took more than a few risks with you both, but now more than ever, we need to be careful.' Robinia shifted her gaze towards me. 'On the day you blasphemed Pax, I was terrified guards would swoop in and take you away. Such an offence would have you locked in solitary confinement and without access to you, efforts to help would be lost. That's the reason why I was so angry.'

Robinia closed the door quickly. 'Quercus is coming,' she said, her tone tinged with caution.

Quercus stepped inside a moment later. 'Technical glitches,' he remarked, his eyes lingering on Robinia. 'At least the light is back on in here, and in the tunnels. Tier one and two also suffered a few shortages. The technicians think it may be an overload on the system caused by the grand lighting in the Justice of Pax. They're doing their best to rectify all matters now.'

'It's good to know they have it under control,' Robinia said.

'Anyway, we've been summoned by the Council members, so we must go at once,' Quercus said. 'Malus would also like to see your case-study on the accused, so you may be gone a while. I'll escort the girls back to their cells after our Council meeting.'

Robinia departed alongside Quercus, without casting so much as a fleeting glance in our direction.

Coral took a deep breath. 'Wow, what a day this turned out to be. Do you think Robinia will be able to prevent our cleansing?' she asked.

'There's still time for you to backtrack, Coral. Convince them you were bullied.'

'You'll never persuade me to do that. I can't imagine life on Ruin without you. I'd be better off dead as it would be a miserable existence.'

'You have Willow. I bet she'll stand by you again.'

'Even if she wanted to, I wouldn't let her. It was bad enough the last time. I'll not put her through that again.'

This was typical of Coral, selfless as always, putting the need of others before herself.

'Anyway, we won't need to worry if Robinia's movement find a way to help,' she said, chewing on her short nails. 'I just wish they could do something for Mary.'

As much as it had been difficult, finding this stolen moment with Coral was uplifting. Especially knowing Robinia was helping from the inside, even if we knew little of her plans. I began to compile questions in my head so next time we had a chance to talk, I'd be better prepared.

* * *

Back in my cell, I lounged on the bed mulling over our new relationship with Robinia. How many were in her movement and how long had they been conspiring? She must pretend to take the drug Control, act emotionless in front of her peers, and was excellent in her deceit. She certainly fooled me.

It was unthinkable, the thought of losing free will, and I knew I would fight to my last breath to hold on to my sense of self.

'*Bravo, Jasmine, and what do you think that will accomplish? They'll slip it in the food or water supply.*'

The unexpected words in my head caught me completely off guard. What startled me more was the realisation they had originated from the Medic himself. I shut my eyes tightly, attempting to summon more. It was hopeless.

The lock to my cell clicked, and as the door opened Salix appeared before me, his presence a welcome sight. The guard who accompanied him vanished, leaving us alone.

'Salix,' I murmured, lifting myself from the bed, gazing at him as if he were the most precious gift in the world. He appeared jittery, surveying the confines of my cell without uttering a single word. Something was off.

'Hey, it's okay. It's me, Jasmine,' I said, with a weary smile.

His eyes held an empty distant look, devoid of their usual spark. 'I know who you are,' he said, his voice as dull as his eyes.

I took a step towards him, halting as he backed away.

Feeling confused and a little rattled, I sank back onto the edge of my bed. 'Is everything okay? Has Robinia sent you?'

He folded his arms. 'No, why would Robinia send me? She doesn't have that kind of authority.'

An imaginary alarm sounded in my head heightening my growing sense of apprehension. 'Since Robinia knows we're friends. I thought she might have sent you.'

His face was a mask of indifference, his beaming smile, the one that never failed to brighten my day was gone. 'We *were* friends. That was in the past, and what feels like a long time ago.'

Why have you come here?' I asked, gripped with a ripple of fear.

'Aconite asked me to visit, as Malus was interested in the history we shared.

They both thought you might want to know what I think of you now?'

Leaning towards him, I held out my hand. 'Why don't you sit beside me, and we can talk. I'll tell you my side of the story.'

He took another step back, unfolding his arms as if ready to push me away. 'What would we gain by that? Do you think I'm interested in hearing anything you have to say?'

I gasped, feeling my eyes brim with tears. 'No matter what happens, I'll always think of you as my best friend, and I'll never let Aconite or Malus take that from me. Don't let them take it from you too.'

I searched his eyes realising it had already been done, they had given him Control. The Salix I knew was buried somewhere deep inside himself. I tried to reason from a different approach. 'Think back to the way we were before all this happened. You were always there for me, making me laugh and giving reasons for me to carry on. In my bleakest moments, *you* gave me hope. How can you say you're not interested anymore?'

I said, my voice thick with sobs. 'Please, don't let Aconite take you from me. I can't bear to lose you.'

'I should go now,' he said, rapping his knuckles against the door.

'Wait, Salix, please don't go. Let's try to talk,' I begged.

His parting words were final. 'I came here under Aconite's instruction, willing to let you know how I feel about you. You mean nothing to me. You deserve to be cleansed. May Pax have mercy on your soul.'

Anger surged like a volcanic eruption, consuming me completely. I charged wildly around the cell, colliding with the walls in a frenzied fury. Bitten-down nails pawed at my scalp and face. With a sturdy kick, I sent the dinner tray flying; mashed potato and meat sprayed the floor. Exhausted, I collapsed on the ground, wrapping my arms tightly round my legs. Tears cascaded down my face, each drop a torrent of anguish, while my broken sobs filled the air.

Malus skulked into my cell, rubbing his chin and wearing satisfaction like a prize badge. 'How the mighty Jasmine has fallen. Your friends don't seem to care anymore, especially Salix. He was extremely keen to point this out and couldn't wait to pay a visit to let you know.'

I kept my head buried in my knees, not wanting him to see the raw wounds on my face.

His voice was tinged with a sinister edge. 'Aconite agreed with me on a small matter we need to bring to your attention.' He paced back and forth with hands clasped at his middle. 'We feel it unfair to ask all our good citizens to be part of history as judge and jury, and have you left out. Pax will demand a special sacrifice from *you*, to help her forgive your misdemeanour. It's been suggested Salix, or perhaps Ash, be taken from Ruin to an Island called Mortem. Here, they will be placed on an ancient alter and sacrificed to Pax. This blood will wash away any future rebellion ensuring the laws of our society. Thereafter, a child will be sacrificed each year on the anniversary of your judgment. This will be your legacy.'

I felt my rage begin to swell, desperate to unleash its destructive presence. As it built in momentum, I thought it would explode out the top of my head. It took much effort, but I held it back, kept it in check, all the while seeing the damage I could do to Malus in my mind's eye. Sitting as still as possible, I kept my voice soft. 'I can understand why you see that Pax would want a sacrifice and I'll accept it. I think the Government would be foolish to ransom two exceptional young men such as Salix or Ash. They have bright futures, and the state needs them.' I no longer cared if he saw my marred face as I looked deeply into his evil eyes. 'Take me to Mortem and I'll willingly give my life to Pax. I'm sure having me on an alter would make amends for all I've done, and would save any other child meeting their death.'

He bared his yellow teeth. 'Sacrificing yourself is not an option. Have a long hard think about who you'll send, Salix or Ash? ... Ash or Salix? I'll come for your answer soon.'

'You'll have a long wait, Malus. I'll never send anyone to their death,' I said, crossing my arms. 'I'm not a murderer like you and your kind.'

His nod was courteous, his words deliberate and measured, carrying an undercurrent of menace. 'Then we shall decide for you.'

22

Overwhelmed by turbulent emotions running riot, I hardly slept. Mary was destined for a dreadful fate. Shock and disbelief still lingered as I contemplated her cleansing, with a deep sadness settling over me. Thoughts of what could have been haunted my mind. If only I had found a better place to hide her – or found Ash earlier. Perhaps I could have taken better action. The weight of unanswered questions and regret consumed me.

Now that Salix was under the influence of Control, he wanted nothing more to do with me. I mourned for him in the same manner I did Mary, as he was lost to me too. Perhaps Robinia could help him. She had an invisible movement behind her, people causing disruption with technical issues. Surely, she, or someone in her movement, would know how to save him?

Adding to my distress, Malus demanded I choose between Ash or Salix as a sacrificial offering to Pax. He had to be bluffing, as there was no way Aconite or the Government would allow such needless loss of life. However, my worry lay more towards the threat of children being offered each year in my memory. Coral and I had spoken of children going missing on Ruin. Was this act already in play, and Malus now using my downfall to bring it into the open? I had reached a point where nothing could astonish me, when it came to the wicked acts executed by our Government.

Robinia arrived with breakfast, her nose wrinkling at the mess of my cell. 'What happened in here?' she asked, handing me the tray. 'You better tidy this up.'

'I'm not hungry,' I replied, absently dipping the spoon into porridge and allowing the dollop to drip back in the bowl.

'Please, don't start all this refusing to eat act again. It's more crucial than ever for you to maintain your strength,' she said, her eyes exploring the scraped wounds on my neck and scalp. 'Oh, Jasmine, what have you done to yourself?' she asked, her tone filled with concern.

'No more than what's already been inflicted,' I said, with a deep sigh.

'I'll fetch some ointment to help ease any pain and stop infection.'

'There's no need.'

Robinia knelt down and began scraping scattered pulp from the floor, forming a little pile. 'This will require proper cleaning. As if we don't have enough to do already. I'll arrange for someone to come and tidy once we're gone. Now, please do as I ask and eat your breakfast.'

In an attempt to appease her, I reluctantly took a small spoonful. It proved futile as I hastily abandoned the tray and rushed to the washroom. With my head lowered over the toilet, my empty stomach retched.

Robinia gently rubbed my back. 'Perhaps a nice warm shower will make you feel better. Let me put it on while you gather yourself together.'

Steam filled the washroom, creating a warm comforting

atmosphere. Robinia helped remove my clothes, wrapping a towel around me.

'I don't want to go to the hall today, Robinia. I don't think I can face it. It's all too much.'

Robinia was aware of a discreet blind spot situated beside the shower, effectively hiding us from the prying eyes of the hidden camera. With a firm grip she guided me to the safe area, and to the sound of running water. 'Pull yourself together. It's important you stay focused,' she said, keeping her voice low.

'Seriously, I can't do it anymore.'

She squeezed my shoulder tight. 'You don't have a choice. If you can't do it for you then think of Coral. She needs you, and you must stay strong for her,'

I slumped against the cubical. 'I don't care.'

Her hand landed forcefully on my cheek, the sharp sting triggering a swell of tears I couldn't stop.

'You don't understand,' I said, rubbing my tingling face. 'Seeing Mary yesterday, battered and broken, it killed something inside me. I can't take any more of it,' I said, my quiet murmur carrying the weight of my anguish.

'Don't you dare give up?' she spat. 'There's more at risk here than you can imagine. Coral would never abandon you and Mary would think you a coward for the way you're behaving now.'

As my body lost all strength, I slumped into Robinia's waiting arms. Her firm hold kept me upright, stopping my fall. Shaking me forcefully, her face hovered close to mine. It was filled with urgency and determination. 'They used Mary to weaken your determination. They want everyone to see you as a pathetic and feeble child. Until now, you've battled like a bold warrior queen from a long-lost world.'

She softly kissed the top of my head. 'They're terrified of you because you're unique. They'll use any trick they can to aid in your downfall.'

'I'm not unique,' I argued, trying to pull back. 'Forming friendships isn't exclusive to me. Salix had the same gift. Even Spindle, when it came to helping Lucy. As for breaking rules, you can't look me in the eye and say others haven't broken any in the past. Why would friendships or breaking rules scare the Government so much anyway?'

Holding me at arm's length, she peered deeply into my eyes, as if searching for something profound. 'Trust me. If all goes to plan, you'll have every answer you seek. But you must believe me when I tell you you *are* unique. Of that there's no doubt.'

I banged the back of my head against the tiles, frustration rising in my voice. 'I need answers now. I'm not any different from Rowan or Lily. In fact, next to them I'm a complete failure. If you tell me your theory of why I'm different now, I promise not to give up.'

Her eyes darted anxiously towards the doorway, her body tense with a sense of unease. 'You don't conform to the rules and regulations of Ruin.'

'Tell me something I don't know,' I said.

'You form solid relationships with people when you shouldn't. All through schooling we should maintain light acquaintances. With you it's all or nothing.'

'We've already been over this,' I said, creasing my brow.

Robinia clenched her teeth, digging her nails into my arms. 'When they start to prescribe Control, you lose the person you once were. You lack any personal feelings and your single unwavering ambition is to serve the state. But, more than that, if Control is pumped into you when you are too young, the side effects and dangers are too much to be ignored.'

We were going round in circles. I knew all this from Mary, Ash, and even Rowan. 'Stop,' I yelled. 'Leave me alone. I'm done with all of you. Let's just end this now.'

Robinia's expression flitted to one of sympathy and regret. 'You've been fed Control since your time in the nursery unit,' she blurted, gasping a huge sigh. 'I didn't know how to tell you and didn't want you to be scared.'

'What . . . I don't understand,' I said, shaking my head.

'You were a troublesome child, and no matter how much punishment you received, you refused to submit. Aconite, the Elders . . . we have been studying you for a long time. We can't understand why Control has no effect, especially with the amount you're given. You're on a dosage nobody should be able to withstand. Yet, it has no impact on you whatsoever.'

'But how? How do they get it into my system?'

Robinia averted her eyes, unable to meet my gaze. 'In the morning, when each Elder or child collects their anti-sickness pills.'

'But I'm not given anything extra.'

'You're not given the same as everybody else. Your tablet is Control, only packaged to look the same as what others take.'

A sudden coldness settled over the washroom, and I shivered involuntary. My head felt strangely vacant, as if all thoughts had drained away. I felt a sense of numbness, unsure of how to process this news, or find the right words to express my feelings.

'Do you grasp the gravity of your situation?' Robinia implored, her voice filled with urgency. 'You can't be controlled, and if there are others like you, it poses an immense problem for the Government. Initially, they contemplated eliminating you . . . putting you down. It was my mentor who convinced them to study you instead. However, the Government now feels you're too much trouble and it's better to be done with you.'

My knees buckled and I felt myself cling to Robinia for support again. 'There must be others like me?' I muttered.

'We haven't found any yet which makes you exceptional. That's the reason they keep a closer eye on you than any other child on Ruin.'

It still didn't make sense. 'If I scare them so much, why did they allow me anywhere near Coral? She should have been mentored by someone else, and then she'd never have fallen into my influence,' I said, raising my voice.

Robinia pressed her finger on my lips. 'They wanted to study your interactions with others, to see if you could manipulate and encourage,' she said, her eyes darting quickly to the doorway. 'After they humiliate and hand out your punishment, they hope it will deter any other citizen from ever thinking about breaking rules. They need to make an example of you for that purpose.'

Robinia paused, the silence giving me a chance to comprehend the magnitude of the situation.

'Is there anything else I need to know?' I asked, my head having gone from empty, to spinning with so many thoughts.

She nodded slowly. 'They study your blood and have tracked down others in your lineage to see if they show the same immunity.'

'What do you mean by lineage?' I asked.

'Those who potentially share the same biological characteristics from the same male and female breeder you were born from.'

I thought of Mary, and her family unit. It had never crossed my mind we could have blood relations among the individuals residing alongside us here at Midpoint.

'Do I share the same blood with anyone?' I asked, 'Do I have family here on Ruin?'

'I've never been privy to that file, so I can't say.'

The thought of having family spiked a rush of adrenaline which helped lift my flagging spirit. Carrying on was the best choice, and I began to feel less battle weary. Now I knew more about myself, it was time to find out about Robinia. 'What made you turn against the state?'

'We'll discuss me when there's more time,' Robinia said,

with a smile. I think she was relieved to see my fighting spark return.

Feeling a sense of advantage, I felt it necessary to make my intentions clear. 'You said it was impossible to help Mary, and although I can't accept it, I do understand. But no matter what, we need to help Salix as he's been medicated with Control. Is it possible you can find a way to help him?' If you can, I promise to fit in to your people's plans without any questions.'

I thought she was going to say Salix was beyond help, or her movement would need to vote on it. I was wrong.

Robinia looked at me thoughtfully. 'Control is a drug that takes affect quickly. The longer it's in you, the stronger its grip. You have to be weaned off carefully, but once it's out your system, you become yourself again. Look at me, I'm proof of that.'

'Can you help him?'

'Right now, we need to concentrate on you and Coral. Salix is a rescue for another time. Now, we really need to get moving.'

'How many are in your movement?' I asked, stepping into the shower.

'Not nearly enough, but we're growing. You know I can't tell you much as I'm sworn to secrecy.'

'Is the Medic, Aspen, part of it? He did something to me and...'

'Robinia, are you in there?' Quercus voice bellowed from the cell door. 'What's taking so long?'

She leapt into the shower beside me, water soaking her ceremonial robes. 'I'll just be a minute,' she called, winking as she left.

Their muffled voices filtered through, and I could hear Robinia recounting a fabricated story, that I had slipped in the shower, bumped my head, and experienced a slight dizziness. The accident wasn't disastrous enough to require medical attention, but she'd managed to get soaked while helping.

Wrapping myself into a towel I tiptoed to the door so I could hear them better.

'Did they say why I've been summoned?' Robinia asked.

'I've only been told there are some concerns the Council would like to discuss,' Quercus said.

'What concerns?'

'If you come with me now, we'll find out together.'

Robinia peaked her head round the bathroom door. 'Ah, good. You've made progress. Get yourself dressed and someone will come for you shortly.'

They headed off, leaving me to fret over the new concerns the Council had about Robinia. Had they heard us, and was Robinia now in danger? Mary, Coral Salix and now Robinia. All those I loved were under attack and there was nothing I could do.

23

Coral and I had been transported to the Justice of Pax early. We watched the procession of individuals trickle in, nodding politely to each other while finding seats. It wasn't long before the hall was packed and the air thick with the rising tide of chatter. Their anticipation of events creating an energetic energy for them, but an oppressive opposite for Coral and me.

The trepidation of facing another day in the Justice of Pax was evident on Coral's face. 'Why do you think they've brought us up early?' she asked.

'They're probably scared your lift shaft will stick again. We can't keep Malus waiting,' I said, screwing up my face.

Seeing how gaunt Coral looked, I made the conscious decision not to tell her about Salix or Malus's visits. It would only add to her worries and shielding her from further distress was the best course of action.

'I found out what the smell is,' Coral said, her smile not reaching her eyes. 'You know that pong as you hit the labyrinth, and the weird sound that comes too.'

The smell and noise were a constant presence every time

we traipsed through the tunnel, but Quercus always refused to discuss it.

'Go on, tell me,' I said.

'One of the offshoots nearby is where the cows are stabled. You think we have it bad, imagine living in their conditions. I don't think I'll ever eat beef again.'

'Don't be silly, Coral, you have to eat. You need to keep your strength up,' I said, which sounded ludicrous coming from me. The number of times Robinia had uttered the same words in my direction.

Coral laughed heartily. 'If we survive this, I'm going to petition, and ask for the cows to be free. They shouldn't be kept underground in the dark, nor should any of the cloned animals.'

Coral plotting her next cause gave me hope Malus hadn't snuffed out her determination.

Salix was the first of my friends to arrive, approaching the front benches with measured steps. He settled in place, his gaze unwavering and fixed straight ahead.

The Elder behind him looked familiar, and squinting for a better look, I realised it was the Medic, Aspen.

A voice resonated loud in my head. *'I told you to frighten her a little.'* Did the Medic say that to me? I shut my eyes tightly, summoning all my focus on the day of my examination, attempting to remember the events of what happened. It all came flooding back. Me, sinking my teeth into his ear, and the taste of iron as his blood stained my lips. The voice in my head belonged to Robinia, but why would she want the Medic to scare me?

None of it made sense. Not even the children I saw when Aspen pulled back the blue curtain. Could it have been a hallucination from the sedative he jabbed in my neck?

The Council of Twelve filed on to the stage, settling in their seats. Robinia looked poised and composed, her knees pressed together and her hands firmly clasped on her lap. Needless to say, her ceremonial robes were dry.

Aconite, with his usual flair delivered a lavish welcome from the pulpit, commanding as much attention as he could before passing the reins of proceedings back to Malus.

Malus rose from his throne with an air of self-assured importance and picked up the microphone. 'We will now hear from those who encountered Jasmine's deceit first hand. Those who graciously forgave her first offence and did their utmost to help keep her pure. Jasmine took advantage of their trust.'

He made a subtle sweeping motion with his hand toward the front bench. 'First we will hear from Rowan. Please do come and share your testimony with us.'

Rowan's eagerness was palpable as she hurried towards the stage, ascending the steps two at a time. Wearing a smug expression on her face, she strutted to Malus's side.

Malus rested his hand on her shoulder. 'Please listen carefully to what Rowan has to say. This young lady is an outstanding citizen and has served the community of Ruin well. She's an excellent example of what can be accomplished here on this island.'

I rolled my eyes. 'Here we go', I said to Coral, my heart racing, the beat echoing in my chest like a drumroll. 'You know how much she likes to exaggerate.'

'Thank you for your kind words, Malus, and for allowing me the opportunity to address our good citizens. I truly believe everyone should know the extent of Jasmine's treason,' she said, with an air of confidence.

The knot in my stomach tightened, and the lump in my throat made it impossible for me to shout out for her to get on with it. As much as I had my differences with Rowan, it pained me deeply to see her stand against me.

Her gaze swept across the Justice of Pax. 'Dear citizens, when I noticed Jasmine stacking her tray with piles of food in the Be Thankful Hall, I thought at first she was guilty of gluttony. However, my suspicions grew when she only nibbled without ever actually eating. One evening her sleep was troubled, and she called out the word Mary,' Rowan said, more than a hint of joy in her voice. She paused, allowing the murmurs from the pews to gather momentum.

Malus hushed them after a few moments. 'And what did you suppose this Mary was?'

'I wasn't sure, but I wandered over to comfort her. When I asked her who or what Mary was . . . she told me . . . she told me. . . ' Rowan touched her brow. 'I'm sorry, I feel a bit faint,' she said, staggering back.

Her knees dipped and Malus caught her in his arms. He looked over to where the Council of Twelve sat. 'Can someone fetch some chilled water please?'

Quercus dove eagerly offstage returning with a plastic cup. Rowan sipped cunningly, knowing she held the whole of Midpoint in the palm of her hand.

For someone supposed to be lacking in emotion, Malus was full of concern. 'Are you okay to continue, Rowan, or would you like to leave it there for today?'

Rowan swooned for a few more seconds. 'I'm sorry, this is extremely difficult, but I'll do my best to carry on. With the good grace of Pax, I'll manage, as I'm sure she'll give me strength.'

Rowan glowed from the loud applause her acting brought, and waited till the end of the very last clap before carrying on. 'She told me she was praying . . . but not to Pax. She was praying to . . . Mary, and told me Mary was the mother of the old God.'

The room fell into a paralytic silence. As if the crowd couldn't be shocked further, Rowan lifted her chin, her voice rising to a higher pitch. 'Before I had the chance to question Jasmine further, she placed her lips on mine, parting them so I could taste her tongue.' She tilted her head towards me, her gaze emanating an unmistakable sense of triumph.

I launched myself at the glass wall, relentlessly pounding it with clenched fists. 'You're lying. You're nothing but a deceitful imposter,' I yelled with ardent frustration.

Coral sprang to her feet too, thumping her cage with all her might. 'How could you betray us like this, Rowan? Jasmine was your friend.'

Malus raised his hand in the air, commanding silence from the ear-splitting uproar filling the hall. 'Order please, as we need to confirm collaboration.' He turned his attention to Rowan, his gaze piercing and commanding. 'Is there any person present who can support your statement?'

Rowan pointed directly at Lily seated in the front row. 'Lily sleeps in the bunk above Jasmine. She saw and heard everything.'

'Please stand and make yourself known, Lily, and confirm if Rowan's account is true,' Malus ordered.

The hall fell into momentary silence as all faces looked for Lily. She shuffled uncomfortably with her eyes glued to the floor. A flicker of hope rose in my gut that she wouldn't bow to pressure, and would snuff out Rowan's lies.

Whispers grew louder as the seconds passed and my hope spiralled too. Malus called to her again. 'Stand and be heard, Lily, or are you a coward afraid to speak her truth?'

Lily looked up, and the torment on her face was evident. Her body looked weighed down by an invisible weight as she stooped instead of standing tall. With a voice filled with reluctance, she mumbled. 'Yes, it's true.'

'Louder please,' Malus called spitefully. 'Let everyone hear.'

Lily's face flushed, and she spoke louder. 'Yes, I can confirm Rowan's account of events.'

The Justice of Pax grew heavy with an air of tension. Although I was devastated, I reasoned Lily had no option in doing what she did as her life was difficult enough, without going against Rowan. Rowan had purposefully instigated the situation leaving Lily little choice. Nevertheless, the entire episode shattered my heart to pieces.

After dismissing Lily, Malus extended his congratulations to Rowan with a commendable tone. 'You've shown due diligence and duty towards our way of life, and to our Goddess Pax. May you be blessed in all you do, and prosper for the good of our one world nation. You may return to your seat.'

As Rowan floated off the stage, brimming with self-worth, Coral couldn't contain her anger. Her words burst out as she shouted loudly, hoping Rowan would hear. 'I hope you cartwheel down those stairs and smack your big fat ugly head, Rowan.'

Just as I was about to reassure Coral not to stress, Malus summoned Salix. A deep pang of sorrow pierced through me interweaving with my nervous unease. It was excruciating to watch him take his formal steps to the stage. His once lively voice now stripped of its cheerful tone because of Control, and replaced by a cold and distant flatness.

'One morning, Jasmine approached me requesting to see my brand. I was taken aback, considering her request outrageous. She didn't persist or bully me, and although I felt uncomfortable, I allowed her to see and touch my wrist.'

It was difficult to listen to, but at least he hadn't lied. Salix was gone, locked somewhere deep inside the confines of his mind. Had it not been for that, I was sure he'd never have turned against me.

'Clearly boundaries have been crossed. Do you have any idea why Jasmine would make such a request? Furthermore, can you explain why you were complicit in her demands?' Malus asked.

Salix didn't answer right away. He shook his head soberly, contemplating his reply. 'I'm sorry, but I've no idea why my brand was of interest to her. I'm even more perplexed with myself for fulfilling her whim.'

Pressing my forehead against the cold glass, I wept for my lost friend. He had done as I asked because he didn't want to disappoint me. This new Salix would never understand or know such a friendship.

Salix's gaze sought out Aconite, who watched sternly from the pulpit. 'I hope my weakness will be forgiven, and our wonderful leaders will look lightly on my folly. I can't offer excuses, but only an assurance if asked now, I would report her actions without hesitation.'

A storm of emotions churned within me, heartbreak, sorrow, regret and profound anguish.

Coral tapping nervously on the glass broke my melancholy. Her brow was furrowed and her voice tinged with confusion. 'What's going on with Salix?'

'It's a long story but I'll tell you when we get back to the pen.' I said, realising. there was no point in holding back the truth.

'Who can confirm this happened?' Malus asked.

Salix cast a glance towards Ash in the front row. 'Ash appeared at the exact moment the incident took place and it was obvious it left him upset.'

My mental state plunged to a new low when Malus called upon Ash and he took to his feet. He looked directly at me when he confirmed the event.

'Everything Salix said is true,' Ash said, his words cutting through the air with resolute conviction. 'It was the way she touched him that confused me.'

'Can you expand on what you mean?' Malus asked.

'It wasn't merely a matter of her gaze or simple touch upon his wrist. There was an intensity in her eyes, a deep longing of something I couldn't fathom. The way her fingers traced delicately along the skin of his wrist, it was surreal, leaving me utterly shocked.'

Once again the Justice of Pax was filled with a mix of hushed whispers, gasps and the sound of listeners moving restlessly, uncomfortable with the news they'd just heard.

My heart, already shattered into countless fragments, seemed incapable of breaking further. My entire being felt as though I was collapsing inward, consumed by an overwhelming sense of implosion.

Coral attempted to offer solace from the confinement of her cage, but I couldn't face her or listen. My attention was solely fixated on Ash, following his every move until he expressed his gratitude to Malus and returned to his seat beside Rowan.

She leaned towards him, her lips brushing against his ear in a whisper, and a deep bitterness flowed through me. As much as I hated Ash, the thought of her being near him was unbearable. My only consoling thought was she'd never truly win his heart. One day, they'd both be subject to Control, and their memories of each other would fade away.

***

Back in the holding pen, Coral did her best to lighten the mood. 'I guess not having friends is a plus as it means nobody can be summoned by Malus to dish the dirt.'

'What about Willow?' I asked.

Coral brushed the thought away. 'Willow doesn't know anything and as much as I call her my friend, I never confided in her. I've spent more time with you than anyone else.'

It wasn't until that moment I truly grasped the lonely existence Coral had on Ruin. Regret washed over me as I realised how self-centred I'd been, oblivious to her struggles. I could've done more for her, to help make life more bearable. The weight of guilt settled on me again, adding another tick to the ever-growing list of remorse.

Robinia appeared in the holding pen, her face etched with worry. 'That must have been tough. How're you feeling, Jasmine?'

'I lost it for a little while, but I'm fine now,' I lied, knowing I was only just holding it together. The state of my gnawed nails and chewed skin told the true story.

Robinia followed my stare. 'You'll have no fingers left if you keep that up.'

I scowled, annoyed she could be so flippant after the horrors I just endured.

'You were going to tell me about Salix. Why was he acting so strange?' Coral asked.

Robinia leaped into the conversation without feeling a need for a cautious approach. 'He's on a drug called Control which makes him compliant. You'll be put on it too if you survive this mess.'

Coral didn't seem bothered by Robinia's directness. Perhaps I was too protective of her and not giving her the credence she deserved.

'Is that the same drug Mary told us about, the one they give when we become of age?' Coral asked.

I took the swift decision to cut Robinia off before she could reply, not wanting her to blurt out I was also on control. 'Salix is another pawn in this sorrowful mess. They've prescribed him the drug simply to get to me,' I said, with a sigh.

Our conversation came to a sudden stop as Quercus strode into the holding pen.

'Today went well,' he said, nodding approval at Robinia.

'Depends whose side you're on,' I said, firing Robinia a wary stare.

She looked perplexed. 'There are no sides here. We serve Pax, and therefore carry out the wishes of her chosen leaders.'

Robinia's eyes roamed my face every bit as mine explored hers. Did she know my fears, that I had doubts about her true intentions?

Coral's voice took on a serious note. 'Can I ask a question?'

Quercus nodded. 'Make it quick as Robinia and I have important matters to attend to. With that in mind, I've organised for one of the guards to escort you both back to your cells today. He'll be here any minute.'

'Do you think Malus would allow Jasmine and me to speak at the trial? Surely everyone should hear our side of the story?'

Quercus grunted. 'That's a big ask.'

'I don't see why not,' Robinia said, her brows furrowed. 'I don't think Aconite would approve, but Malus may be open to the suggestion.'

A chuckle escaped my lips, and I couldn't help but shake my head in utter disbelief.

'What is it?' Robinia asked.

'You said a few minutes ago we didn't have sides. We simply serve. So why would anyone be interested in what we had to say. What is it Robinia, sides or no sides, because you can't have it all ways?'

Coral's jaw dropped. 'Jasmine, what's gotten into you?'

I was on edge, frustrated I couldn't confront Robinia about the encounter with Aspen. 'Sorry, I guess what we've gone through has made me a little tetchy.'

Robinia nodded. 'That's understandable,' she said, before turning to Coral. 'I'll approach the Council with your request and see what they say. Asking won't do any harm.'

* * *

We followed the guard along the dark tunnel towards the labyrinth, with the voice in my head offering advice. *'You could take him out – two of you against one of him. Find a way out through the tunnels and escape.'*

Coral jolted me back to reality. 'What's up with you and Robinia?' she asked. 'You were a bit frosty, and remember, she's trying to help.'

'I guess today got to me more than I realised, and I took it out on her. Anyway, what's all this with you wanting to tell your story at the trial.'

Coral's smile was huge. 'If I get to say my bit, everyone in Midpoint will know what a conniving bitch Rowan truly is.'

24

The hazy form of the crowd materialised as my eyes adjusted to the blinding brilliance of overhead stage lights. An energetic buzz of conversation from the benches reached the stage; Aconite and Malus seemed oblivious, concentrating on the handheld monitor Malus shared.

Malus glanced in our direction, his cold stare sending shivers through me. His stern expression spoke volumes, showing the depths of his animosity. Aconite's eyes remained fixed on the monitor, his face full of purpose, deeply committed to whatever it was they were looking at. Together, clad in official robes, and Malus proudly wearing his peruke like a prize, they offered a complex insight into everything that was wrong with our governance.

'What do you think they're up to?' Coral asked, in a hushed tone.

'Knowing them, it won't be anything pleasant,' I said, doing my best not to worry. Each day had blurred into the next with more and more people I'd never met before coming forth to give accounts of my shady dealings with them. The only good transpiring from the whole circus was I got to spend time with Coral.

'Perhaps they're thinking about letting us represent ourselves,' Coral said, ever the optimist. 'If we do get the chance, I won't hold back.'

I raised an eyebrow. 'Do you really think anything can be gained by us telling our truth? Not only that, do you think they'd listen or care?'

Malus tapped on the microphone; the loud thudding noise reverberated through the hall, catching everyone's attention. 'Good morning citizens, and welcome once again to the Justice of Pax. Today, we'll hear from Birch, known to all of you as the Giver of Goods. Birch is an Elder held in high regard with an exemplary record until it was tarnished by the accused.'

There was no need to call Birch forward as he stood proudly in place by Malus's side, by the time Malus had finished his long-winded introduction. 'Birch, please tell our good citizens of the audacity, duplicity and scheming imposed upon you.'

Birch's rigid demeanour softened as he gave a curt nod, revealing an air of confidence. With shoulders squared and his gaze focused, it was evident there was more to him than I gave him credit for. He spoke slowly and clearly. 'The older girl, Jasmine, appeared at the warehouse along with one of her comrades,' he said, pausing to scan the front row. On finding Ash, he signalled for him to join him on the stage. However, Ash remained firmly rooted to his seat.

Malus paced the stage, hands behind his back. 'And what was the reason for their visit?'

'Ash claimed his furs had been lost and was issued with a new set. The incident was reported to the Council of Twelve, and Ash willingly served his punishment without complaint.'

Malus looked puzzled, his pacing stopped in front of my cage. 'Can you tell us, Birch, what does any of this have to do with the two girls who stand accused of the highest treason?' he asked, rubbing his chin, his eyes fixed on me.

'Later investigation found Ash didn't lose his furs, only pretended to. He then took the blame for Jasmine, who was the true culprit. If you ask me, she manipulated the whole event.'

Ash sat still, keeping his head bowed, his face hidden from my view.

Malus scanned the front row and sought him out. 'Please come forward, Ash, and take your place beside Birch.'

Each step Ash took towards the stage was like a needle stabbing into my heart. My mind was a mangled mess of mixed emotions. This time, his gaze didn't fall in my direction, even though my eyes were firmly fixed on him.

'Can you verify you misled the Giver of Goods, acquiring furs you didn't need?' Malus asked.

Without a moment's hesitation, Ash's voice rang out. 'I'm sorry to admit it, but yes, I did deceive Birch.'

Malus folded his arms, his face a mix of concern and disappointment. 'Why would you do such a thing?'

His response didn't come immediately. Instead, his eyes wandered around the Justice of Pax, scanning the faces of the crowd, finally settling on me.

'Get it over with,' I screamed at him, my fist colliding with toughened glass. Pain shot through my hand as the bones cracked on impact, a sharp jolt of agony ran through my arm.

Ash didn't flinch at my anger, he merely returned his attention to the waiting crowd. 'Jasmine approached me after our evening meal and begged me to go with her to the Warehouse. She was afraid of receiving punishment for losing her furs and asked if I'd take the blame on her behalf,' he said. 'She pleaded with me, saying I wouldn't receive any punishment due to my impeccable record. Even if a punishment was assigned, it wouldn't be half as bad as any she'd be given.'

I let out a low groan, the weight of his betrayal settling

heavily on me. It was as if my entire being was detached from the present, as if I were an outsider looking down at my own shattered reality. Another friend, another painful lie. Sagging limply against the glass wall, I hugged my chest to keep my heart from breaking all over again. Ash was Mary's grandson and would never know the extent of his disloyalty.

'Why would you, a young man of such calibre, allow Jasmine to manipulate you like this?' Malus asked.

I was desperate for Ash to recant his lies, to tell the truth and proclaim his love for me. It was inexplicable, but a deep longing for him remained, even within the deep hatred I held for him.

Ash pondered the question, his brow furrowing. 'I can't make excuses for my actions, but I want you to know I'm sorry. There was a past incident where I had reported, Jasmine.' He hesitated, as if saying my name out loud brought a flash of guilt and made him want to stop. For a brief second our eyes met, but I couldn't find any warmth in them. 'I reported her to the Elders, and she was whipped badly. She knew I felt guilty and perhaps used this to manipulate me into lying about losing my furs. I was weak and allowed myself to be influenced.'

Malus mumbled softly in acknowledgement. 'Did anyone else witness her come to you and ask this request?'

'Rowan and Spindle,' Ash said, nodding as though his words needed some form of emphasis.

I stole a fleeting glance at Spindle, who appeared completely absorbed in his own thoughts. With a distant gaze, it was as if he were peering into an unseen realm, totally uninterested in the trial's proceedings. It didn't surprise me, as Spindle was never interested in anything I did, and probably wished we were at the cleansing part already.

Malus singled Spindle out. 'We've already heard from Rowan a few times. Spindle, would you like to add anything to Ash's statement?'

At the mention of his name, Spindle's eyes refocussed and his brow relaxed. He shuffled slowly to his feet and I waited for him to confirm Ash's lie too.

'I'm sorry, Malus. Both Ash and Rowan can vouch for the fact I've never liked Jasmine. I sort of switch off when she's around, so I can't confirm or deny what happened.'

It came as an unexpected surprise, leaving me a little perplexed. This moment had given Spindle an opportunity to act upon his dislike for me, yet he opted to tell the truth. Even though he didn't say anything in my favour, I was grateful he didn't add to the lie.

Rowan leapt promptly to her feet, before Malus had a chance to ask her. 'I can confirm Spindle and Jasmine never jelled. However, every word Ash said is true.'

Malus nodded, a satisfied expression finding his face. 'At least Spindle wouldn't have fallen into Jasmine's trap of leading boys astray.'

Soft murmurs from the crowd began to spread. The hushed voices mingled, creating a sound that began to swell.

'Thank you, Ash, you may return to your seat.' Malus said, redirecting his focus back to Birch, and capturing the attention of the crowd. 'There was a further incident in the warehouse, Birch, where you received a visit from both the accused. Is this correct?'

'It is, indeed.'

'Please, tell us what happened,' Malus asked.

Leaning in closer to Coral's cage, I kept my voice low. 'This should be good if he tells the truth.'

Birch's eyebrows arched upward, a flicker of revulsion crossing his features as he cast a quick glance at Coral. 'Both girls came to the warehouse claiming they required a pouch to hold sapling seeds,' he explained, his tone laced with frustration. 'On leaving, the smaller one, Coral, created a disruptive scene, insisting the pouch was damaged. When I began to investigate the matter further, Jasmine excused herself, claiming she would return to the table and find another pouch.'

His words hung in the air, painting a picture of deceit and manipulation. The Justice of Pax hummed with an air of intrigue.

'Did she find one and bring it back to you?' Malus asked.

Birch shook his head, his unease obvious. He wouldn't want to admit we'd fooled him. 'No, Malus, she didn't.' Falling silent, he tugged nervously on his ear while a red glow spread from his neck to his cheeks.

From every corner of the hall, the side-long glances of spectators converged, their whispers charged creating an atmosphere of intrigue and speculation.

Malus recognised Birch's distress, reached out and lightly patted him on the back. 'Continue, Birch. None of this is your doing and you're not to blame for the preposterous antics of the accused.'

'While tending to Coral, and doing my best to deal with her concerns, Jasmine sneaked to my monitor and called up files with past transactions.'

'What proof do you have Jasmine did such a thing?' Malus asked.

Birch sucked in a sharp breath, causing a faint snort to escape through his nose. 'After the girls left, I returned to my monitor to log a report of damaged goods. However, the screen was on an item of stock already distributed, which shouldn't have been the case. The stock search had taken place when I was with Coral and could only have been called up by Jasmine.'

The lack of foresight was my error, and I cursed for having landed Coral in another treacherous situation. 'Oh Coral,' I said, with regret, meeting her stare. 'I didn't realise I left a trail.'

Malus prowled the length of the stage again. 'This is certainly a strange accusation, and one would wonder why anyone would want to search past transactions. Please tell us, Birch, what was it Jasmine had been looking at?'

'It was the transaction of the furs supplied to Ash on her previous visit with him. His brand and records were on screen. If you want my opinion, I think she was there to gloat, and to brag of her manipulation skills to the younger child. Perhaps she was mentoring more than the Council could have imagined,' Birch said, with an air of disgust.

'Can you think of any other reason why Jasmine would be looking for this particular transaction?' Malus asked.

'Perhaps she has a brand fetish. Was she not fixated with another boy's brand too?'

Throughout the entirety of the hall, glances shifted from person to person, as they absorbed Birch's account. A detonation of laughter erupted, the hearty peals echoing around the hall, leaving the Elders on Control shouting for order. A dawning realisation washed over me, as apprehension settled in. History would remember me as much more than a breaker of rules. I'd be remembered as a brand stalker too.

'Thank you, Birch. You may take your place back among your fellow comrades,' Malus said delighting in my humiliation.

As Birch departed Malus called on Ash. 'Do you have any idea why Jasmine would search this transaction?

Ash shook his head with such a force I'm surprised his neck didn't snap.

Rowan raised her hand, bringing a murmur of anticipation from the crowd. 'May I say something?' she asked.

'Yes, Please do.' Malus said.

'I totally agree with Birch. I believe Jasmine does have a fetish. She openly flaunted herself at Ash and Salix, who were unable to reject her whims. She is a danger to our morality. We can't blame Ash or Salix, they were bewitched by a temptress.'

Shouts, and lots of them echoed loudly round the hall.

'*Burn the witch.*'

'*Death to the temptress.*'

'*Hang the sorceress.*'

Malus quickly asserted his authority, calming the fervor. 'We now know Jasmine's furs were never lost. It was all a lie as she willingly gave them to the cave dweller and were found with her when captured. Rowan is correct in her assessment. Jasmine bewitched Ash, the same way she cast a spell on Salix,' Malus said, summing the matter up.

While Malus rambled on, Aconite skulked from the pulpit, sought out Robinia and whispered in her ear. Rising awkwardly, she followed him from the Justice of Pax.

'Where do you think they're going?' Coral asked.

I shook my head. 'I don't have a clue, but I don't like it. The other day, Quercus pulled her from my cell, advising the Council had concerns, but with everything else going on, I never found time to ask her about it.'

We didn't have long to wait before finding out. Aconite returned signalling to Malus who abruptly ended his ramblings.

'Good citizens of Ruin, can I ask you to make your way in an orderly manner to the Cleansing Chambers,' Malus said, a glint in his eye.

A cold dampness settled on Coral's brow. 'Do you think our time's up?' she asked. 'Are they going to cleanse us now?'

'No, I don't think so,' I said, trying to keep calm, hiding the quiver in my voice. 'They've said all along the citizens will pass judgement and they haven't been asked for a verdict yet. I think it's another tactic to scare us.'

I hoped I was right, that Aconite hadn't decided to make judgement on his own. Surely, he didn't have such authority over Malus. The trap doors opened, and our cages sprang to life.

As my cage began its descent into the lift shaft, I saw Ash;

his fingers grazed his chin in a thoughtful manner as he spoke to Spindle. Whatever he said, both turned in unison to look at me. Ash held a look of genuine surprise, while Spindle appeared utterly shocked, his mouth slightly ajar.

* * *

Robinia and Quercus waited in the holding pen, ready to release us from the confines of our cage.

'What's going on, Robinia?' I asked, doing my best to keep the tremor from my voice.

Her eyes appeared red and blotchy, as if she'd shed recent tears. She moved stiffly round the holding pen and didn't meet my gaze. We trailed behind them in our shackles as they led the way from the holding pen, out into the tunnel and towards the labyrinth.

'Are you sure you're okay,' I heard Quercus ask her.

'It's just a reaction to the smell down here. I'll be fine,' she said.

Her voice sounded raw and carried a hint of vulnerability and emotional strain. The way she said it sparked my panic. Tears sprung to my eyes at the thought of walking to our death. I hoped we'd be unshackled so I could hold Coral all the way to the end.

Sensing my dread, Coral sobbed quietly beside me, and I couldn't comfort her in fear of losing the little control I had left.

The mob gathered in the walk lanes venting their anger, landing blows and spitting as we passed. Robinia blew on a whistle, the high-pitched sound alerting guards who suddenly appeared forming a protective wall. However, the angry shouts and chants continued to follow from behind.

An even greater crowd congregated at the Cleansing Chamber, their raised fists and contorted faces fuelled by a shared need for justice. As the mass of bodies surged forward, the army of guards did their best to hold them in line, securing a safe and open space for Aconite and Malus to deal with Coral and me.

We were pushed to our knees in front of Aconite and Malus. Coral leaned against my arm, and I took solace from her, tilting my neck and gently resting my cheek against her head. Those deep in the crowd without a view watched our distress on the plasma screens. Not one person in Midpoint would miss our execution.

I barely registered Malus's ranting or the shrill clamour from the crowd, it sounded distant, faint. So many emotions collided together. Fear, despair, but mostly an overwhelming sense of injustice. The sudden realisation I wasn't ready to die, even though I had told myself otherwise.

We were seized from behind, our bodies roughly hoisted up, and pushed forward towards the Cleansing Chamber.

With a mechanical hum, the colossal steel doors of the chamber parted, sliding open.

In the far-left corner of the concrete block, Mary huddled in a pitiful heap, her frail body broken and bruised and sickly pus seeping from one black eye which had swollen closed. Both her hands and legs were tightly bound with rope, which seemed farcical. Even if her body had been fit to run, where could she have escaped to.

Time warped in a paradoxical manner, happening exceptionally fast, yet unbearably slow. Sparks erupted from the gas rings beneath the grated floor, setting ablaze mesmerising hues of orange and yellow. As the flames roared to life, an intense heat followed, both creeping across the concrete floor and charred walls towards Mary.

Beside me, Coral unleashed a frenzied struggle, desperately attempting to break free from the grasp of the guard who held our chains. Her tiny frame strained with effort as she pushed and tried to shake herself forward to no avail. Her screams fell on deaf ears, as Aconite and Malus ignored her heartfelt pleas.

Paralysed with grief and helplessness, I found myself frozen on the spot and detached. It was as though my body had disconnected and I looked down at the cleansing from a place above. My screams came from within, trapped and unable to escape my lips, echoing noisily within the confines of my mind.

Mary didn't beg for her life, or call for help. Her lips moved slowly as if in prayer, until the billowing flames and fiery furnace engulfed her.

My head spun and a dark mist drifted over my eyes. I didn't feel the thud as I fell to the ground.

* * *

I'm not sure how long I was out but I woke on the floor of the cage with a dizzy haze clouding my senses. I could hear Coral's voice faintly nearby, but couldn't place where exactly.

'Sorry,' I muttered, trying to push myself up but my body wasn't connecting with my brain.

Malus peered through the glass, his face distorted and blurry, his voice distant. 'This is your last chance. You won't be given another opportunity to tell your account of what happened.'

Coral pleaded too, her voice near but far. 'Pull yourself together. Everyone is waiting for you. It's the only chance you'll get.'

I faded further into the fog, trying to nurse my sore hand through the shackles. Laughter floated from all around, drowning out Coral's cries. Someone was in the cage beside me, pressing their hand on my brow.

'We should have taken her straight to the Medic. I want it recorded my suggestion to do this was disregarded,' Robinia said. 'If it was only a slight faint as you suggested, Malus, she would have recovered properly by now. Immediate medical attention was the correct course of action. Not being carried through tunnels back to the holding pen and carted back to the Justice of Pax.'

'Perhaps we should have her examined,' Aconite said, his face appearing at the glass.

'Have her taken to the medical station right away. But, I stand by my conviction. This was her only opportunity to address the crowd. She won't have another.'

I tried to swallow but my throat was parched and painful. The bright lights above stabbed at my eyes, so blinking sluggishly I hid my head from them, shying away from Robinia too. Curling up into a tight ball, I drew my knees up to my chin. My mind had tried to shield me from Mary's cleansing, but the haunting image of her burning came flooding back. My body convulsed uncontrollably as the darkness took me again.

* * *

Shadows formed in the gloom and floated with me. Rowan emerged, her large green eyes taunting. I drifted past without a second glance gliding towards Ash. He pushed me away, so I soared further into the pitch-black void.

Fingers pressed down on my neck. 'Can you hear me, Jasmine?'

'*Ignore them. Don't go back.*' It was Mary. '*Stay in the dark. Stay here with me and no harm will come to you.*'

Smelling salts. Their pungent, sharp odour penetrated the dark veil. Not only did I smell them, but tasted them on the back of my throat too. I gagged as my eyes flickered open. Aspen hovered above holding a sick bowl at my chin while my gullet burned as I coughed up bile.

'Welcome back,' Aspen said, his hand touching my sticky brow. 'How're you feeling?'

'I'm thirsty,' I replied, hardly recognising my own voice.

Robinia wiped my face with a damp cloth before helping me sit up and sip some water.

Once my thirst was quenched, I pushed Robinia away. 'Don't come near me,' I said, my breath rattling. 'You're plotting against Coral and me, giving us false hope.'

'Easy now,' Aspen said, her voice tender. 'You don't want to bring on another panic attack. We've only just got you back from the last one,' he said, stripping off rubber gloves and flinging them in the waste bin.

'What have you done to me,' I asked, my heart racing.

'It's okay, he's a friend,' Robinia said. 'Look, he fixed your sore hand.'

Sure enough, when I glanced downward, my left hand was coated in a pristine white bandage.

'It's not broken, just badly bruised,' Aspen said.

The panic in my voice was impossible to hide. 'He did something to me the last time I saw him, and he's done something to me again,' I argued.

Aspen handed me a white tablet. 'It's a sedative and will help you relax.'

Robinia smiled reassuringly. 'We won't force you to take it, but I promise it'll help if you do. You've been through so much.'

No longer caring, I gulped the tablet back. Its magic didn't take immediate effect, but I soon began to feel a warm glow spread over me bringing a floating sense of calm.

'Your blood pressure's still a bit high, but not as bad as it was. It's not surprising. What you witnessed was horrendous.'

I tried to get up, but my head was still giddy and hollow.

'It's okay, you don't need to rush. I've told Malus you won't be fit to go back to the Justice of Pax today,' Aspen said, shining a light in my eyes. 'I won't let Malus or Aconite near you while you're here.'

'I take it they can't hear us?' I asked, blinking from the thin beam of light.

Aspen swept his hand across the room. 'The medical equipment plays havoc with the microphones, so we're okay.'

My gaze shifted towards the open blue curtain, revealing the machine pumps humming with a suction sound. Yet, the beds lay empty. Had my imagination conjured the tiny infants?

'I remember stuff,' I said. 'I heard your conversation the last time I was here before blanking out. Why were you trying to frighten me?'

Robinia and Aspen exchange glances, as if a certain unspoken understanding connected them. Scraping a chair over, he positioned himself next to me on the bed.

His tone was solemn. 'None of us know how safe we are right now and to give too much information could endanger our movement. Our main concern is to keep you alive and find a way to smuggle you off this island. We need to study your blood, to see why Control doesn't affect you. You are an asset in our fight to provide an antidote. Can you imagine if we had a pill that blocked their conditioning? People would have free will by the masses and freedom would follow.'

Robinia reached out and took my good hand in hers. 'That's the reason you're so special. You don't have any sickly effects from the drug, but one thing we've noticed is your rage. Anger is a trigger, but it keeps you focused, as if you relish going against the norm. That's why Aconite is terrified. He can't afford any more children on Ruin growing up to be like you.'

Robinia had already told me I was immune, but I had never fully realised the implications. 'Do you work with the people from the caves on the mainland? I know people rebelled and fought to quash our Government over many generations. Mary told us about them. She was one of them.'

A terrible sadness washed over me as I spoke of her, my heart breaking for the family who waited her return. 'We need to tell Mary's people what happened to her, and how brave she was.'

Aspen shook his head. 'We have always been aware of the rebellion led by those in the caves. We've just never been able to establish contact. That was another reason why you, Mary and this trial became important.'

'Mary told Coral and me Government ranks had been infiltrated.'

Robinia squeezed my hand before letting it go. 'Then we need to find out where they are and work with them. The caves on the mainland are vast, stretching for hundreds of miles. The rebels are good at hiding, and I've heard some say they operate like ghosts.' Robinia paused, taking a moment to reflect before resuming with a thoughtful tone. 'One of the main issues we face is our networks are splintered. We have factions on most of our islands, but nobody ever truly knows who they can trust.'

Aspen sighed. 'It's true, the network of caves is complex. If only Mary had put her trust in me sooner, I may have got more information from her.'

My eyes widened. 'Wait, you spoke with Mary?'

'Yes, but not as much as I'd have liked, and we were rarely alone. I'm sorry we couldn't save her. She loved you and Coral like her own and worried what fate would befall you. She took strength knowing our movement was here in the background.'

He removed Mary's small wooden cross from his pocket. 'Robinia gave me this to give to her, but she wouldn't take it back. She said to give it to you when you were free. We still have much work to do to make it happen, but take this now and hopefully you'll find comfort.'

With a trembling hand, I clutched the cross tightly and brought it to my lips. Robinia held me close as tears spilled down my cheeks. Aspen waited patiently until I managed to compose myself before carrying on.

'Mary shared details of her grandson, advising you and

Coral had a plan to find him. She wanted you to tell him everything, about his mother, and their life in the caves.'

After everything that happened Mary still hoped we'd find him. No matter how much they tortured her, her graciousness triumphed. Overwhelmed with her tremendous loss, I held her cross to my heart.

'Is that why you were examining brands?' Aspen asked. 'Did Mary provide you with clues about colour and shape, leading you to suspect it might be Salix or Ash?

A long sigh escaped me, and I nodded in confirmation.

'Which of the two was her grandson?' Robinia asked.

Biting my lip, I hesitated, contemplating whether Ash deserved to know given his actions. After a moment of brooding, I responded. 'No, I was simply ruling both of them out. We were still looking for him when we got caught.'

I didn't feel guilty about the lie. If I was ever fortunate to meet with Mary's people, how could I reveal to them it was her own grandson who secured her terrible fate.

'Not that it matters, if all goes to Aconite and Malus's plan, but should I be concerned about Control?' I asked, a tinge of worry creeping into my voice. 'What if it suddenly kicks in and I lose my mind. I don't even know what side effects to look for?'

'If given too young, it causes problems in reproduction, which means less breeders for the state. Other recorded side effects are blinding migraines, tearing of blood vessels and blood clots in the brain. Don't worry. We have x-rays of your head and you are perfectly healthy,' Aspen said.

Robinia produced a small vibrating disc from her pocket, similar in size to the frequency blocker she used in the holding pen to cut the sound feed to the systems. 'Someone's coming,' she warned, as Aspen followed her gaze to the door.

Aspen was in the middle of sounding my chest when Aconite burst in. 'What's taking so long?' he asked.

Momentarily taken aback by the interruption, Aspen

removed the stethoscope ear pieces and addressed Aconite. 'What can I do for you?'

'I want to know what's taking so long?'

'Do you want the girl fit for trial?' Aspen asked.

'Her wellbeing is imperative,' Aconite confirmed.

Aspen's facial expression was one of sharp concentration. 'Then you must call a halt to proceedings for today. Jasmine has been traumatised by events, so much so, her brain has switched off. My suggestion would be to resume in two or three days to give the mind time to heal, in the short term.'

Aconite wavered, his rapid response fazed by the time scale given, and his face awash with disbelief. 'We don't have two or three days. The trial will resume in the morning.'

'As you wish,' Aspen said. He turned to Robinia, 'Let it be noted for the records that my recommendation was dismissed.'

Robinia nodded curtly. Watching them interact was extraordinary. Aconite flashed so many sentiments blowing hot and cold while Aspen and Robinia were passive and demure.

'Are you done with her,' Aconite asked, casting me a grim look.

'Yes, she may return to her cell, but I insist she rests and is not unduly disturbed.' Aspen said.

* * *

That night, the inside of my left arm began to itch. While I rubbed the irritated skin, I felt something small and sharp imbedded just below the surface. Upon closer examination, I saw the faint trace of a delicate scar.

Could I truly trust Aspen and Robinia?

25

The following morning, Coral's face lit up with delight when Quercus delivered me to the holding pen. Her beaming smile stretched wide, filling the slightly chilly room with warmth. Our conversation remained sparse until Quercus shackled me up, then left.

'I'm so glad you're okay. What did the Medic say was wrong.'

I didn't get the chance to reply as we were catapulted to the hall above. At least I was. Coral's cage stuck in the lift shaft again.

Malus ambled over, gesturing for Aconite to join from the pulpit. Malus leaned over the edge of the trap door, looking down into the lift shaft, engrossed in the conversation flowing from the engineers below.

'You really need to get the runner inside Coral's lift shaft fixed, Aconite. It's not good enough,' I said, as he joined Malus and hovered by his side.

He ignored me, but I could see his agitation mounting. Clenched fists and the tension washing over his face gave him away.

'Did the engineers say how long it would be, Malus? We really need to keep to our schedule,' he said, his voice elevated.

'No more than ten minutes,' Malus replied, taking Aconite by the arm and leading him towards the Council of Twelve.

Gazing across the expanse of the Judgement of Pax, I pondered at the influx of individuals coming in. What was happening to their daily tasks? Were all lessons suspended? Did the same people come every day, or were the given access on a rota?

I caught sight of Robinia and wondered again if I could truly trust her. Ash arrived and hurried to his seat. He startled Rowan by tapping her lightly on the shoulder, their shared moment of surprise had them burst into laughter. His gaze roamed from the stage to the confines of my cage, and our eyes locked for a fleeting moment. It was me who looked away first.

Malus strode confidently to the centre of the stage, his voice blasting through his microphone. 'Good morning everyone. We have a technical glitch with Coral's lift shaft. It should be fixed soon and then we'll begin.'

Malus had done everything in his power to humiliate me and break my spirit. Yesterday, he had invited me to brief the hall when I was at my lowest ebb, having lost my mind to grief. Today, I wasn't going to give up without a fight.

Coral's cage rolled up and Malus clapped his hands. Before he got one word out, I took a deep breath and roared. 'Malus is the giver of death. He worships a false Goddess and steals your free will. If this isn't true, have Pax strike me down dead right now.'

The atmosphere became charged with tension, especially from those in close proximity who overheard my comments. Malus kept a rigid stance, his chest swelling with defiance as he strode toward my cage.

Standing tall with my feet firmly planted on the ground, my breath created a fog on the glass as I bellowed, hoping my words would reach as many ears as possible. 'You belong to a bloodline who harnessed the Sun, bringing cosmic disorder. Pax didn't bring The End of Days, it was man. Pax is a false Goddess made up to flip the narrative, to scare people so they won't disobey.'

Malus's eyes narrowed revealing a steely determination. He pounded on the glass, directly at the level of my face. Although I squirmed, it was only a physical reaction, and not one of fear.

'Why not invite your family over? I'm sure everyone would love to meet them.' I continued to yell.

'Jasmine, what're you doing?' Coral asked.

'That's right, Malus. The family you and your cohorts keep secret while we are taken from breeders, to be turned into slaves. You and your accomplices live a life of leisure in hidden homes.'

A surge of anger coursed through me, rising like an unstoppable wave. As I found my voice, an increasing sense of confidence welled too. I jabbed my finger defiantly on the glass wall. 'The family unit was destroyed, and we live this horrible existence without love or nurture. You continue to make a mockery of humanity with your web of lies to this very day.'

Murmurs of my outburst from the front benches rippled, gradually spreading further back through the hall. Intrigued by the commotion, more and more citizens crammed closer to the stage craving to hear of the trouble I stirred. I could hear their questioning murmurs as they pondered my accusations.

'Please show some respect for Malus who has come here to do his job.' Robinia scolded, stepping over to my cage.

Malus's eyes blazed with fury, his fists clenched so tightly his knuckles turned an eerie shade of white. My gaze stretched beyond him, my attention shifting to Aconite who now had the microphone and was busy lulling the viewers back to their seats, numbing their desire to know the truth, and stealing my victory.

'Children go missing on Ruin. Is it because experiments have gone wrong,' I raged, trying to shout above Aconite's booming voice. It was no use. I had lost my audience, but I still wasn't ready to give in. 'Where do you hide their bodies?' I asked Malus.

'Silence,' Malus roared. 'This behaviour is outrageous.'

Robinia's eyes darted nervously from Malus to me. 'Enough, Jasmine,' she said.

Aspen joined my little group on the stage wearing an air of concern. 'Would you like me to administer some relaxant?' he asked.

Adrenalin surged through me like a flooding dam. There was no way I'd let them hinder my mission of getting my message out. 'There's no love or nurture on Ruin, only a grim reality with hidden enslavement, and you say we should be thankful.'

Malus looked over his shoulder, making sure Aconite still held the crowd. 'Lower the cages,' he called frantically. 'And someone fetch a muzzle to shut her up.'

Even as the cage descended, I continued to shout defiantly, my voice echoing all the way down to the holding pen. I was relieved Coral's cage didn't stick on the way down as I knew we wouldn't have much time.

She stared in amazement. 'Where did all that come from?'

'I'm not sure, but it doesn't matter. Coral, you need to know about the Medic.' I said. 'He's one of Robinia's friends and he's been secretly helping us. He gave me Mary's cross back,' I said, pulling it from my pocket and holding it up so she could see. 'Listen carefully. I told him and Robinia we don't know who Mary's grandson is, so they don't know about Ash.'

She tilted her head. 'Why lie?'

'It was his betrayal that led to Mary's cleansing. He can never be allowed to know of her,' I spat.

Coral scowled. 'Are you keeping him a secret to protect him?'

I shook my head forcefully. 'No way. Why would I protect him? I hate him.'

Coral wasn't convinced. 'I think if Ash finds out the truth and the extent of what he's done, it'll destroy him. I think deep down you know this, and you don't want that for him. You're protecting him and that's not fair. He deserves to know.'

I might have agreed with Coral's comments when I thought I was falling in love with Ash, but now my feelings were different. 'Ash is dead to me, and if I had the chance, I'd fling him in the Cleansing Chamber and light the flames myself.'

I averted my gaze, unable to meet her eyes, yet I felt the weight of her intense stare bearing down upon me.

'We don't know for certain if it was Ash who reported us. We came to that conclusion ourselves. We never had any real evidence,' Coral argued.

I stiffened, annoyed we were wasting time on a matter already decided. 'It was him, Coral, I just know it.'

The arrival of Robinia and Quercus brought an abrupt end to our conversation, their disapproving glances casting a shadow over the already tense atmosphere.

'Your manners are terrible,' Quercus said. 'I've never known such insolence.'

Faking a yawn, I put my hand over my mouth. 'Well, Quercus, I've never known such a boring Elder like you. Next time I need a sleeping pill, I'll just ask for you to come and sit by my bed. Your presence would knock any insomniac out for weeks.'

I was ready to rant full blast again, but Robinia intervened.

'Quercus, would you please go and fetch the Medic? It seems Jasmine requires a sedative to prevent her escalating into another episode of heightened agitation.'

Quercus offered a brisk nod as he bolted for the door. 'Gladly. I'll bring him immediately.'

Robinia waited a few minutes to make sure he was gone. Her tone was mixed with a sense of urgency and concern. 'Have you any idea what you've done?'

'Other than tell Malus a few truths. Had I not freaked out yesterday, I'd have done it then.'

She sucked a sharp breath as her eyes roamed my face. 'With that outburst, you've just signed your death warrant quicker. While we're doing our best to slow proceedings down to allow time for planning, you're doing your best to speed it up.'

I leaned against the glass wall and almost smiled. 'Was there really ever going to be a different outcome. At least I'll go knowing I said what had to be said. Perhaps they'll have pity on Coral, realising what she was up against having me as her mentor.'

Robinia placed the palms of her hand on my glass cage. 'What good are you to our cause if you're dead?'

'Don't you get it, Robinia? This trial is a spectacle, and we were going to be cleansed regardless. And really, what could you have done? Sneaked us out and hid us. Where would we go?'

Robinia's jaw clenched as she lost all composure. 'Nothing was finalised, but we were making progress. People were risking their lives for you, and you've stamped all over their efforts with your stupid, fiery ego. Does Coral not deserve better from you? Ask yourself that. You've let her down more than the rest of us.'

As I attempted to form words, my lips parted, but silence filled the air instead. The weight of my foolishness and the gravity of it sank in. Coral, overcome with emotion, began to weep.

Aspen's arrival did little to brighten the mood, and the gloomy atmosphere persisted. He handed me a tablet through one of the air holes. 'It shouldn't be too difficult to swallow without water,' he said, his eyes dulled with a deep sadness. 'It will help keep your temper at bay.'

I placed it on my tongue, rolled it to the side of my mouth and pretended to slug it back.

'Can you find out what's happening in the Justice of Pax?' Robinia asked Quercus.

While everyone's attention remained fixed on Quercus's departure, I discreetly spat the sedative to the floor and swiftly crushed it under the sole of my foot.

Aspen looked at me as if I were his enemy. 'This is not good. Malus is in a foul mood and the outcome is even more perilous.'

'I've already told her,' Robinia said, her anger now gone. She appeared deflated, and I found myself at a loss for words, or for actions that could make it right between us.

Aspen rustled in a bag and took out two blue pills, passing one to Coral and me through the cut holes in the glass. 'I need you to take these and hide them. Only take it if you are put in the Cleansing Chamber. It will numb your nervous system and you'll fall asleep quickly without any pain.'

As I studied the deadly medication between my finger and thumb, Robinia gritted her teeth. I could tell this wasn't easy for her.

'If the verdict goes better than we hope, destroy it right away,' Aspen advised. 'You can't have these found on you, or the Elders will know I'm not who I seem to be.'

'You gave Mary one, didn't you? That's why she didn't scream with pain,' I asked, tucking the pill in my pocket. It snuggled comfortably beside the small wooden cross.

He smiled sadly and nodded.

'Thank you,' I said. 'For making it easy for her.'

I shifted my gaze towards Coral. 'If my outburst condemns you, I'll...'

'Stop it,' Coral interrupted before I could finish. 'What's

done is done and I wouldn't change anything. I only wish I was as brave, facing up to Malus the way you did.'

My eyes swam with tears. 'Coral, I've said it a hundred times, but you're the bravest person I know.'

Her unexpected bout of laughter had us all puzzled, and unsure of what had triggered it, it drew me in. Perhaps it was a nervous reaction, but even Aspen and Robinia giggled.

'What's so amusing?' I asked, pulling myself together.

A gleam of pride danced in Coral's eyes. 'Nothing really, it was just a silly thought. You realise in a hundred years from now, the children of Ruin will be hearing about us in history. Bet they'll call us the rebels of Ruin.'

Quercus arrived back, and if he'd returned a minute earlier, he'd have caught Robinia and Aspen in mid chuckle. His brow glistened with sweat, and his breath came in rapid, uneven gasps. 'Malus has proclaimed that Pax has waited long enough for appeasement. If the sedative won't work within the next ten minutes, he'll have Jasmine muzzled.'

Aspen pulled out a pocket watch suspended from a delicate silver chain. 'Five should be ample. I'll wait with Robinia and make sure Jasmine is completely calm before the cages lift.'

'I'll be glad when all this is over,' Quercus said, leaving again without saying goodbye. It made me wonder what type of person he would have been had he been allowed to live freely. I felt sadness he had played his part in all of this without realising the wrong he did. It wasn't his fault.

Robinia dabbed her eyes with the back of her hand. 'I wish I could change your fate,' she said. 'We had great plans for you both in our movement and I'm sure we would've accomplished great things together.'

With time slipping away, the luxury of waiting for answers to questions eluded me. I found myself compelled to ask, driven by an urgency to finally having peace of mind. 'Most probably, I'll be gone from this world soon. Would you both do me the favour of answering some of my questions?'

Aspen glanced fleetingly at Robinia. 'I don't see what harm it can do,' he said.

Robinia smiled kindly. 'What do you want to know?'

I struggled to pinpoint a definitive starting point. 'Why is it we can't recollect our early years in the nursery?' I asked, trying to find the right words without causing offence. 'I've experienced sporadic flashbacks, but the memories are fragmented. I'm convinced we were subject to harmful experiments carried out on us during that time.'

A hint of unease flickered across Aspen's face. 'I won't deny we run tests. They're hardly experiments, and the children come to no harm. Some are unpleasant, therefore memories are erased afterwards, to protect the mind,' he said, folding his arms against his chest.

'Tests for what purpose?' I asked. 'I recalled a memory of Spindle convulsing on the floor. You were there,' I said, pointing accusingly at Robinia. There was a gravity to my words, reflecting the importance of my concern. 'You slapped me. I also recalled another where you beat Spindle brutally with a cane.'

I anticipated an explanation from Robinia, but was met with silence. Instead, it was Aspen who took the lead, weaving a web of fabricated excuses.

'What we do makes sure the immune system is strong, no matter which virus presents itself. Everything we do is for a reason, to make the body invincible against any form of attack.'

His reasoning was shameful, and I shook my head forcefully. 'It doesn't matter how you justify it. Putting alien substances into children isn't running tests. It's experimentation, and its wrong.'

'Think logically,' Aspen argued passionately. 'Look at yourself and all those you've grown with. All of you are healthier and stronger than any previous generations because of the work we do, and what has been done.'

The stark contrast between my own principles and the opposing beliefs held by someone who was supposed to be on my side left me bewildered. I rubbed a hand over my face, keeping my anger in check. The last thing I needed Aspen to know was I hadn't taken the sedative to keep me calm. 'It's awful and I'll never bend to your view,' I said.

Aspen shrugged. 'It's happened since time began, even from the old world, so what we do is nothing new. Our movement may want a change of governance, but as well as bad, great things have been accomplished since the End of Days. Nobody can deny that.'

'The first time we met, what were you doing to the four children behind the blue curtain.' I asked. 'I caught a glimpse of them when you attended to your ear.'

My question made him gasp. 'What children? You must have been hallucinating.'

'But, I saw them,' I said, my voice unwavering. 'They appeared as though they'd been dipped in oil.'

I stole a glance at Robinia. Her discomfort was palpable, as she nervously twisted her fingers together.

Coral, who had been listening attentively all the while, made the decision to share her thoughts with Aspen. 'Something strange happened with Lily and Willow. Lily's mental state is screwed to say the least, never mind the added rumours of her finding the body of a child. Before we were locked up, Willow told me any time she tried to remember the events of what happened, she got a blinding ache at her temple.'

Robinia sounded irritable. 'Girls, do you really want to spend the little time you may or may not have left debating the rights and wrongs of what might and what might not be true.'

Aspen decided to have the last word. 'Lily was bogged down with stress, nothing more. Did Willow claim she saw a body? I don't think she did. You have to acknowledge nothing is ever black or white. All matters bring a shade of grey or something in-between.' He extended his hands, palms facing upwards. 'We're all learning as we try to make life better, but mistakes will always be made along the way. Please don't judge too harshly.'

'Can the Sun be unharnessed?' Coral asked, surprising us all. 'If that could be done, then it might allow the Earth to heal properly, which would help in making a better world for everyone.'

'That would be a question for the scientists,' Aspen said. 'I don't think it's as simple as removing the harness, but it's certainly a worthwhile discussion for leaders of the future.'

My yearning for a better world pulsed within me, almost tangible in its intensity. However, an underlying unease began to gnaw at my conscience. It stemmed from a thought that Robinia's movement, while aiming to replace corruption, still harboured shades of darkness and hidden complexities of its own.

I hoped I was wrong, and was leaving this world to people who would make a true difference. Even though I still craved many answers, I no longer had the energy or desire to ask. Coral took up my mantle.

'Why can't we live like the people from the caves? Mary told us how wonderful it was,' Coral asked.

Aspen was quick to answer. 'Free will can be every bit as dangerous for a society as being oppressed.'

'What do you mean by that?' Coral asked. 'Surely to be oppression free should be our goal.'

'Take Jasmine for example,' he said sweeping his hand in my direction.' You all saw me give her a sedative. It was given with good intention and to help her. However, Jasmine, thinking she knew better, spat it out and crunched it underfoot, hoping no one would notice.'

'Why's it an issue?' I asked, annoyed I'd been caught.

Aspen chuckled under his breath. 'With full free will, there will always be some who'll work against others building a greater society, thinking they know better. Our movement is looking for a balance. Please don't blame us for that. Let me also be clear though, we aren't against people living a life with choices, we simply can't risk it going too far to the detriment of what's achieved breaking down.'

Disheartened, I sighed. 'I'm sorry. I don't want my last moments in this world to be medicated. I want to leave on my own terms.'

He smiled sincerely. 'And that's why you'd have been a fantastic asset to our movement. You don't need to apologize.'

I struggled to decipher both Aspen and Robinia's true intentions. Despite my earnest efforts, a lingering sense of wariness persisted.

After a short pause, Aspen took on a sombre tone. 'I need to make a confession and if you can't forgive me, I hope you'll at least try to understand. When I examined you, I kept some of your blood which I've hidden. I'm going to use it to find an antidote for Control. You won't need to worry what history's account of you will be. When our movement takes power, you'll be known as the heroine who freed humanity from bondage.'

'As long as you use it to free *all* people, and not a selected few,' I said.

His face slackened. 'I'm sure however it works, we'll all be grateful.'

'You must be calm when you return to the Justice of Pax,' Robinia said. 'You can't let them know you're not sedated and risk exposing Aspen.'

Time was running out and we'd soon be hoisted to the hall above, but there was one more subject I wanted to tackle. 'What were your plans for Coral and me? Were you going to sneak us out of Ruin to some other island?

Coral grinned. 'Can you imagine Aconite and Malus if that happened.'

As the minutes passed, a sense of doubt overshadowed my expectation of receiving an answer. Robinia's smiled, a radiant expression that lit up her face and caused her eyes to crinkle at their corners. I had never saw her look so beautiful. 'We're all sounding like defeatists. Until the doors of the Cleansing Chamber close, there may be hope. Even as we sit here, our movement makes ripples. However, you ask something I can't answer because I truly don't know. Our instructions are simple - always be ready. Signs come, or words are spoken, and we know what to do. We all hold a piece of a code, and as we see it come together, we work it out. The term we have coined for it is action in motion.'

If only I possessed the energy, I'd have confronted her directly, exposing her feeble tactics as lame and futile. A shiver ran through me, and I wrapped my arms around myself seeking warmth. As I gently rubbed my arms to generate heat, I remembered the tiny scar on my left forearm. What did you inject into me?' I asked, rolling up my linen sleeve.'

Coral sprang from her seat, her voice filled with urgency. 'Let me see. I've got one too, look right here,' she said, exposing bare skin.

Quercus had a knack for choosing the wrong moments. He burst into the holding pen, his cheeks flushed and his breath laboured. 'It's time. Aconite has called for a return to the hall.'

Aspen plucked a small medical torch from his pocket. 'Go on ahead, I'll do a final check to make sure the sedative has taken root.'

Robinia nodded. 'Tell Aconite I'll be along in a few minutes too. I want to make sure all is in order, so we don't have another episode like what happened before.'

'That would be wise,' Quercus said, casting a last dismissive look. He rushed off leaving the four of us staring at each other.

Robinia's expression reflected a deep sense of gravity, and her words carried a hint of sadness. 'None of us really know what will happen next. Everyone is guessing Malus will bring matters to a quick close because of his fury. Please be strong and know I'm with you both in spirit. Take strength from that.' She placed the palm of her hands against the glass wall, one on each cage. Coral and I emulated her touch.

Aspen put the torch away and placed his arm tenderly on Robinia's shoulder, her head fell back against his chest. This show of affection took me by surprise, giving hope that love would surface no matter what happened.

Our cages rumbled to life. Aspen stepped forward, his tone urgent. 'Remember, don't take the blue pill until you're put in the Cleansing Chamber. It's only to be used if the outcome is death. It will act quickly bringing a numbness, and take your life before the fumes or flames will have a chance.'

'What do we do if we're not to be cleansed?' Coral asked.

Her unwavering optimism brought a bittersweet smile to my face. Coral was being Coral right to the end, and my heart was a mixed bag of love and guilt.

'We'll work something out,' Aspen called, his voice filtering up through the darkness of the lift shaft.

Even if we did have time, I doubted Robinia or Aspen would have revealed their plans or true intentions. Their movement lacked organisation, working on impulses, waiting on signs.

Coral and I never stood a chance under their charge. We were moving forward and towards our death.

26

The Justice of Pax hummed with an unprecedented level of activity, surpassing any previous proceedings. The atmosphere crackled with tension, driven by the eager anticipation of the spectators. Their excited chatter sounded throughout the hall, amplifying the palpable energy. A few scuffles broke out, over individuals wanting a seat closer to the stage. Elders stepped in, leading those responsible from the hall, and trying to instil a sense of calm.

Plasma screens displayed a massive throng of people clamouring on the steps outside, their bodies tightly packed together, creating a commotion. Elders wearing bright green sashes over their black tunics mingled with them, keeping order. It was obvious this proceeding was the big one, the grand finale not to be missed.

Malus fixed me with a malevolent glare as he stepped on the stage, and I realised that to remain submissive would be a daunting task. I thought of Aspen and the need for his safety, took a deep breath and swallowed the desire to provoke or allow anger to surface.

Coral sat motionless, her gaze fixed in a vacant stare, while

Malus glided confidently over the polished stage with his microphone firmly in hand. Every word uttered had a pithy punch, making sure his speech would be remembered for years to come. His gaze swept callously over to our cages. 'Before judgement is passed, Jasmine has one final task to perform.'

I felt my cheeks warming, and although I hadn't a clue what was coming, I knew it wouldn't be good.

Malus's words dripped with a twisted delight. 'Jasmine has been asked to select one of her friends as a sacrificial offering to Pax. Two names have been given to her, and she must now confirm who will go to their death. Rather than be transported to Mortem, the sacrifice will be made here and now.'

A suffocating silence filled the hall, it was charged with anticipation as the crowd waited for me to seal someone's doom.

'Who will it be, Jasmine?' Malus goaded. 'Ash or Salix?'

At the mention of their names, the crowd erupted in a discord of shocked murmurs, collective gasps and whispers. I stole a look at the front bench. Ash's face was a contortion of anguish and disbelief. Salix simply sat staring straight ahead.

Rowan, Spindle and Lily jumped from their seats, circled both Salix and Ash in a display of support and comfort.

Rage burned inside me, rendering me motionless. Malus seemed to relish the moment, biding his time until the murmurs in the hall subsided.

'We need an answer. If you can't give one, then we shall choose for you,' Malus said, a malicious smile stretching across his face.

Salix stared hypnotically at the stage, as if transfixed by an invisible force. With deliberate slowness, he rose from his seat. In a voice stripped of its usual warmth, he called out with an unsettling detachment. 'Take me, I will die willingly for Pax.'

An agonising scream clawed its way up from the depths of my being, choking at the back of my throat, I couldn't breathe.

Once again, I found myself frozen to the spot, watching from outside of myself, as Salix sombrely ascended the steps.

Quercus emerged on stage, clutching a crimson velvet cushion with a gleaming dagger on top. Salix accepted it without hesitation.

'It's heavier than it looks,' he said, his finger skimming the raw edge of steel drawing blood.

Quercus placed the red cushion at Salix's feet.

A gloomy mist crept to the outskirts of my vision while my brain began to close down. 'Please don't do it, Salix,' I whimpered, feeling as if I were shrinking inside of myself.

Coral's voice reached my ears from a distance, as though we were separated by hundreds of miles. She begged for mercy, pleaded for them to stop, but it was no use.

Salix fell to the floor, his knees resting on the velvet padding. A haunting silence fell over the hall, the crowd mesmerised by his willingness to die, as he aimed the sharp tip of the dagger at his stomach.

'When you're ready, Salix,' Malus said, placing a hand lightly on his head. 'Make it quick and it will be less painful.'

Salix took a sharp intake of breath, and clenched his teeth. He swiftly plunged the dagger deep into his stomach. Blood seeped from the wound, his face contorting with pain as he twisted the blade, pulling it upward, falling on his side to face me.

As the life ebbed from him, and his eyes grew dim, the shadows closed in on me and I found myself in the darkness once again.

If only I could have remained in the confines of my blackout.

'Are you okay?' Coral asked as I surfaced.

Crimson stains smeared the floor where Salix's body had lain. I blinked heavy tears from my eyes. 'How long was I out?'

'Ten minutes at most. Aspen tried to stop proceedings but

Malus wouldn't have it.' She paused, stared dejectedly. 'You can't blame yourself for Salix, and he wouldn't want you to. I think Malus knew he'd volunteer.'

Noticing I was back from the brink of hopelessness, Malus's voice grew louder. 'Cleansing is the only way to appease our gracious Goddess.' His head inclined upwards as if looking directly at Pax herself, his arms extended wide. 'We live in constant fear of your wrath, and we beg you to be merciful. In sending the offenders to be cleansed, we ask you look kindly on all loyal followers and allow us to continue our courteous servitude to you.'

A ripple of appreciation swept through the Justice of Pax. Malus embraced the moment and allowed it to linger and settle naturally.

'It's now time for you, the children of Ruin, to have the final say in this matter. The back of each bench contains monitors which will now be switched on. You'll notice the option tabs showing all forms of punishment. I'll draw your attention to the tab for cleansing and should you wish the offenders to burn, please select that icon.' Malus said. 'Cast your votes wisely knowing punishment could befall all of us if we don't see justice carried out correctly. For those who are standing, and those on the walkways, you will be able to vote on hand held monitors. Please see the Elders among you with green sashes who can help you with this.'

I remembered seeing the tiny screens in my first visit to the hall. Little did I realise then our fate would be held in them with a tick box choice. As participants engaged in intense discussions, their animated voices heightened the tense and charged atmosphere.

Coral leaned back on her bench, her blue eyes wide filled with so much sorrow. I wanted to shatter the glass of the cage, bridge the gap between us and hold her close. 'How're you holding up?' I asked.

'I can't believe they can do this,' she said. 'That they're able to convince people so easily to condemn us to death for a simple act of humanity. It's understandable for those on Control, they don't know any better. But, there's no excuse for the others.'

As the Council of Twelve didn't have pews in front of them, their votes were cast on hand held monitors. I watched Robinia, her concentration fixed on the small screen and wondered what she'd choose. Hopefully something not too painful.

Engaging in a calm conversation with Coral amidst the impending vote to determine our fate felt surreal.

With a glint in his eye, Malus addressed the crowd. 'We'll have a short recess while we take the choices made into consideration,' he said. 'I'd like to take this moment to thank all of you for your good conduct during the trial and for your wonderful hospitality. I'll go back to the mainland with glowing reports. Our leaders will know our future world will be passed on to good hands.'

My fingers found and brushed the small blue pill hiding in my pocket with Mary's cross. They offered comfort, and I was happy I had them. While votes were counted, Coral and I made a pact we'd hold the blue pill in the side of our cheek and swallow together before the flames ignited.

It felt as though time had stretched to an eternity, the weight of each passing moment palpable, yet accelerating at the same time. Malus was soon on centre stage once again unable to hide his excitement.

'Good citizens, you've listened to accounts of treason and deceit committed by the accused. Although Coral was under Jasmine's influence, she lacked any signs of regret and continues to defy our teachings. Had she been sorry, she'd have pointed the finger long ago and condemned her mentor, in the same timely manner Jasmine's inner circle did.'

Each word escaping Malus's lips felt like a dagger to my

heart. The harshness of his tone and the unyielding expression on his face made it clear there would be no mercy granted to Coral.

'A unanimous vote for cleansing has been delivered and I therefore condemn Jasmine and Coral to be burned. May the holy flames of Pax singe the sin from their souls.'

The collective jubilation of the crowd erupted with a roar of deafening cheers. The applause clapped like thunder, intermingled with a rumble of stomping feet. It was over, and drained of energy, I slumped against the cold glass wall of the cage feeling a numbness creep in.

'It's okay. It'll soon be over, and we'll find peace. We'll be with Mary,' Coral sobbed, her voice choked.

Tremors wracked my trembling hands as I clenched them tightly together, trying to find a way to anchor myself. I felt if I didn't call out with rage, I was going to pass out. Robinia's gaze met mine, her eyes filled with empathy as she mouthed the words, '*Be strong*'.

Malus's commanding voice sliced through the air. 'Having been witness to such a historical moment, it's only fair I should offer an invitation for anyone who would like to say a few words? To give reason for their conviction.'

There was a sudden flurry of motion as hands rose and waved in the air, the individuals calling out for a chance to be heard.

'Goodness,' exclaimed Malus, his voice filled with surprise. 'I didn't expect so many.' As he extended his finger in a commanding gesture, ready to appoint a person of his choice, a voice bellowed from the crowd, overpowering his intention. It was Spindle.

'Cleansing is too quick for Jasmine. After everything she's done, she should be sent to suffer in the mines and worked to death.'

Since Salix's sacrifice, I couldn't summon the courage to

steal a glance at the front row where my friends were seated. They would blame me solely for his death and the immense guilt I carried was overwhelming, without the added anguish of seeing it reflected on their faces.

'I'm certain Salix would have been a future leader, someone of profound significance,' Spindle expressed solemnly. 'Jasmine's actions robbed him of his future. Surely, her purification doesn't even begin to pay back such an immense loss. Coral should die in the mines too, her actions are every bit as unforgivable'

I had always been aware of Spindle's animosity towards me, understanding it, after my recollection of our nursery years. His hatred towards me must have reached a more profound depth, if burning me alive was not sufficient in his eyes.

People turned to one another, engaging in hushed conversations about Spindle's new proposal. The concept ignited intrigue and spread through murmurs and whispers, eventually finding their way to the forefront of the stage.

The hall fell silent when Malus cleared his throat and began to speak. 'But, the votes have already been cast and Pax will await the cleansing.'

Spindle stood tall, his shoulders squared and his chin held high in the air. I had never witnessed him display such confidence before, as he had always been overshadowed by Ash and Salix. He turned his back on the stage and faced the hall.

'Burning Jasmine and Coral alive won't purify them. Only hard labour in the most gruelling conditions will. Think back to our lessons, where we learned of the dismal existence of criminals and rebels being worked to death. Imagine Jasmine and Coral deep in the belly of the earth, sunlight never touching their skin again. Each day toiling in thick suffocating dust till they drop and die of fatigue. With every painful choking breath, they will remember, and be sorry for the crimes they committed.'

It started with a low ripple, one word over and over until it grew louder and louder. 'Mines . . . mines . . . mines.'

Rowan attempted to tug Spindle back to his seat as he pivoted towards the front. Rather than sit, he stood firm, raising his fist in the air, he spearheaded the chants, igniting a further surge of energy among the crowd.

'I didn't realise Spindle hated you that much,' Coral gasped.

'I never knew he could be so assertive,' I said, shocked. 'Did you see the displeasure etched on Malus's face. And as for Aconite, I thought he was going to self-combust on the pulpit.'

Ash swiftly rose to his feet, joining Spindle's side. 'Spindle's right, send them to the mines,' he said, with unwavering determination.

One by one, individuals rose from their benches till nearly all who gathered inside the Justice of Pax stood.

Aconite rushed from the pulpit, urgently beckoning Malus to join him by the side of the Council of Twelve.

Somone near the front called for us to rot in the mines, and the one word mantra changed from mines to rot. It came thick and heavy, blasting in from the steps outside and the walk lanes too.

'What's Spindle and Ash playing at? You'd think he'd be happy to see us burn.' Coral said.

I sought out Robinia, desperate to gauge her reaction, on whether this new development was good or bad. It was clear the crowd's uproarious behaviour had unsettled not only Malus, Aconite, and the Elders , but also left me pondering the potential implications this situation would bring.

Malus retreated from the Council, directing a look of disgust towards Coral and me. Abruptly, he turned to face the restless crowd. 'If this is your wish, then who are we to stand in the way of the will of the people. Your choice comes with a cost, and I need confirmation you are willing to pay the price for what you now want?'

Robinia evaded my gaze, unable to hold my stare, as the unified calls of acceptance reverberated throughout the Justice of Pax.

'What do you think is happening now?' Coral asked, with a look of despair. 'What more can they do to us?'

'Nothing. They can't hurt us anymore. Justice has been passed and we're going to the mines. This is just further bluster because Malus didn't get his way.'

It couldn't have been more distant from the truth. Malus pursed his lips, evil seeping from his ugly black heart. 'I would like to invite Lucy and Willow to come forward.'

'What's he going to do to them?' Coral cried despairingly, her face pressed against the glass.

Malus stood in-between Lily and Willow, his arms snaking around both girls shoulders. 'Pax must have a cleansing. As Jasmine and Coral will not burn today, it has been agreed by the Council of Twelve and Aconite, Lily and Willow will meet the flames instead.'

Spindle sprung to his feet, his cheeks flushed, his voice sharp. 'Surely sending Jasmine and Coral to the mines is appeasement enough,' he exclaimed. 'Why would Pax require additional sacrifices. Hasn't she already claimed Salix?'

Malus voice bellowed with contempt as he spoke. 'There shall be no further demands entertained in the Justice of Pax today,' he sneered. 'My word is final and absolute.' He removed a whistle and blew on it hard. Two guards appeared from back stage. 'Kindly escort this young man out of the proceedings before I subject him to the same fiery fate.'

Lily's legs gave way beneath her. Malus gripped her tight, stopping her from falling to the floor. Willow stared at Coral, her look reflecting a mixture of resignation and acceptance. Tears streamed down our faces as we succumbed to uncontrollable sobs, overcome by grief and despair.

'No. You can't do this,' I roared at the top of my voice unable to contain my rage any longer. I pounded my body against the glass wall, yelling as loud as my vocals allowed. 'I'll kill you, Malus. I'll break free and kill you.'

He no longer cared about my outburst. 'You'll have to escape from the mines first,' he said.

As the guards closed in on Spindle to remove him from the hall, our eyes locked for a brief moment. I couldn't read if it was hate or sorrow I saw in them. His actions to condemn me further had inadvertently triggered Lily and Willow's cleansing. After all that happened, my heart welled with sorrow for him, knowing firsthand the burden of guilt, and how difficult it was to carry.

With his head low and his steps heavy, he departed with a guard on each side, to the whispers of the crowd, murmuring their own interpretations of the unfolding events.

Malus cut the murmurings short. 'When we commit a crime against the state, not only does it undermine our laws, but breaks the very heart of Pax. Jasmine has never been able to grasp how much her actions have caused pain. Salix offered himself willingly as a sacrifice but Lily and Willow are forced. Let's see how Jasmine copes in the mines knowing the innocent suffered on her behalf. She'll be eaten by guilt, praying every day for a quick death.'

Malus blew on his whistle once more, summoning two additional guards who swiftly materialised beside him. 'As both girls are blameless, their cleansing will be a private affair. We owe them that at least.' Malus said.

My voice was raw but I continued to scream loudly and bang on the glass wall. I called out directly to Robinia. 'Do something to stop this,' I implored. 'Please, anybody, do something.'

Coral slumped on the bench, her chin drooping to rest upon her chest. The guilt of Willow's cleansing overwhelming her and landing a burden beyond what she could bear.

Gripped by an icy chill, I watched in horror as Lily and Willow were escorted from the hall, aware of the horrendous death awaiting them. Each step they took echoed the weight of all our emotions

Malus delivered one last devastating blow in his closing speech, leaving me reeling from the impact of his words. 'Coral will no longer accompany Jasmine to the mines. Instead, she'll be transported to the island of Mortem to be sacrificed on a holy alter, as a peace offering to Pax.'

In an instant, my heart skipped a beat, and I turned swiftly to her. 'Coral, I won't let them separate us. I'll find a way to break free and come get you,' I said, through a clenched jaw. I promise, we'll be together to the very end.'

Raising her head listlessly, she gave a low grunt. 'After what just happened, I don't care anymore,' she said, her sorrowful eyes meeting mine. 'They can do what they like.'

As our cages rumbled to life, pulling us back into the darkness, we departed from the resounding roars echoing throughout the Justice of Pax, bidding farewell to the unbridled clamour for the final time.

27

Coral's cage hadn't materialised, and there was no sign of Robinia or Aspen either. I curled up on the cage floor, wrapping my arms tightly around my legs, to try and quell the tremors that shook my body. A sense of abandonment crept in as the minutes ticked by.

Whenever I closed my eyes, the haunting image of Salix sprawled in a pool of blood invaded my mind. The loss of my dear friend broke my heart, and the inability to properly mourn his passing intensified my anguish.

Lily and Willow had left the Justice of Pax, making their way towards the Cleansing Chamber. My hope clung to the possibility Robinia was by their side, intervening to halt their burning, and save them from such a terrible death. I couldn't bear the thought of losing them too.

The absence of Coral sent an icy wave of apprehension coursing through me. Normally, I would hear the clanks and bangs from the mechanics inside her lift shaft, working hard to bring her back to the pen. However, this time, there was nothing but an eerie silence, the stillness allowing my mind to wander to unsettling thoughts.

Island of Ruin

As the door slid open, I was surprised and shocked to see Ash standing there, hesitating on the threshold, unsure of whether to enter or retreat.

'What're you doing here,' I asked. 'How did you find your way down here?'

'I had to see you,' he confessed. 'I followed Quercus one morning, so I knew the way. They're all in a frenzy up there,' he added, rolling his eyes upwards. 'So, I knew it was now or never. Ever since I witnessed you being dragged through Midpoint, I've wanted to visit. I'd sometimes walk past your cell, hoping someone would enter, so I could try and catch a glimpse of you.'

'So, you've come to gloat,'

'No,' he said, stepping inside and striding toward the cage. 'I've been torn in two since all this started.'

Despite the glass wall separating us, I instinctively backed away.'

'What happened to your hand?' he said, his eyes falling to my bandage.

'It's nothing,' I muttered, even though it was done in anger during his testimony. I didn't have the energy to tell him, and it was as if him being here was sucking every last piece from me.

We stared at each other, he looked bewildered, at a loss for words. I felt an angry calm, despising the conflicting emotions welling inside of me. He eventually broke the silence.

'Look what you've done,' he said.

My throat felt tight, and the words came out in a snarl. 'What I've done? 'No, Ash, it's what you've done. All this is on you because of the twisted way your mind works. I hope you feel it's been worthwhile.'

My anger didn't faze him. 'I'm sorry. They made me say those things about you. I didn't want to stand with Malus . . . honest.'

Lunging at the glass I banged it hard. 'You think I'm mad

because you stood with Malus. You think it's that simple? Why don't you stop for one minute to think how we got here in the first place.'

'None of this is simple,' he said, rubbing a hand over his head. 'It's all a mess. If only I didn't care about you the way I do. You're in my thoughts, my dreams and I can't explain why.'

There was a time I'd have given anything to hear those words. I'd have plucked them straight out of the air on leaving his lips and pinned them on my heart.

'Everything that's happened is your fault. I'll hate you forever, which isn't nearly long enough. I should never have trusted you, but that's on me. I just don't understand why you had to tell.'

He looked confused. 'Tell who what?'

I laughed cynically. 'Come on. Don't play the innocent here. I know it was you who told them where to find the old woman.'

Ash frowned. 'You've got this all wrong. I never told anyone.'

His lies only added to my fury. 'You've so much blood on your hands. Mary, Salix, Lily and Willow. All dead because of you.'

His nose was inches from the glass, his breath blowing a foggy mist that settled on its surface. 'I'm still trying to process the death of Salix. You've no idea how I feel about that, or Lily and Willow. But, if you want to play the blame game, take a long hard look at yourself. I warned you over and over where this was headed, but you didn't listen. You can't blame me, or anyone else for that matter. Your actions brought this whole sorry mess to where it is now.'

His words cut through me like a searing blade. 'Is that why you sided with Spindle, to have me sent to the mines?'

'What?' he shook his head furiously. 'No, I couldn't bear to watch you burn, Jasmine. When Spindle gave an alternative, instinct took over. You'd still be alive in the mines and with life there's hope. Don't be angry at me for that.'

'You think I want to live, after what they did to Mary and Salix,' I said ,baring my teeth. 'I'm not just angry. I'm filled with hate. I hate everything about you. You conned me into believing you had feelings for me. Yet, stood in the Justice of Pax and lied about everything. How could you?'

Defiance flashed across his face. 'None of us had a choice. We were forced to say the things we said. You've no idea the pressure I've been under because of you. Anyway, you would've done the same.'

The laughter escaping my throat was a wild, high-pitched gurgle, untamed and brimming with an instinctive ferocity. 'The pressure you've been under. Try sitting on this side of the cage and you'll know pressure. Poor you, Ash.' As for you thinking I would lie against any of my friends, you obviously never really knew me.'

'Not just me. Pressure was put on all of us. Rowan, Lily, Spindle and Salix.'

'Don't you dare mention his name,' I yelled.

Exhausted, my brain screeched to a halt. I slid slowly down the glass wall slouching to the ground hiding my head in my hands.

Ash's tone took on a softer note. 'I kept your secret, no matter what you think. I'm sorry about the old woman. She obviously meant a lot to you, but she was a rebel from the mainland and should've stayed there with her own kind.'

I inhaled deeply before meeting his eyes. 'She wasn't just a cave dweller. Sadly, you'll never know the importance of her, and what she was to your life. You don't deserve her, and she certainly deserved better than you.'

'What are you talking about? None of that makes any sense.'

'Just go,' I said. 'Before they come and find you here.'

We stared at each other for a few seconds before Ash tipped his forehead against the glass. 'I'll find a way to contact you. I've been promised a position with the Government on the mainland, so I'll have access to files. I'll never stop looking for you.'

His hands clung tightly to the glass, as if trying to imprint warmth and dispel the coldness I felt for him. With a heavy sigh, he turned away, heading towards the door. He cast one final glance, our eyes met, and then he was gone. It was only then I looked at the hidden camera, and smiled for Malus.

Left alone, I pondered Ash's words, and his foolishness. If Aconite and Malus saw the footage, the promised position on the mainland with the Government would be taken from him. Regardless, we were coming of age and he'd be prescribed Control. I would become a distant memory lurking in his consciousness. I'd also be dead.

28

It was bitterly cold at the docks, and I huddled into my furs waiting on the watercraft that would carry me across the Pewter Sea to the Mainland.

The sky loomed heavy with dark clouds promising black rain; a haunting silence hung in the air. Apart from a solitary guard and a few Elders tending nets, the pier was empty. The trial was over, my sentence had been delivered, and I was no longer worthy of interest.

In a distant cove, two children worked on tasks. My heart ached as I watched their antics, reminding me of my time with Coral, and how life once was. Her cage never returned to the holding pen on the day of our judgement, so we never got to say goodbye. I can only presume she was taken to Mortem immediately, while I had to wait a couple of days for my watercraft to arrive.

Robinia made a solemn promise to keep me informed on any news regarding Coral, if possible. However, due to her limited contact with those living on Mortem, she warned of getting my hopes up to high. The grim reality was Coral likely had already been sacrificed, although I found myself unwilling to confront that painful truth just yet.

I still possessed Mary's small wooden cross which nestled safely in my pocket beside the blue pill. As much as the voice in my head often begged, I could never swallow it nor find the courage to destroy it either.

Haunted faces of infants stalked my dreams. It was as though they were calling to me, reaching out to warn of sinister deeds. Missing children and experimentation were not a fantasy, as Robinia would have me believe, but a truth of something malevolent running deep on Ruin.

It was one of the accusations I threw at Malus in an angry outburst, and a flicker of fear danced across his face. I sensed a hint of unease and apprehension, suggesting my accusations did not fall wrong. Hopefully, someone someday would find strength to expel the evil the End of Days spawned.

It was the same evil that took Salix from this world. At least his death released him from their grip and the life of servitude they planned. It was bittersweet, but I knew in my heart Salix would never have wanted to live such a life. He'd been my saviour, and the best friend any person could have had. If an afterlife existed, I hoped he would find Coral and Mary. Hopefully, I would find them all too.

Melancholy had me think of Lily and Willow. Both could have shined if given a proper chance. Robinia assured me their ending was swift and painless. Aspen had saw to that. However, I still harboured the guilt of their passing, knowing this also destroyed Coral. It wasn't Spindle's fault, and I'm sure he would carry the guilt unnecessarily until the drug Control would numb his consciousness and take it away.

Spindle had always maintained his distance from me, and I was relieved upon finally uncovering the root of his hate. However, it was during his defining moment in the Justice of Pax I witnessed a different side of him. As he rallied the crowd against Malus's desires, he displayed true leadership and a connection with people. If only he were on the right side, his potential as an inspiring figure would have been remarkable.

It was no surprise my demise and the part Rowan played fast tracked her career. Robinia told me the Elders already discussed the great position prepared for her on the mainland under Malus's watchful eye. Her desire to be someone of great importance fulfilled, but the glory she felt would fade when drugged with Control. She didn't realise her life would be a monotone existence, without ever really having lived at all. My anger hadn't waned, and if Robinia's people succeeded in bringing an end to the current regime, Rowan would find herself rotting in a cell.

The watercraft arrived banging against the soaked stone of the port wall. It was an early model, a measly metal rectangle stuck on wooden logs with a lofty mast. Hopefully the small engine would kick in to carry us over hefty waves. The steering wheel was protected under a canvas roof, giving shelter to the trader who'd guide the rudder. I on the other hand would be open to the elements.

The trader jumped on the pier, his thick arms pulling a huge rope tied to a concrete post. He placed a wooden plank between the craft and dock that creaked loudly while he unloaded hessian sacks and tattered crates.

Once done, he held out his hand and guided me onboard, placing me on a cold damp bench. The boat swayed abruptly, the murky water below promising a rough sail.

I arched my back freeing it from kinks while my guard secured the shackles on my ankles to a ring on the deck. At least my hands were free letting my fingers find warmth in the pocket of my furs. Once done, he passed the key to the trader, trusting him to hand me over to guards who'd escort me to the mines.

I sat quietly while cargo for the mainland filled empty space around me. The brisk breeze whipped my face while sea salt stung my lips. Eventually, we were cast free and a niggle of fear rose as we glided slowly towards open sea.

Until now, I'd held Ash from my thoughts, confused by his denial of betrayal. Had I been wrong? If it wasn't him, then who? My trust had been fractured regardless, with his testimony of lies, which had cut deep. He would soon become of age, and his recollection of me would be as the traitor tried in the Justice of Pax. I doubted he'd even remember my name, never mind the emerging feelings of love we shared, an emotion banned to all people.

Thunder rumbled from an angry sky bringing streaks of lighting zig-zagging through the gloom, bursting the heavy storm clouds. I tilted my chin upwards feeling the black rain pelt against my forehead and cheeks, mixing with my tears.

An insufferable itch tingled along my left forearm, and peeling back my sleeve, I studied the tiny scar. A faint flickering glow blinked beneath the skin at its surface. Was it a symbol of hope planted by Aspen? It no longer mattered as I was heading for the mines.

As we sailed far from the speckled shoreline, venturing further into the boundless expanse of the Pewter Sea, my eyes caught sight of a lone figure perched on an outcrop of rocks. He stood there, in a backdrop of flickering lightning and pounding black rain, a solitary sentinel watching my departure.

It was Spindle.

ACKNOWLEDGMENTS

Where to begin? I am immensely grateful to all the family and friends who have made it possible for me to pursue my writing dream and transform this book into a reality.

First and foremost, I want to express my heartfelt love and appreciation to my incredible husband, Martin, and our two remarkable adult children, Rebekah and Sam. Their unwavering support and encouragement never faltered, even during the darkest moments when I contemplated giving up.

I am incredibly grateful to Wendy H. Jones, whose belief in me and endless support propelled me forward on this incredible journey. Her guidance and encouragement have been invaluable, and no number of thank yous can truly convey my appreciation for the time and dedication she has given to our friendship, and to this book.

I would also like to extend a special shout-out to my colleagues on the Council of the Scottish Association of Writers, as well as our remarkable membership. It has been an honour to be part of such an amazing writing community. Needless to say, I must also extend a special thank you to everyone in Ayr Writers and History Writers. The meetings and sessions I've managed to attend have been instrumental in my thought process and approach to the finished piece.

I'd like to mention two extraordinary friends who deserve special recognition. To Linda Brown and Kirsty Hammond, I am immensely grateful for your presence in my life. Thank you for being there to bounce ideas off, lend an ear during my moments of frustration and celebrate with me when everything comes together.

My deepest gratitude also goes to Heather Wilson, who has been by my side since the first line was written. Thank you from the bottom of my heart for our wonderful friendship and invaluable support.

Finally, to all those who have played a part in my journey, you know who you are, I extend my heartfelt thanks.

ABOUT THE AUTHOR

About the Author

Marti M. McNair resides in the heart of Ayrshire alongside her husband, Martin. With eleven years' service on the Council of the Scottish Association of Writers, she presently holds the position of Vice President.

In addition, Marti is a valued partner in the esteemed Auscot Publishing and Retreats, uniting writers from diverse corners of the globe. Through this collaborative venture, Marti contributes to the creation of an inspiring and nurturing space for writers to come together and thrive.

The dream of becoming a published author in the Young Adult genre has always burned brightly. With her debut novel now in your hands, she eagerly hopes you thoroughly enjoy her fictional endeavours.

The next book in the trilogy, Rebels of Ruin, will be available by Christmas 2023.